BEYOND THE BEYOND

'Poul Anderson never had a dull idea, never wrote a dud story,' said the *Yorkshire Post* of *Time and the Stars*: and in this collection of stories he shows once again what control he has of his medium, and how skilful he is at depicting the background of future millennia. There are five novellas in the volume, all substantial enough to provide a really satisfying development of plot and situation.
Packed with imaginative detail of outer space, this collection shows Poul Anderson at his ingenious best.

Beyond
The Beyond

Poul Anderson

CORONET BOOKS
Hodder Paperbacks Ltd., London

Copyright © 1969 by Poul Anderson
These stories have appeared in a somewhat different form,
as follows:
'Memory' (under the title 'A World Called Maanerek'),
Galaxy Science Fiction, July 1957. Coypright © by Galaxy
Publishing Corp., 1957.
'Brake', Astounding Science Fiction, August 1957.
Copyright © by Street and Smith Publications, Inc., 1957.
'The Sensitive Man,' Fantastic Universe Science Fiction,
November-January 1954. Copyright © by King-Size
Publications, Inc., 1954.
'The Moonrakers', If Worlds of Science Fiction, January
1966. Copyright © by Galaxy Publishing Corp., 1966.
'Starfog', Analog Science Fact-Science Fiction, August
1967. Copyright © 1967 by The Conde Nast Publications, Inc.
First published 1970 by Victor Gollancz Ltd.
Coronet edition 1973

Printed and bound in Great Britain for
Coronet Books, Hodder Paperbacks Ltd,
St. Paul's House, Warwick Lane,
London, EC4P 4AH
By Hunt Barnard Printing Ltd.,
Aylesbury, Bucks.

ISBN 0 340 16337 2

CONTENTS

MEMORY

TORREK

THE GILDER FOLLOWED the slope of Kettleback Fell, caught an updraught rising from Brann's Dale, and swung towards a blued-silver sky of twilight clouds. Above the cold white brawl of Skara River there lay a chill hazy air mass which sucked it down again.

Vilyan's hands were briefly frantic on the controls. Then he had crossed the river and was once more upborne, until presently he went above the timberline.

"We are close now, oath-brother," he said. "Best you make ready."

Torrek nodded, left his seat, and crawled down the narrow length of the fuselage. He felt the light fabric, oiled cloth drawn tight on a frame of hollow canes, shiver to his touch. It resounded with the noise of the great booming winds.

Reaching the little trapdoor, he peered through its glass inset, down at a savage barrenness streaked with snowfields. He tested his arrangements—the coiled rope knotted to a crossbar, the three knives sheathed at his waist, the net which bound his long yellow hair to keep it from his eyes. Otherwise he wore only a loincloth, for he dared weigh no more than he must on this errand.

He was a big and supple young man, with a harsh bony cast to his face that made him an alien among the handsome people of Dumethdin. And the name they had given him, Torrek, meant more than simply "stranger"—it hinted at a degree of monstrousness, for he alone of all folk under the Rings could not even guess at his parentage. Nevertheless, Clan and Lodge emblems were tattooed on his face.

"There's the nest!" Sweat leaped out on Vilyan's forehead, pearling the blue symbol etched there, the sign of Sea Bear

Lodge, in which he found sworn brotherhood with Torrek. His hands jerked, a bare trifle, on the sticks, and the glider shuddered.

They had climbed high, until now they were slipping along that gaunt dark mountaintop called the Skara Man's Hat. On a windy crag overlooking three thousand feet of cold sky, there was raised an enormous, disorderly heap of branches, welded with the decay of centuries into one fortress mass. As far back as tradition remembered, krakas had nested here.

Certain Elders, far down in Diupa, thought it an unholy work to slay the kraka, for she had been there so long, and her mothers and grandmothers before her, reaving the valleys below. If the kraka sat no longer on the Skara Man's Hat, menace brooding over Fenga Fjord, there would be an emptiness in the sky.

Folk whose livestock and small children had been carried up to these unclimbable heights thought otherwise.

Vilyan's dark reckless face split in a sudden grinning tautness. "There she comes herself, oath-brother!"

"Good," grunted Torrek.

"May Ellevil and the Moon Lady ward you—"

"Hold her steady now," Torrek interrupted harshly.

One who did not know him might have been offended at such surliness, even when death beat upwind to meet him, but in Diupa they thought they understood their changeling. You could not look for ease, or mirth, or even much courtesy from one whose life had been so hideously uprooted. His brain, they thought, must still be ploughed with the scars of memory torn loose, five years ago.

Therefore Vilyan only nodded. But when Torrek had left the glider and Vilyan was bringing it back towards the fisher town —for he could not hover in this home of the warring winds—he sang the Long Faring Song for those who have gone away to battle and are not likely to return.

Torrek opened the little door, threw out the rope, and slid down its length. One of his daggers was gripped between his teeth.

For long, ghastly minutes he swung like a bell clapper, more than a mile above the fjord. Now he could hear the wind, a huge hollow roaring through the blue dusk. Its force streamed him ahead at the rope's end.

The challenge of the kraka cut through to him. She came threshing upwards from her nest, blind with murder, for at this time of year she had young in the nest and that thing of stiff wings dared fly over them! Almost, she hurled herself straight at the glider—her mother had thus crashed one, a man's lifetime ago. But then, as Torrek had planned, she saw him dangling like bait on a fishhook, and she veered and plunged towards him.

The man felt a final tightening of nerve and muscle. His eyes seemed to gain an ultimate clarity, his ears to be whetted until they heard the crashing of Smoky Falls where Skara plunged down the Steeps, time to slow until the onrushing kraka poised in midair and he could count the stripes on her tawny hide after each giant wingbeat. But he was not afraid. In a bare five years of remembered life, there is small time to learn the habits called fear.

Then the kraka struck.

She was a little smaller than he, discounting the thirty-foot span of leathery wings and the long rudder-shaped tail. But her four feet ended in talons which had been known to split men at one blow, and her muzzle held sabre teeth. Few people, hanging one-handed from a cord, could have kept from pitching downwards to escape.

Torrek drew himself up, at the last instant, into a ball. As the winged thunderbolt shot below him, he let go. His legs closed around the lean belly, his left arm around the neck, and his right hand thrust a dagger into her throat.

She screamed.

For a few wild seconds she threshed and bucked and writhed in the air, seeking to hurl him off. His knife was torn from his grasp and sparkled meteoric downwards. He needed both arms and every draining drop of strength to keep his place.

Then his weight became too much for her, and they slid down the wind towards the sterile slopes. Her wings, flailing the sky, slowed that fall somewhat, turned it into a long glide . . . and meanwhile Torrek had drawn another knife and was slashing methodically at her vitals.

He felt no pity for this most splendid of animals—there were too many small bones up on Skara Man's Hat. But he had a moment in which to think that she was brave.

And a moment, incredibly high in the air, to look over the misty woods and the green depths of Brann's Dale, across Smoky

Falls and the narrow fields that men had ploughed between the cliffs and the fjord to Diupa town.

More: he could see across Fenga Fjord to Holstok and the White River Delta, a low rich land fair for the harvest. He could see the narrow end of the bay and follow its windings northward between sheer rock to the mouth. There, where the Roost foamed with an incoming tide, lay those guardian islands called the Merry Men; and Torrek thought he could even see the grim walls of Ness, the fort on Big Ulli which watched lest the beast-helmeted pirates of Illeneth descended again on Dumethdin.

But now the kraka was weakening, her blood spattering the blue twilight air, and as her wings beat less frantically, her fall became the faster. Clench-jawed, Torrek thought she would have her revenge by painting his flesh on the Steeps of Skara next to her own.

Then, with a wobbling convulsion, she staggered eastward again, and the updraught from the warmer ploughed fields gave her a final helping hand, and it was the fjord into which she plunged.

Torrek dived from her just before she struck. He split the water with a force that drove him down and down into greenish depths until his eardrums popped their protest and a coraloid spear raked his flank. When he had finally struggled back to the surface, his lungs seemed ready to explode. It was a long time before his gasping ceased.

The kraka floated not far away, upborne by her enormous wings—dead. And the early lamps of Diupa glimmered within easy distance.

"Well, old girl," panted Torrek, "that was friendly of you. Now wait here and be so good as not to let the ollenbors find you and clean your bones—I want that striped hide!"

He strode out for the town, wearily at first, but his strength came back with the swiftness he knew to be abnormal. Sometimes, alone with his own truncated soul at night, Torrek wondered if he were human . . . or what?

There were canoes putting out from the pier. His landing had been dimly espied by the townsfolk. Lean outriggered shapes clove murmurous waves, a hundred paddles struck the water in unison, and the coloured paper lanterns hung at the stem posts were like seeking eyes.

"Ohoyohoa!" A conch lowed after the cry, and the brass throb of gongs took up an underlying rhythm. *"Ohoyohoa!* May the sea give you up. Oh my beloved! May the sea surrender you living, *ohoyohoa!"*

"Here I am!" called Torrek unceremoniously.

The nearest boat veered. Muscular hands drew him up, and soon the conches and gongs and voices roared victory.

By the time the fleet had come back, dragging the slain kraka and bearing Torrek on a captain's dais, the Diupa people had all swarmed to the dock.

Masked and feather-cloaked, shaking their rattles and their weapons—crossbows, axes, war-mattocks, halberds, blowpipes—the young men of Sea Bear Lodge danced out the pride he had given them. Grave in their embroidered robes of scarlet and blue, his adoptive Clan Elders waited under glowing lanterns. Between the long, low, airy houses of painted oilcloth and carved wood panels and peaked shingle roofs, the children and the maidens strewed flowers for him.

Even the humblest farmers, artisans, fishermen, with no more finery than a bast loincloth and a feather headdress, lifted their tridents and shouted his honour when he stepped among them.

High over the mountains the thin evening clouds broke apart. The sun was down, though it would not be dark for hours yet, here in the warm latitudes of the World Called Maanerek. But the sky showed an infinite clear blue, with two of the moons riding high, nearly full. And enormous to the south lifted the rainbow arch of the Rings, most holy bridge.

It was the usual thing that the clouds of the long warm day—forty hours while the sun strode over the Islands—should disperse as evening cooled towards night. Yet Torrek, with the fjord's chill kiss still tingling on his skin, imagined that all-kindly Rymfar must be with him, to draw the curtain from the sky just as he stepped ashore to his people.

His people. Now, for the first time, he felt a thawing in himself. These lithe, dark, high-cheeked folk had made him their own when they found him speechless and helpless in the fields, had taught him with the same patient kindliness they showed their children, had forgiven him the blunders and breaches inevitable to one not raised from birth in their ways.

In return he had sailed in their canoes—yes, fished and hunted and ploughed the fields, had fought in their lines when the robbers of Illeneth forced the Roost and entered Dumethdin.

And the folk had given him rank according to his growing abilities, so that now he rated Pilot.

But he had still been the waif. He had not truly bought back his life from them . . . until today.

"Drink," said Elder Yensa, handing him the ancient silver Cup of Council.

Torrek went to one knee and drained the thin spiced wine.

"Let your name be written on the scroll of Harpooners," said Scribe Glamm, "and when next the Fleet goes forth after the sea snakes, may you wield a goodly spear and be rewarded with the share due to your work."

Torrek bowed. "I am unworthy, Reverend Uncle," he said.

In fact he knew very well he deserved the elevated rank. He had expected to gain it, if he lived. Now—

He straightened, and his eyes went to the young women, respectfully waiting on the edge of lantern light.

Sonna saw him and looked down. A slow flush crept up her cheeks. She lowered her head until the long dark garlanded hair hid the small face from him.

"Reverend Uncle," said Torrek, bowing to the grey man of Korath Clan who watched him from shrewd eyes, "a Harpooner is of rank sufficient to speak as friends with the child of a Captain. Is it not so?"

"It is so," agreed Baelg.

"Then have I your consent to go into the mountains with your daughter Sonna?"

"If she is willing, that is my will," said Baelg. A grin twitched his short beard. "And I believe she is. But you must rest yourself first."

"I will rest in the mountains, Reverend Uncle."

"A mighty man indeed!" said Baelg, while the young men flashed teeth in admiration. "Go, then, and if the will of you two be later for marriage, I shall not look askance."

Silently Torrek bowed to the elders, to the Scribe, to the Councillors of Diupa and the Viceroy of the King of Dumethdin. Sonna fell behind him, matching his long strides. In a few minutes they were beyond the town, on a road which wound through fields up into the mountains.

* * *

"I could have stayed for the feasting, Sonna, if you wished," he said awkwardly. "Perhaps I was too hasty."

"You were not too hasty for me," she answered with an enormous gentleness. "I have been waiting a long time for this night."

The road became a narrow trail winding upward between great cool fronds, under soughing leaves. There was a damp green smell in the air and a rushing noise of waterfalls. Here many caves were found, and a young man and woman could lie in their shelter on beds of gathered blossoms, eating wild fruits and splitting the hard-shelled skalli nuts, through all the long night of the World Called Maanerek.

As their trail, a ledge which tumbled down through a deepening purple twilight, led them briefly out of the forest, Torrek and Sonna saw the Inner Moon rise and go hurtling across the sky. There were four outer moons visible now among the few soft stars, as well as the shuddering bands of the Rings, and they built sharded bridges of light on Fenga Fjord and across the ocean beyond.

Distantly, inaudibly from here, a lacy curtain of white spray broke around the Merry Men as one of the tidal bores which guarded Dumethdin and challenged her sailors came roaring in through the Roost.

Sonna sighed and took his arm. "Wait a little," she said quietly "I have never seen it so beautiful before."

A curious, angry emotion stirred in Torrek. He stood stiff and savoured the bitterness of it until he knew what it was; a resentful jealousy of others who had trod this path with her.

But that was a crazy, ugly thing to feel, he told himself in bewilderment—considering a woman, an unwed girl who had pledged herself to no man·as yet, to be property; to rage when she acted like a free human creature as he might rightly rage at someone who used his personal flensing tools!

He bit off the insane feeling and spat it out, but the aftertaste remained, a grey doubt of himself.

Who am I?

"There is grief in you, Torrek," murmured Sonna.

"It is nothing," he answered.

Why am I?

"No . . . I can feel it in you. Your arm became suddenly like wood." Her fingers stroked down its muscled length, tickling the gold hairs which also set him off from the brown smooth men of Dumethdin. "It is not right that you should know grief."

"Let us choose a cave," he said in a voice that grated like a hull on a rocky reef.

"No, wait, Torrek." She searched his moonlit face with dark oblique eyes. "I will not spend a night with rage and sorrow up here . . . not beside you."

He felt a dizziness. In spite of Baelg's words, it had been too much to hope that Sonna would ever—

"Ever wed a nameless man," he mumbled without thinking.

She smiled, a smile of victory, but stepped past the main issue to say: "Not nameless. You are fully adopted, Torrek. You know that. And after today's work—"

"It is not enough," he said in returning despair. "I will always be the one without roots, the torrek whom they found in the ploughed fields five years ago, speechless, kinless, memoryless. I might be a child of hill trolls, for all I will ever know!"

"Or a child of the Rymfar," said Sonna, "or of the black Flitters they tell of among the mountain tribes. What of it? You are yourself and only yourself."

He was shocked. The idea of a human existing as a single creature, self-sufficient, part of no Clan or Lodge or Nation, and with no need to be a part, was unheard of. Sonna was a woods-witch to voice it!

And then, as if a bolt had clicked home, he understood the rightness of the idea. It was not that he lost his wistfulness—he would always long for a blood kinship that had been denied him—but his lonely status was no longer a monstrosity. He was different, yes, even crippled in a way, but he was not unnatural.

For another slow moment he stood wondering why Sonna's carelessly tossed-off words, whose implications she could not really have grasped, should so bite into him. It was almost as if she had touched and awakened a memory of—

"No more!" he exclaimed, laughing aloud. "The night is not so long that we can stand here wasting it."

"No," breathed Sonna demurely. Her hand stole into his.

There came a humming in the sky.

Briefly, Torrek was puzzled. Then as the noise grew and he heard the whine of sundered air behind it, the hair stood up along his back.

He had only brought his remaining knife for a weapon. It

jumped into his hand. He shoved Sonna roughly against the cliff wall and stood in front of her, peering upwards. Moonlight dazzled him.

The black shape crossed the Rings and slid down an invisible wire, and one end of the wire was pegged to him. It came too fast for thought, too fast for a dash back into the woods. Torrek had not yet grasped the size of the thing, twice the length of a longboat, when it halted by the ledge.

It hung there and speared him.

No other word—he was *held*, pressed against the cliff by a rubbery force he could not see. When he roared and hurled all the weight and strength he owned against that net, it threw him back on to Sonna with a fury that knocked a gasp from her.

"Torrek," she whispered. Her hands groped at his waist, blindly in the pitiless unreal moonlight. "Torrek, do you know—"

He did not. He had no memory of this lean, dully black fish shape . . . and yet it did not quite seem a thing from nightmare, not quite the vengeful ghost of the kraka. Somehow he could accept it, as he might accept a new and deadly kind of animal.

"It's not a glider," he said through clenched jaws. "No wings. But it's been forged or cast—metal."

"The Flitters." Her voice shook.

He gave it some thought, standing there pinned in the racking earthquake of his own heart. The Flitters were a tale, a rumour, a recent mumble among the inland barbarians. This had been seen, that had happened, strange flyings and curiously dressed men . . .

A circular door opened in the flank of the—ship? Beyond it was a similar one which also opened. A metal gangway protruded, tongue-fashion, to the ledge.

Torrek could not see inside, but the light that spilled forth was hellishly brilliant. It so stunned his eyes that those who walked over the gangway became no more than shadows.

When they reached him and stood staring, he could see a little better. They were big men, with something of himself in their features and colouring. But they were wrapped from boots to neck in drab one-piece garments, and they wore massive round helmets.

Behind him, Sonna whimpered.

The men talked to each other. It was a language Torrek had

not heard, a choppy unmusical tongue, but there was no great excitement in the tones. These men were doing a routine job.

Through a haze of anger Torrek saw them reach some kind of decision—it seemed to involve Sonna rather than him—and go to work. They cast supple cords into the unseen force-mesh, nooses that closed on him and were drawn taut until he was trussed up like a woolly for slaughter.

One of them waved an arm in signal. Torrek fell to the rock as the force died away. Sonna sprang past him, spitting her fury. A man grinned, sidestepped her rush, and grabbed an arm, which he forced behind her back. She went to her knees with a cry and was quickly bound.

"What are they doing?" she called in alarm. "Torrek, beloved, what do they want?"

"I don't know," he said.

He was slowly overcoming his own helpless wrath, forcing it to the ground as if it were his opponent in a wrestling match. A great chill watchfulness rose in its place.

"Oh my dearest—" wept Sonna.

It cracked across Torrek's heart. He mumbled some meaningless comfort or other. Inwardly he thought of knives for these grinning, chattering bandits in hideous clothes. He thought of hanging their heads in Diupa's smokehouse.

Sonna writhed and tried to bite when they picked her up and took her inside the ship. It earned her nothing but a stunning cuff. Torrek conserved his strength, watching the metal bleakness through which he was borne.

Lashed in a chair, he had a view of the sky and the Steeps through a kind of—no, not window, nor telescope—image-maker? He focused on that, ignoring the alienness of furnishings around him. Even when the ship rose noiselessly into heaven, and the highest peaks fell out of sight, and Sonna's courage broke in a raw scream, Torrek remained watching the view.

But when the stars harshened and came forth in their hundreds, when the great bowl of the world turned into a ringed shield dazzling against darkness, and Sonna clenched her eyes and would not look . . . he had an eerie sense of homecoming.

Almost, he *knew* the monster mother ship would be waiting there and would draw this little boat into herself.

Was it only the speculations of Diupa's philosophers, or did he remember as a fact that the World Called Maanerek was merely a single one of unaccountably many?

He shivered at a ghostly thought, a thin frightened wisp of—recollection?—of how cruel and alien those worlds could be.

Torrek whirled in the narrowness of the cell where they had caged him. One hand snatched for his knife. When he remembered it was gone, his teeth clicked together, as if closing in a throat.

Sonna caught his arm. "No," she said.

He came back to humanness like one awakening from a dream. The carnivore light faded as he looked down at her.

"What?" he asked vaguely.

"It is no use to fight them," she said. "Not till we know more."

He nodded stiffly, as if his neckbones creaked. Then he held her in his arms and glared at the men who were opening the door.

The younger one raised a weapon. At least Torrek supposed it was a weapon, shaped like a very small blowgun, but grasped in a single fist. This person, or troll, or whatever he was, seemed healthier than his fellows: his skin had a normal weather-beaten look, not the dead paleness of the others, and he moved with a muscular assurance. He was almost as big as Torrek, with the same yellow hair cropped short, but with a beak of a nose and a rigid set to his lips.

He spoke. It was a heavily accented version of the Naesevis tongue, the common mercantile language of the Islands. Torrek was not expert in it himself, though so wealthy a nation as Dumethdin naturally attracted many traders, but it was near enough kin to that spoken along Fenga Fjord for him to use.

"Best you do not attack me. The *gun*—this weapon shoots a—it can put you to sleep instantly. Awaking from such a sleep is painful."

Torrek spat on the floor.

"You do understand me, do you not?"

"Yes," said Torrek, "I understand you." The pronoun he chose was insulting, but the stranger did not seem to know the difference.

"Good. I am Coan Smit. This man beside me is the learned Frain Horlam."

The other was little and old, with thin grey hair and blinking watery eyes. Like Coan Smit, he wore a plain greenish coverall, but lacked the young man's insignia.

"What do you call yourself?" Smit asked.

"I am Torrek, a Harpooner of Diupa, adopted to the Bua Clan and an oath-brother in full standing of Sea Bear Lodge, pledged to the King of Dumethdin."

It was another insult: anyone who knew Naesevis should have been familiar enough with the symbology of the Islands to read Torrek's allegiances off his tattoos. Once more it made no impression.

Not at all offended, Smit grinned briefly and said something to Frain Horlam, who nodded with a curious eagerness. Then, turning back to his prisoners, Smit went on in a careful tone: "Thank you. I want you to understand, Torrek, that we are your friends. We are, in fact, your *people*, and you are about to be given back your rightful heritage."

As from an immense distance, Torrek heard Sonna's indrawn gasp. He himself felt no great shock. The knowledge had been growing within him since that sky-boat came through darkness to grip him fast. In part it was that he looked like these folk. But in a deeper part, lying beyond all words, this was something he simply knew.

It was a cold and poisoned knowledge.

"Well, what have you to say further?" he demanded curtly.

"If you will come with us, we will take you to a place where it can better be explained."

"I will do so, provided this woman comes with me."

"No, it is best she stay. There would be too much trouble; even without her, it will be hard enough to make things clear to you."

"Let it be so, my dear one," mumbled Sonna. There was a beaten weariness about her. She had seen and suffered too much in too short a time.

Torrek saw how the unhumanly stiff manner of Coan Smit, a manner of metal, broke open as his eyes drifted down the girl where she stood. Almost, then, Torrek seized Smit in the grip of a wrestler, to crack his spine across a knee.

He choked back his rage and the icy wariness that replaced it was so unlike Dumethdin's warm folk—it branded him so sharply as one of this witch-race—that he slumped and grew saddened.

"Let us go," he said.

As he followed Horlam down a glaring bare corridor, with Smit and Smit's weapon at his back, he turned over his last glimpse of Sonna: a small figure at the barred door, all alone in a cage.

It was not to a room where he could look out on the arrogant stars and the cool ringed shield which was his home that they took him. Their walking ended down in the guts of the ship, in a great chamber which was a flashing, blinking, quivering, humming wilderness of philosophic apparatus.

"Sit down, Torrek," invited Smit.

The Diupa man crouched back from the chair, for it was an ugly thing of wires, instruments, and shackles.

"On the floor, perhaps—not in that," he answered.

"You will sit in that chair," Smit told him, hefting his weapon, "and permit yourself to be bound into it. Whether you do so freely or let me knock you out with this gun is your affair."

Torrek snarled at him. Smit was standing too far, too ready for a leap. Therefore Torrek yielded. As Horlam closed the steel bands which locked him by wrists, waist, and ankles, to the chair, his lips moved, invoking the nine evils on Coan Smit.

Horlam lowered a grid of wires and less comprehensible things on to Torrek's head and began adjusting it in various ways. Smit pulled up a chair for himself, sheathed his gun, and crossed his legs.

"Well," he said, "this will take a little time—to adjust the *circuits*, I mean—so I may as well tell you what you wish to know." He grinned wryly. "It is hard to figure where to begin. Some nations of men understand that the world is a round ball spinning about the sun and that the stars are other suns. I do not know if in your country—"

"I have heard such tales," grunted Torrek.

Till now the imaginings of Diupa's learned men had not seemed very plausible to him. But now he knew—beyond all reason, without needing as proof the fact of this ship—that Smit spoke the truth. But why did he know it so surely?

"Very well, then," said Smit. "It is a great distance from sun to sun, greater than men can truly understand. And there are more suns than have ever been fully counted. Nevertheless, men learned how to cross such distances in ships like this, overcoming the barriers of space, time, heat, cold, weightlessness, airlessness. Spreading from one world, very long ago, they strewed their seed on thousands of other worlds.

"Then the Empire went down in wreck and men forgot," Smit continued. "On *planets* like yours, far removed from the old centres of civilization, thinly populated at the time of the disaster—on such worlds, hardly a memory remains of the Empire and its fall."

Torrek shivered. It was not alone the weirdness of the tale, but this sense of having been told it once before, in some forgotten dream.

He said slowly: "There are legends concerning those who existed Before the Rymfar."

Smit nodded. "Of course. Not all knowledge was lost. On some worlds, a kind of civilization survived. But only slowly, through numberless agonies, has it struggled back. The Empire has not yet been rebuilt; there are many separate nations of planets. Most of the *galaxy* is still an unexplored wilderness—But I am talking beside the point.

"All right. This is a scout ship of a certain nation, your nation, which lies an enormous distance away. We have been cruising through this region of space for a number of years, mapping, studying . . . preparing the ground, in a way. Five years ago we discovered your planet and tested a new procedure.

"You are Korul Wanen, an officer of this ship. Your memories —all your memories of your entire life—were stripped from you. You were left to be picked up by the Island folk. Now we are taking you back."

Smit turned and waved an imperious arm at one of the grey-robed men who stole meekly about, serving the switches and dials of the great machine. He let Torrek sit there with sweat spurting out on the skin while he gave an order. Then he faced back, grinning.

"You don't like it, do you, Korul Wanen?" he said.

"It's a lie!" croaked Torrek. "How could you have found me if—"

"A good question. But I fear it will not disprove my assertions. You see, a small *radiating*—signalling unit, drawing its power from your own body, was implanted in a bone of yours before you were put down. We could locate you from many miles away."

"But no one would be so stupid!" roared Torrek. "I might

have died! The folk you say you left me with might have been cannibals and eaten me! What then could you possibly have gained?"

"Nothing," said Smit. "But neither would we have lost anything—except one expendable unit of the crew."

There was a certain avidness in Smit's pale eyes. He was not telling this because there was any special need to, Torrek saw. He was telling it because he wanted to watch his prisoner squirm.

Torrek stiffened. It was hard to remain calm when his heart beat so heavily and his mouth was so dry.

Why, he thought in a remote, astonished part of his brain, *I am afraid! This is what it feels like!*

The grey-robed person came back with a black cylinder the size of a man's forearm and gave it to Smit, who handled it as one handles heavy objects.

He smiled at Torrek. "In here," he said, "is the ghost of Korul Wanen."

Torrek clamped lips together. He would not ask!

"He will live again in his own body," said Smit. "But first, of course, Torrek must be rubbed out."

That drew a howl. "No!"

"Yes," said Smit eagerly.

He passed the cylinder to Horlam, who fitted it into the machine next to another one.

"You might turn over your memories one last time, Torrek. They will soon be nothing but a scribing in a tube."

Torrek struggled, uselessly, until he thought his muscles would burst. If they but would, he prayed in anguish, if he could only know clean death!

As the dizziness and the darkness closed in on him, the machine screaming inside his head until he felt it must rack his brain apart, he saw Smit lean closer to peer at him. The last thing of which Torrek the Harpooner had awareness was Smit's look of enjoyment.

KORUL WANEN

He hefted the cylinder. "Five years!" he murmured.

"Oh, it could hold several centuries' worth of experience, my boy," said Dr. Frain Horlam. "When you use individual molecules to store information—"

Wanen looked up from the cylinder, across the desk to the ageing psychologist. He was not certain how to act. On the one hand, the old fellow was a non-Cadre civilian; as such, he rated scant respect from a lieutenant in the Astro service. On the other hand, Horlam was in charge of the major scientific undertaking of this expedition, and on an exploratory trip, such work was subordinate only to the gathering of militechnic data.

Therefore Wanen said with a carefully noncommittal courtesy: "The theory of this never was explained to me. As long as you only wish me to make conversation, with no subject assigned, perhaps you would be kind enough to instruct me."

Horlam's grey head lifted. "In a rough way, if you like," he said. He leaned back and took out a cigar. "Smoke?"

"No!" Wanen collected himself. "You know I am an Academy man and therefore conditioned against vice."

"Why?" Horlam tossed the question off so casually, between puffs on his own cigar, that Wanen answered without thinking:

"In order to serve the Hegemony and the Cadre which guides it more efficiently—" He jarred to a halt. "You're deliberately baiting me!"

"If you say so."

"These are not joking matters. Don't make me report you."

"This ship is a starvish long way from home," said Horlam, with no obvious relevance. "Seven years now since we left. Nobody back there knows where we are—we didn't know ourselves just where we were going. The stars have changed position so much that the old Imperial astro data are no use at all, and space is so big, and there are so many stars—if we don't come back, it will be hundreds of years, probably, before another Hegemony ship chances to come exploring around this way again."

Wanen's uneasy puzzlement grew. It might only be the lingering strangeness of his experience. He had wanted to report for duty as soon as he awoke in the sick-bay cot, but they had made him rest for a while and then sent him to Horlam's office. An informal talk was to probe his restored self and make certain he was once again fit to serve. But this was *too* informal!

"Why do you say these things?" Wanen asked in a very low, controlled voice. "They're platitudes, but your tone . . . somehow, it all borders on deviationism."

"For which I could be given anything on the scale of corrections, from a reprimand, up through death, to lobotomy or memory erasure—eh?" Horlam smiled around his cigar. "Never mind, boy. You must also know that there aren't any secret police aboard to whom I could be reported. The reason I'm saying all this is that there are certain things I must tell you. I want to cushion the shock. Your first deep-space voyage?"

"Yes."

"And you only had two years of it. Then you were mind-blanked and deposited on that planet. The rest of us have been batting around this part of the Galaxy for five years more. Things change under such conditions. There has to be a certain adjustment—a loosening of discipline, a letdown of idealism. You'll see it for yourself. Don't be unduly shocked. The Cadre knows the phenomenon well, allows for it."

Wanen realized suddenly that this was why deep-space men never returned to the home worlds of the Hegemony. When you had made your first really long voyage, you were never allowed closer to the Inner Stars than a year's journey; your home became the great naval bases. You knew this in advance, and were told it was a matter of quarantine, and accepted the sacrifice as a small offering to make for the Cadre.

Now he saw that the disease he might conceivably be carrying, against which the people of the Inner Stars must forever be protected, was not a physical one.

"Very well," he said, smiling his relief. "I understand."

"Glad to hear it," said Horlam. "Makes things that much easier."

Wanen laid the cylinder on the desk. "But we were discussing this, were we not?"

"Uh, yes. I was explaining the fundamental idea." Horlam drew a breath and set forth on a lecture. "Memory patterns, including the unconscious habit patterns, are taken to be synaptic pathways 'grooved' into the nervous system—if I may speak very loosely. The personality at any instant is a function of basic heredity, physical constitution—health, diet and so on—and the accumulated total of these synaptic paths. Now the paths, being physical, can be scanned, and, of course, whatever is scanned can be recorded.

"Inside this cylinder is a complex protein whose molecules are selectively distorted to record the scanned data. But that's detail.

Whatever can be scanned can also be selectively heterodyned, cancelled, rubbed out—call it what you like—leaving the adult body a memoryless, mindless hulk. But such a body relearns with astonishing speed; it becomes a new, wholly functioning personality in less than a year.

"If these new memories, such as those you acquired in the past five years, are scanned and cancelled, the recording of the old ones can be 'played back', so to speak—reimposed on your nervous system. And thus Lieutenant Korul Wanen returns to life."

The young man scowled. "I know all that," he protested. "You explained it to me yourself when I got this assignment . . . but perhaps you've forgotten. After all, to you it happened five years ago. What I was interested in now were the more technical details: the type of signal used, for instance."

"I can't tell you much," said Horlam regretfully.

"Classified? I'm sorry I asked."

"It's not that classified. No, first is the fact that you would have to learn three new sciences for me to make sense to you. Second, it's an ancient Imperial technique, totally lost during the Dark Ages. An exploratory ship found a wrecked machine and a set of handbooks in the ruins of a city on Balgut IV about thirty years ago. Slowly and painfully, the research unit to which I belong has rebuilt the psychalyzer, as we call it, and learned a few things about it. But we're still mostly groping in the dark."

"This record here—" Wanen nodded at the cylinder, which stood on the desk like some crude idol—"you intend to study it, I imagine?"

"Yes, but as an electronic phenomenon, not as a set of memories *per se*, which it could only become by being reimposed on a living brain, which I suspect could only be your brain. But with our apparatus, we can make a point-by-point comparison of his record with the record we have of yourself as Wanen—run statistical analyses and so on. I'm especially interested in trying to find out precisely what patterns in the recording correspond to the learned elements of personality.

"This was a totally new kind of experiment, you understand. Never before has the same body experienced two totally different cultures. Now we can really separate out the significant factors.

Give my computers—and me—a few years to chew all the data, and I may actually begin to know something about the human brain. Yes, you've performed a real service to science."

"I hope it is also a service to the Hegemony," said Wanen.

"Oh, it is. Consider what might be done about deviationism. At present, the psychalyzer can only wipe out the total memory of a nonloyal unit. The process of re-education from the ground up is slow and costly; lobotomy and reduction to low civilian rank is a waste of good human potential. If we knew how, deviant tendencies could be corrected much more neatly, without sacrificing the deviant's skills and experience. In fact, perhaps conditioning could be made so thorough that no one would be physically able to have nonloyal thoughts."

It was such a splendid vision that Wanen jumped to his feet and blurted: "Thank you! Thank you for letting me serve!"

Horlam knocked the ash off his cigar and nodded in a slow, somehow old fashion. "You're all right," he said in a dry voice. "You may report for duty."

Coan Smit had changed in five years. He was no longer quite the steel-hard, steel-proud Academy youngster who had forever left the Inner Stars in order to serve them more fully.

Wanen grew only slowly aware of it in the course of hours when they stood watch by the Number Five boat-launcher, as they had done so many times before. Smit was still deft, crisp, neat. If his face had darkened, that was an honourable badge, given him by the sun and wind of the ringed planet. Wanen himself, after all, was even more deeply tanned, and added thereto was a barbarian tattoo.

But Smit was not *absolutely* Academy. The creases in his uniform were merely knife-edged, his boots did not blind the eye. He stood properly straight, but without actually straining his muscles. He walked with the regulation pace, but was there the faintest hint of a swagger?

When they were finally relieved, Smit yawned in a most un-Astro fashion. "Good to see you again, Lieutenant," he said.

"Thank you, Lieutenant," said Wanen formally.

"Let's get a cup of coffee. I want to talk to you."

Their hard heels clacked on metal as they went down the passage towards the junior officers' wardroom. Wanen found himself noticing the enlisted men he passed. The had grown sloppier than the officers, not outrageously so, but it was there; and when they saluted his insignia, he sensed an air of cringing.

Many punishments must have been ordered aboard the "Seeker" in the last five years: sweatbox, nerve-pulsing, and worse. But that should not have been necessary ... or should it?

Wanen sighed in confusion. They raised you from birth to serve—his mind recited the comforting Hierarchy: *The unit which is called I serves the unit called the Ship, which serves the Fleet, which is an arm of the almighty Hegemony and of the Cadre that guides us all towards the New Empire; there are no other loyalties.*

You were bred and raised for one purpose only like all units below Cadre level. Your particular purpose was to serve in the Outer Fleet. And that, of course, was right and good; but it was a narrow education that did not prepare you for the sudden impact of strangeness.

For two years, while the "Seeker" hurtled through unmapped hundreds of parsecs, he had seen a little of the otherness which is deep space—just a little. Then five years dropped from his life, and here he was again, in a ship which for half a decade had had the cold wild otherness seeping through her armour and—

They entered the small wardroom. No one else was present. Smit dialled for coffee and, when it came, sat cradling the hot cup in his hands for a while, as if he were chilled.

"I saw you, of course, a good many hours ago," he said finally. "But you wouldn't remember that. You were still Torrek then."

"Torrek?" Wanen raised his brows inquiringly.

"That was your name, you said. Oh, you were a proper savage, I can tell you!" Smit chuckled. "Beautifully easy to bait, too. I hope you don't—*Hey!*"

Wanen yanked himself back barely in time. His hands were still crooked claws. He looked at them numbly, and it came to him that they had curved to fit a man's throat.

"What are you *doing*?" gasped Smit.

"I don't know." Wanen sat down again heavily and stared before him. "All of a sudden, a derangement. I wanted to kill you."

"Hm." Smit recovered with the rapidity of disciplined nerves. He sat a little farther away, but his face grew calm again. After a moment he said in a thoughtful tone: "Some underlying disturbance—yes, I suppose that's it. A residual effect of the transformation you've undergone." He shrugged. "Well, why not? This is a new kind of experiment. You'd best see Horlam again, but I don't imagine it's anything too serious."

"Yes." Wanen stood up.

"Not now, you idiot! Relax. Drink your coffee. I want to discuss matters with you. It's important to our whole mission."

That brought Wanen back into his chair. "Proceed," he said. If his heart still shivered, he kept it under control.

"I hope the doctors can get that ugly tattoo off your face," complained Smit. "It bothers everybody."

"It's no worse than combat scars," said Wanen huffily.

"Oh, yes, it is. It stands for something different—something none of us wants to be reminded of." Smit glowered into his coffee for a little while longer before resuming: "You recall that we found only two inhabited planets, both of them the usual wretched, uninteresting places, before coming on Ring here. That's the nickname the crew have given it: Ring. It's important and exciting enough to rate a pet name.

"You must also remember that our preliminary scoutings showed it to be an unusually fertile planet with a human population which had lost all traces of Empire civilization—but had, on the other hand, built up a rich variety of cultures for themselves. The highest society, technologically speaking, is in the Islands, the big subtropical archipelago. They're just on the verge of printing and chemical explosives and could easily come up with a scientific-industrial revolution. That's the people we dropped you among."

"Yes," said Wanen. "I remember seeing it from the air. They told me that was the place—" His voice ran on, almost as if another mind were musing aloud. "There was a deep fjord, and towns along it, and mountains with long valleys like green fingers reaching down to the water and—No, I'm not sure." He rubbed his eyes. "Did I see clouds floating under a high peak? There was something about a peak, like victory. No, I can't recall."

He grew aware that Smit was regarding him oddly, but the sense of exaltation remained within him.

"Continue," Wanen said. "You were bringing me up to date."

"Yes. I was. Well, then, we left Ring, and for nearly five years more we've been prowling this part of the spiral arm."

"What did you find?"

"Planets. Some with people on them. Nothing to compare with Ring. About six months ago, therefore, we came back. I and some others went down on ethnic survey in the Island region. I suppose you've heard something about the techniques. Kidnap a native, use accelerine and hypnosis to get the language and basic cultural information from him in a hurry, then dispose of him and go out yourself. Claim to be a foreigner from some other country. It works pretty well with societies that know there are other nations 'beyond the horizon' but don't know exactly what they're like."

"What's a Boats man doing in ethnic survey?"

"You're Boats, too, Lieutenant."

"That's different. There were certain physical qualifications needed for the experiment, to give the blanked man a chance of survival, and training was, of course, irrelevant. But you—"

A bleakness crossed Smit's face. "We're short of ethnic specialists," he said, "and war boats aren't needed hereabouts. I had to fill in. So did a number of others."

"High casualties elsewhere?"

"Yes."

"But—from primitives?" Wanen was startled. "I thought they weren't even supposed to know there were observers among them —let alone get unnecessarily antagonized—let alone kill our men with—with spears!"

"All those things happened," said Smit grimly. "The loss of quality—competence, adjustedness, efficiency, even loyalty—the decay of the entire crew was incredible. In the case of the ethnic men, it was disastrous. See here, Lieutenant—half the casualties among survey teams were due to our having to shoot the men ourselves for radical deviationism."

Wanen sat as if struck on the head. "No," he whispered.

Smit bared his teeth. It was not a smile, nor quite a snarl. "Yes. I've felt the tendencies in myself. What did you expect? Seven years of metal walls and celibacy!"

"But we have Antisex. We have loyalty rallies—"

"Mere suppression of overt symptoms. Frustration continues to build up underneath, until it breaks loose in sheer destruction and negativism. Even a lifetime's conditioning can't survive that kind of pressure."

"But this can't be the first time—"

"Of course not. It always happens on a really long voyage.

When the first troubles arose, the captain explained the phenomenon to all us officers."

"Well, then!" Wanen leaned back, sighing his relief. "So there must be a procedure in the Classified Manuals."

"There is," agreed Smit. "After casualties due to such causes exceed a certain percentage, the ship is to find a backward planet. A certain small area is to be occupied. Built-up aggressions may then be freely vented on its men and children. Antisex is discontinued and the local women made generally available."

Wanen felt a curious, sick reluctance within himself. He couldn't understand it. Even from an altruistic viewpoint, such measures were for the good of the barbarians, too, since the procedure was obviously essential to the expansion of the Hegemony, and the Hegemony would come at last to include all mankind everywhere in the galaxy.

Nevertheless, he could hardly get the words out: "So Ring has been picked?"

"No," said Smit. "The tension release I spoke of took place months ago, on the last planet we stopped at."

A second's inexplicable relief was followed by a new tightness of soul. "Then why are we still here?"

"Problems! A dilemma!"

Smit shoved his empty cup away, got up, and started pacing the floor. It was not the act of an Academy man, taught never to show uncertainty to the world.

"You see, the Classified Manuals further recommend that a ship return to base immediately after such release has been effected. Otherwise—well, just consider the ordinary insignificant little enlisted man, the faceless unit among hundreds of other interchangeable units. For a few weeks he has been a conqueror, killing, whipping, flaying, burning, raping, drinking himself stupid every night. Resuming ship discipline and Antisex isn't easy. In fact, if he isn't pointed back towards normal surroundings at once, the Cadre alone knows what deviationism can arise."

Wanen said, "Having recovered me, why don't we go home?"

"We've got to occupy Ring," said Smit shakily. "Not for the —the previous purpose. For militechnic reasons."

"What? But I thought this was only a survey."

"Oh, it is. Or was. But look. The average backslid planet is a pretty miserable affair. It's just naturally so hostile to human life that when the Empire broke up and all the artificial gadgets and props were destroyed, or rusted away, civilization went to maximum entropy in an obscene hurry. On most planets man simply became extinct. In the cases where adaptation was possible, the normal outcome was savagery.

"Ring, though, is a world where men can really feel at home. They've flourished! There are millions of them, and they include some extremely able, sophisticated races. It's almost as good a conquest as a unified planet with full industrial culture.

"And remember, Lieutenant, we have mortal enemies. The Republic, the Libertarian League, the Royal Brotherhood, the High Earls of Morlan—there are a dozen other civilizations spreading into space, each with its own idea of what the New Empire should be like. We don't dare let one of their scouts stumble on Ring. Whoever garrisons it first has got possession of it, at this distance from all naval bases."

"Easy now!" said Wanen. "What are the odds of their finding Ring? A hundred billion stars in the Galaxy and this one to find among them all."

"And the G-2 stars are always investigated first," Smit said, "and they're not too common in this spiral arm, and we *know* there are League ships mapping it, too. It's a finite chance, certainly—I know that—but one we dare not take. We *must* plant a garrison down there; it's in the Manuals. Then we head back to base, report our find, and have a task force sent which can take over the entire planet, fortify it properly, civilize the inhabitants, and so on.

"But it'll take us nearly two years to get home—a year to organize the task force, probably—two more years to come back—

"Five years! Can we trust a garrison for five years?"

Horlam began unclipping the electrodes from Wanen's head and body. His lips were pursed, and he frowned, thinking.

"Well?" exclaimed Wanen. Only after half a minute of silence did he realize how un-Astro it had been for him to reveal emotion before a non-Cadre civilian. *What was wrong with him?*

"Well," said Horlam presently, "according to every known encephalographic and neurographic technique, you have no surviving memories of your stay on Ring."

"Are you certain?" insisted Wanen. "There must be something to account for—for—Look here." He forced the words out, one by one. "On my way to your office, I looked out at the planet. I have never seen anything so beautiful in my life. I loved it as I ought to love only the Cadre. I had to run from there before the tears came." He felt pain in his hands and unclenched them; the nails had bitten into the palms. "Something about the experience must have changed me. I'm *deviant.*"

"See here," said Horlam patiently, "it's my specialty, not yours, to know what memory is. It's a permanent alteration of protoplasm as the result of a stimulus. The memory patterns are all in the brain, except for a few habits which are synaptic patterns in the nerves proper. Well, I've just run a comparison of the Wanen record we have, your cylinder, with the Wanen record in your own nervous system. This is an absolutely objective process, a tracing out of electronic patterns of flow, resistance—it makes an electronic map of your entire nervous system."

He finished releasing the younger man, sat down on a corner of his workbench, and took out a cigar. "The difference between the two patterns, my friend, is insignificant—a few additional traces caused by your experiences since your normal personality was reimposed. You've been telling yourself an old-time ghost story, with lingering traces of your Torrek memories in place of the ghost. Now forget it. I assure you that there are *no* such traces."

"But then what's making me have these fits?" Wanen felt himself almost cringing back.

"I'm not certain," shrugged Horlam. "I told you psychalysis is still a half-science fumbling in the dark. But at least I've proved your trouble is nothing very basic to yourself.

"Tentatively, my diagnosis is minor glandular upset. You've spent five years on an alien planet, eating its home-grown food. Perfectly good, nourishing food for a man, but there are doubtless subtle biochemical differences—hormone traces, vitaminlike compounds, and so on. Your body adapted. Now it's having a little difficulty re-adapting to ship rations. The slight chemical imbalance is expressing itself as irrational surges of emotion."

Wanen nodded. His tension began to ease. Chemical neuroses were not unheard of in this service, and easily correctible. "If I'm not actually deviating towards nonloyalty—"

"Not enough to matter," drawled Horlam. "These glandular-digestive hooraws do sometimes express themselves queerly. For instance, this desire to kill Lieutenant Smit that you mentioned, or your feeling towards Ring the attitudes appropriate only to the Cadre. And—let's see, have you had dreams the last night or two?"

Wanen shuddered. "Nightmares. I saw my own crewmates being killed—atrociously."

"An obvious expression of resentment towards them—towards the entire Hegemony culture," said Horlam casually. When Wanen jerked, half leaping to his feet, the psychologist laughed. "Take it easy there, son. You're not nonloyal, and nobody is going to shoot you. It happens all the time and doesn't mean a thing."

He got his cigar going. "After all, man evolved as a creature of forests and open air and—intimacy, shall we say? A family animal. Our civilization forbids all this, locks us indoors with machines, selects our mates for us, whom we seldom see, and takes our children away to raise in crèches. Naturally our instincts revolt. The good unit will not deny that he has bestial instincts—rather, he will accept the fact and use his strength to overcome them."

Wanen found the slow voice relaxing. He even began to feel warm. "I see," he answered. "Thank you. What treatment do you plan?"

"None, unless your symptoms get worse. And I expect they'll improve by themselves. Now you're dismissed. The exec wants you to report to him for special assignment."

It was curious, the thick pounding of his heart as he walked towards the door. The austerity of the ship, blank hallways and neat little cubicles, eternal white glare of fluorescents, gave the mind nothing to seize. It was thrown back on its own sick fantasies.

Wanen rehearsed his orders—any escape from the chaos and the sullen feeling of rebellion that lay coiled in his skull. The trouble was, his orders were so indefinite. In Astro you were necessarily encouraged to think for yourself to some extent. Even an enlisted man was no use on a spaceship if the critical faculties were electrically burned out of his brain, as was done for the lower ranks of civilians in childhood. But this was too much latitude for a plain lieutenant of Boats. What was he supposed to *do*?

"This young woman who was picked up with you. She was the first of a series of prisoners we intend to take, to furnish more detailed information about the country. But she's proven too savage, even dangerous, to be of help. All that's been accomplished is to teach her the Cadric language by psychalysis, under accelerine. What information we have about her people suggests that none we might capture is likely to be of much greater value to us. However, since she was accompanying you, Lieutenant, she may be more co-operative if she is left alone with you. Persuade her to assist us.

"Our ground-fighting forces are not so large nor so well equipped that we could easily hold an island against the determined opposition of the archipelago nations—especially since deviationism is anticipated among the garrison, which may culminate in open mutiny if there is a strong enemy to whom the mutineers could desert afterwards. Therefore it will be necessary, if we are to occupy even one island, that we exterminate all natives throughout the archipelago. The information she can furnish would be of value in conducting such an operation efficiently."

"The Intelligence men—did they try coercion, sir?"

"On the woman? Of course. She stood nerve-pulsing till she fainted, so that's no help. The so-called truth drugs disorganize the mind too much; we need systematic information. We could try mutilation, or the threat of it, but I doubt if it would work either; her culture seems to set a high value on intransigence. Either you persuade her, Lieutenant, or we discard her completely and fish for other prisoners."

"Yes, sir. But if it is permitted me to ask, why should we attack the Island at all? There must be more backward areas, even desert regions, which could more easily be occupied."

"No doubt. But it so happens that the Islands are the only part of the Ring which have been studied in any detail. That is because the ethnic officers were naturally most interested in the planet's most advanced culture. Now we do not have enough ethnic or cartographic specialists left to map any other region soon enough."

"I see. Thank you, sir."

"Service to the Cadre! Dismissed."

"Service to the Cadre!"

Wanen halted at the door.

He was, he realized with a cold shock, afraid of what lay beyond.

Then, mumbling a curse, he palmed the lock. It opened for his prints, and he went through. The door clashed shut behind him.

She sprang from her bunk and stood for a moment without stirring, as if frozen. And yet, he thought dizzily, the lines of her were fleetness itself. He had never in all his memory seen so wild and lovely a creature as the one which poised in the steel bareness of this little cell.

(Yes, he had—as Torrek. But Torrek had been peeled from him, like a skin taken off living flesh.)

She wept and ran to his arms.

As he held her, he felt again the sensation which had risen in him when Ring swam across the stars. Only it was a deeper thing this time, a knife twisting inside him and a summer's breeze in his hair, trumpeted victory and a long blue twilight where they two walked alone. Almost, he carried her to the bunk—

But only almost.

He remembered in barest time that there was a spy-scope mounted somewhere. It brought him back to a sense of his duty, but with the heaviness of a world oppressing him.

She babbled endearments in a language he did not know, until at last he put a hand under her chin and tilted her face up towards him (where had he learned the gesture?) and said with an overwhelming tenderness: "Speak Cadric. I have forgotten."

"Oh—" She drew a little away from him. His arms would not release her, not entirely, but he saw terror in her eyes.

"It's all right," he said. "It's only that I have forgotten what happened on—in the Islands. You see, I have been returned to my people."

"*Your* people!" She said it slowly. The unfamiliar language was stiff on her lips.

"Yes." He let her go and stared at the floor, feeling obscurely ashamed. She did not run from him, but there was no place to run to. He ploughed ahead: "I regret any inconveniences you may have suffered, but it was necessary. We've come for the good of all mankind."

"It—may be." She eased a trifle and whispered: "But you have forgotten everything indeed, Torrek. They have shorn your mind like your hair?"

"I don't even know your name anymore," he said wryly.

"Even—I am Sonna, Baelg's daughter." A slow flush crossed her cheeks. "We were going into the mountains together."

He remembered acutely that he had not yet been issued his Antisex tablets. But it was hard to define his feelings towards the girl. She was more than a means of relieving tension, more, even, than a coprocreator of loyal units.

Surely his trouble went deeper than Horlam admitted!

"Don't you remember how you killed the kraka?" she asked him wonderingly. Her fists drew together. "It was unfair to take that from you!"

"It's all right," he said. "After all, I have regained so much more. I remember my—well, my first indoctrination, instead of—oh, say, my first fishing trip— Never mind! You simply wouldn't understand."

"What is your name now?" she asked.

"Korul Wanen."

"I shall always think of you as Torrek." She sat down on the bunk, smiling unhappily. "Come, join me, at least, and tell me about your people."

He did. It was mostly an astronomy lesson, with a sketch of history since the Empire died and a lecture on the New Empire of the future. He spoke in a most dry, uninspired tone and looked straight before him.

"Yes," she said finally, "it is a glorious vision, to make all men brothers again. I think Dumethdin will be pleased to make an alliance with you."

"An alliance?" he stumbled. "That's not just what—what we had in mind."

"No? What then?"

Being trained only to guide spaceships, and in combat to operate one of the small boats which guarded a major formation, Wanen proceeded to tell her.

She grew altogether still.

"It is, of course, for the best," he said.

She stood up. "Get out."

"What? But I was explaining—"

"I know I cannot kill you. But get out before I dirty my hands by trying!"

"See here—your own self-interest—loyalty to the Cadre is expected of *all* humans—"

She did something then which told him how alien her homeland was and he himself had been. She sat down, cross-legged, and ignored him. She erased him from her private universe of perceptions. He realized only slowly what she was doing; afterwards, he wondered why he understood at all. He had never heard of such a thing before, except in his cancelled Torrek incarnation.

But when it penetrated his mind, he turned and ran from her, shaking with fear.

"You have been an idiot," said Coan Smit. They sat alone in the wardroom, after coming off Boats watch once again.

"How was I to know?" asked Wanen miserably. He stared at his cup without really seeing it. "Diplomacy isn't my field. I'm not an ethnic man, for Cadre's sake! The exec himself said he could not reprimand me."

"I can. An Academy man isn't some stupid civilian—we're not only allowed versatility, it's expected of us. You've let down the Academy, Wanen."

"Shut up!" The emotion within Wanen exploded in a roar. "Shut up or I'll wring your neck!"

"Lieutenant!" Smit sprang erect. "Your behaviour is deviant."

"For your information," said Wanen between his teeth, "my rank is equal to yours. I'm going to file a criticism of your language."

"And *I* am going to file a suspicion of deviationism," Smit retorted. "Horlam is another idiot. He should have turned you inside out. Just because your trouble isn't due to lingering memory traces doesn't prove that you have no trouble."

"I am also physiologically and biochemically checked out," snapped Wanen. "Any imbalance is a question of micro quantities. When were you last investigated? And what business is it of yours, anyway?"

" 'Anyone's business is everyone's business.' "

Wanen had heard the slogan often enough. He had cited it

himself now and then, in a past which seemed impossibly remote. But all at once it tasted like brass in his mouth. He hunched over his coffee cup, smouldering.

"We're too far from home," said Smit, more gently. "If we don't return, it may be centuries before a Hegemony ship comes this way again. An enemy scout may find Ring meanwhile. *Anything* might happen. Better to dispose of you on suspicion than risk our entire operation."

"Yes," said Wanen automatically. "That's the obvious solution."

"Not that I really think that'll be necessary." Smit was fairly bedewed with good-fellowship now. He came around the table and laid a brotherly hand on the other man's shoulder. "Actually, I myself believe your trouble is just some trivial thing. A few shots of hormone, perhaps some conditioning, and you should be as good as new. Or—wait. Now that I come to think of it, you've gone a full seven years without tension release!"

"I was on Ring," mumbled Wanen. "I was a man of—what did she call it?—a man of Dumethdin. We didn't need to do such things."

"No doubt. But now you've forgotten. Hm." Smit paused.

Looking up, Wanen saw him thoughtfully rubbing his chin and realized with an illogical resentment that the fellow was trying to be helpful.

"I have an idea," Smit went on. "It'll have to be approved, of course, but I don't see why it shouldn't be. And if all you need is release, this will certainly provide it."

"What will?"

"This girl, the one we captured. Since she just won't cooperate and a total reconditioning isn't worthwhile, I understand that she'll be lobotomized and turned over to the enlisted men for a few days. Now if you were allowed to watch the operation and then have her first and throw her out of the air lock yourself when she's no use anymore—why, it should be as good as a six months' furlough!"

Wanen sat very still. After Smit had gone out, he remained in his position, crouched over the wardroom table. His heartbeat had slowed so much that he could no longer feel or hear it. Once, vaguely and indifferently, he wondered if he were dead.

Then he realized that he was insane.

*　　　*　　　*

The Boats watch was changed every four hours, with the same men taking it every fourth time round. Between such duties, one ate, slept, studied, participated in loyalty demonstrations—but there was also a certain amount of time to oneself, at least on the officer level. The young men played ball in the gym, or gambled in the wardroom, or perhaps they sat and talked.

At any rate, there would be nothing suspicious about an off-duty lieutenant walking through almost any part of the ship.

Wanen was counting on that. There was a curious peace within him. He knew he was mad. In view of Horlam's exhaustive tests and their uniformly negative results, it was the only possible explanation. The strain of changing personalities clearly had cracked his mind open. He was crazy, and he expected to be killed somewhere along the way, and it didn't matter greatly. Nevertheless he took no unnecessary chances.

He forged his squadron commander's name to a Special Orders slip and presented Lieutenant Rosnin with it when that conscientious young man went on Boats watch.

"Full combat lading for Seventeen, including fusion missiles?" Rosnin's brows went up. "What's going on?"

"Classified," said Wanen briskly. "Don't you see this is a Special form?"

Rosnin might have wondered why any junior officer should be entrusted with Classified orders and, simultaneously, present the directive in so casual a fashion. But he was not a man of great curiosity nor given to annoying his superiors with questions. Wanen had remembered that from the outbound voyage and counted on it.

"It shall be done. Service to the Cadre!"

"Service to the Cadre."

Wanen wheeled and marched to the issue room, where he checked out a Mark IV sidearm with an extra clip of explosive bullets. Normal ship routine would force him to account for his action in about six hours, when a higher-up looked over the day's requisitions. But Wanen didn't expect to be around that much longer.

He had to walk fast now, being already late for his appointment. He was depending on the fact that never before in all history had a properly conditioned unit gone deviant to the point of treason without first showing overt symptoms. He himself was at present considered merely to be under tension. But too fast a gait might attract attention.

No matter. To entropy with it. Korul Wanen was already a dead man on leave.

He came to sick bay and was passed by the armed guard. The damned ship swarmed with guards, he thought irritably—guards, paper work, anything that might keep a man too busy to think.

Well—

Frain Horlam waited, surgically gowned, in the operating room. There were two husky meditechs to assist.

The old man looked coldly at Wanen. "I never knew anybody to be late for tension release," he said.

"I was busy," snapped Wanen. "Get on with it."

Horlam switched on the sterilizers. One of the techs went out. He brought in Sonna, strapped to a wheeled cot. Her eyes were blank with a terror she could not choke off, but when she saw Wanen, she spat.

"Is the spyscope turned on?" he asked.

"Not to my knowledge," said Horlam in an acid tone. "Everyone else is too busy right now. It's you who needs a thrill."

"I only wondered."

"While we sterilize the surroundings—it wouldn't do to have her get sick, would it?—you will probably enjoy explaining what is about to be done to her," said Horlam. He did not look at Wanen; he washed his hands over and over again, with exaggerated care. "Also, of course, we must take the hair off her head before we open the skull. That should provoke an interesting reaction all by itself. Most primitive women are quite proud of their hair."

"Stop that," said Wanen.

"I'm only outlining the pleasures you have in store," Horlam explained, his voice rusty. "We can do the operation under local anaesthesia, so that she'll be conscious through most of it. Naturally, once she's been made docile, you'll have to wait a few days for her to heal up enough—" He broke off.

"Go on, Lieutenant." One of the meditechs said it urgently. His eyes were very bright, fixed on the girl. "Go on, tell it to her like the doctor says."

"Well," suggested Wanen, "both of you fellows come stand

here beside her. There, that's right."

Sonna stared up at him. He could imagine her thoughts, he told himself emptily. She would be wishing she could faint, wishing she could die, but there was too much life in her. Torrek must have had such wishes, right at the end, before they peeled him off Wanen and locked him in a black cylinder.

Wanen walked up behind the techs, laying a hand on the shoulder of each. "I suppose you boys are getting some release, too."

"Yes, sir!"

"Good." Wanen's hands slid upwards, palming their heads. Then the muscles which had wrestled the kraka smashed their skulls together.

They went down like stones, but he kicked them deftly behind the ears, to make sure. Mostly his attention was on Horlam. He yanked the gun from beneath his coverall and turned its staring eye on the old man.

"Don't move," he said. "Take it easy or I'll kill you."

Horlam's face drained of blood. "What are you doing?" he gasped.

"I am going to break out of here. Yes, I am deviant. I am also nonloyal, obstructionist, and homicidal. My greatest wish is to shoot my own dear shipmates one at a time. Please don't make me start on you. Gently now—very gently—keep your hands and feet in plain sight. Come up here and let the girl go."

For a minute he thought that Sonna had indeed fainted. But when Horlam had unstrapped her, she wavered to her feet.

"Torrek," she whispered. "Torrek, *elskling*."

"I am going to take you home, Sonna," he told her.

There was a curious expression on Horlam's thin face. The shock had passed; mostly, now, he looked interested.

"Do you really hope to get away with this?" he asked.

"No," said Wanen.

"Hitherto, this sort of thing has been a clinical impossibility. By all objective tests, you were functioning within the limits of normality—"

"Shut up. Get a surgical gown and mask for the girl. Help her put them on ... Very well. Now, Horlam, you go first out the door."

The clumsy disguise did not get them past the sentry outside. It did slow his comprehension a little bit—long enough for Wanen to shoot him as he grabbed for his rifle.

Thereafter, they ran.

Twice it was necessary to kill men who got in the way. By the time Wanen and Sonna had reached Boat Seventeen, the whole ship was one great clamour of sirens and shouts and hurrying feet.

His explosive bullets mopped up the guard by the launching robot. But as he was setting it to eject the boat, he saw Coan Smit burst from a side passage. Wanen fired once and missed. Then Smit made a dive, tackled him by the ankles, and his gun went flying.

"Go through that door, Sonna!" Wanen ordered.

Smit's hands groped after his vulnerable spots, in the standard Academy in-fighting technique. Wanen blocked him with the same automatic procedure. But then, somehow, Wanen's arms and legs were going through motions unknown to any civilized folk. He broke Smit's back across his knee.

A spatter of bullets rang down the hall. Wanen got up, threw the launcher lock switch open, and followed Sonna.

The boat's combat-ready motors roared as he shoved up the main bar. He vaulted into the pilot chair and grabbed for the controls. Sonna crouched behind him, cramped, bruised, and screaming a call that was somehow familiar to him.

Boat Seventeen leaped from the mother ship and hurled starlight back from her flanks.

"They'll hunt us down—" It was an unexpected groan in Wanen's ears.

"No, they won't!" he said roughly. "I thought of that, too."

He slammed a lever. The fusion missiles leaped from their tubes.

"Cover your eyes!" he shouted, and accelerated brutally to escape.

When the soundless explosion was over, only an incandescent gas cloud remained. It glowed for a moment, unbearably bright, before it expanded and cooled. Darkness gulped it down.

Wanen pointed his boat towards the beautiful ringed planet. He began to weep.

Sonna reached across the narrow cockpit. There was alarm

in the gesture. Horlam stopped her.

"No," he said gently. "Let him get it out. He's just denied his entire lifetime."

She sank back. Through the transparent canopy, the swelling lambent planet tangled its many coloured-luminance in her hair.

"Why are you here, old man?" she breathed. "You could have dropped behind easily enough as we fled. You did not know he meant to destroy the ship."

"I might have guessed," said Horlam dryly. "Or—let us say that I have been a trifle deviationist myself for a good many years, and when the opportunity came— It was my task to detect emerging humanness in men and uproot it. But there is a very ancient saying which asks, Who shall watch the watchmen?"

Ever so faintly, Sonna's fingers brushed the blond head which lay shuddering before her. "Has Torrek come back?"

"Not in the way you hope," said Horlam. "The open, overt memories of Torrek—the deeds done, words spoken, things seen —I'm afraid they went forever with the ship. But there is another kind of memory. Our theories don't allow for it—but then Hegemony science is almost as narrow and mechanical as Hegemony life. You can't, after all, separate the brain and nerves from the rest of the body: from muscles, veins, viscera, skin, blood, and lungs and bones. The living organism is a wholeness.

"Apparently your way of life, down there in the Islands, is a biologically sound one. It suits man's deepest instincts, as ours does not. Therefore, five years of it made a deeper impression on our boy here than the twenty-odd years of slogans and exercises before that. When we brought him back, the psychalyzer wiped out the memories, yes. I even thought it had removed the habits.

"But it didn't touch the *true* habits—those deep reactions, perhaps on an actual cellular level, which we call emotional patterns. Wanen could forget that he had been an Islander. He could not forget what it meant to be an Islander—pride, freedom, decency—whatever it *does* mean. His body remembered that for him!"

Horlam smiled. "I was not without slight suspicions of this," he finished, "but I was already deviationist enough not to report it. I was curious to see what would develop. Now I know, and I'm not sorry."

The girl leaned over the seat and rubbed her cheek against Wanen's. He lifted his head and wiped his eyes, pathetically, like a child.

"What are we going to do now?" she asked.

"Return to your country—our country," Wanen said with a gathering strength. "Warn them. We have a long time yet to make ourselves ready, invent our own science, build our own ships, and find our own allies among the stars—my knowledge and Horlam's will help with the first beginnings, but it will take many lifetimes to finish. It's a good work for a man."

"Oh, Torrek, my poor hurt Torrek—everything you have forgotten!"

"I remembered what was important, didn't I?" He twisted around to face her. "The rest I can learn over again. Will you teach me?"

BRAKE

IN THAT HOUR, when he came off watch, Captain Peter Banning did not go directly to his cabin. He felt a wish for uninhibited humour, such as this bleak age could not bring to life (except maybe in the clan gatherings of Venus—but Venus was *too* raw); and remembered that Luke Devon had a Shakespeare. It was a long time since Banning had last read *The Taming of the Shrew*. He would drop in and borrow the volume, possibly have a small drink and a chinfest. The Planetary Engineer was unusually worth talking to.

So it was that he stepped out of the companionway into A-deck corridor and saw Devon backed up against the wall at gun point.

Banning had not stayed alive as long as this—a good deal longer than he admitted—through unnecessary heroics. He slid back, flattened himself against the aluminium side of the stairwell, and stretched his ears. Very gently, one hand removed the stubby pipe from his teeth and slipped it into a pocket of his tunic, to smoulder itself out. The fumes might give him away to a sensitive nose, and he was unarmed.

Devon spoke softly, with rage chained in his throat: "The devil damn thee black, thou cream-faced loon!"

"Not so hasty," advised the other person. It was the Minerals Authority representative, Serge Andreyev, a large hairy man who dressed and talked too loudly. "I do not wish to kill you. This is just a needler in my hand. But I have also a gun for blowing out brains—if required."

His English bore its usual accent, but the tone had changed utterly. It was not the timbre of an irritating extrovert; there was no particular melodrama intended; Andreyev was making a cool statement of fact.

"It is unfortunate for me that you recognized me through all the surgical changes," he went on. "It is still more unfortunate for you that I was armed. Now we shall bargain."

"Perhaps." Devon had grown calmer. Banning could visualize him, backed up against the wall, hands in the air: a tall man, cat-lithe under the austere stiffness of his Order, close-cropped yellow hair and ice-blue eyes, and a prow of nose jutting from the bony face. *I wouldn't much like to have that hombre on my tail,* reflected Banning.

"Perhaps," repeated Devon. "Has it occurred to you, though, that a steward, a deckhand . . . anyone . . . may be along at any moment?"

"Just so. Into my cabin. There we shall talk some more."

"But it *is* infernally awkward for you," said Devon. "'Is it a world to hide virtues in?'—or prisoners, for that matter? Here we are, beyond Mars, with another two weeks before we reach Jupiter. There are a good fifteen people aboard, passengers and crew—not much, perhaps, for a ship as big as the 'Thunderbolt', but enough to search her pretty thoroughly if anyone disappears. You can't just cram me out any convenient air lock, you know, not without getting the keys from an officer. Neither can you keep me locked away without inquiries as to why I don't show up for meals . . . I assure you, if you haven't noticed, my appetite is notorious. Therefore, dear old chap—"

"We will settle this later," snapped Andreyev. "Quickly, now, go to my cabin. I shall be behind. If necessary, I will needle you and drag you there."

*   *   *

Devon was playing for time, thought Banning. If the tableau of gunman and captive remained much longer in the passageway, someone was bound to come by and— *As a matter of fact, son, someone already has.*

The captain slipped a hand into his pouch. He had a number of coins: not that they'd be any use on Ganymede, but he didn't want to re-enter Union territory without beer cash. He selected several of nearly uniform size and tucked them as a stack into his fist. It was a very old stunt.

Then, with the quick precision of a hunter—which he had been now and then, among other things—he glided from the companionway. Andreyev had just turned his back, marching Devon up the hall towards Cabin 5. Peter Banning's weighted fist smote him at the base of the skull.

Devon whirled, a tiger in grey. Banning eased Andreyev to the floor with one hand; the other took the stun pistol, not especially aimed at the Engineer nor especially aimed away from him. "Take it easy, friend," he murmured.

"You . . . oh!" Devon eased, muscle by muscle. A slow grin crossed his face. " 'For this relief, much thanks.' "

"What's going on here?" asked the captain.

There was a moment of stillness. Only the ship spoke, with a whisper of ventilators. The sound might almost have belonged to that night of cold stars through which she hurtled.

"Well?" said Banning impatiently.

Devon stood for an instant longer, as if taking his measure. The captain was a stocky man of medium height, with faintly grizzled black hair clipped short on a long head. His face was broad, it bore high cheekbones, and its dark-white skin had a somehow ageless look: deep trenches from wide nose to big mouth, crow's-feet around the bony-ridged grey eyes, otherwise smooth as a child's. He did not wear the trim blue jacket and white trousers of the Fireball Line but favoured a Venusian-style beret and kilt, Arabian carpet slippers, a disreputable old green tunic of possibly Martian origin.

"I don't know," said the Planetary Engineer at last. "He just pulled that gun on me."

"Sorry, I heard a bit of the talk between you. Now come clean. I'm responsible for this ship, and I want to know what's going on."

"So do I," said Devon grimly. "I'm not really trying to stall you, skipper—not much, anyway." He stopped over Andreyev and searched the huddled body. "Ah, yes, here's that other gun he spoke of, the lethal one."

"Give me that!" Banning snatched it. The metal was cold and heavy in his grasp. It came to him with a faint shock that he himself and his entire crew had nothing more dangerous between them than some knives and monkey wrenches. A spaceship was not a Spanish caravel, her crew had no reason to arm against pirates or mutiny or—

Or did they?

"Go find a steward," snapped Banning. "Come back here with him. Mr. Andreyev goes in irons for the rest of the trip."

"Irons?" Under the cowl of his grey tunic, Devon's brows went up.

"Chains . . . restraint . . . hell, we'll lock him away. I've got a bad habit of using archaisms. Now, jump!"

The Engineer went quickly down the hall. Banning lounged back, twirling the gun by its trigger guard, and watched him go.

Where had he seen the fellow before?

He searched a cluttered memory for a tall blond man who was athlete, technician, Shakespearean enthusiast, and amateur painter in oils. Perhaps it was only someone he had read about, with a portrait; there was so much history— Wait. The Rostomily brotherhood. Of course. But that was three centuries ago!

Presumably someone, somewhere, had kept a few cells in storage, after that corps of exogenetic twins had finally made their secret open, disbanded, and mingled their superior genes in the common human lifestream. And then, perhaps thirty years ago, the Engineers had quietly grown such a child in a tank. Maybe a lot of them. Almost anything could happen in that secret castle on the rim of Archimedes Crater, and the Solar System none the wiser till the project exploded in man's collective face.

The brotherhood had been a trump card of the early Un-men, in the days when world government was frail and embattled. A revived brotherhood must be of comparable importance to the Order. But for what purpose? The Engineers, quasi-military, almost religious, were supposed to be above politics; they were supposed to serve all men, an independent force whose only war was against the inanimate cosmos.

Banning felt a chill. With the civilization-splitting tension that existed on Earth and was daily wrung one notch higher, he could imagine what hidden struggles took place between the many factions. It wasn't all psychodynamics, telecampaigning or parliamentary manoeuvre: the Humanist episode had scarred Earth's soul, and now there were sometimes knives in the night.

Somehow an aspect of those battles had focused on his ship.

He took out his pipe, rekindled it, and puffed hard. Andreyev stirred, with a retch and a rattle in his throat.

There was a light footfall in the corridor. Banning looked up. He would have cursed the interruption had anyone but Cleonie Rogers appeared. As it was, he made the forgotten gesture of raising his cap.

"Oh!" Her hand went to her mouth. For an instant she looked frightened, then came forward in a way he liked: the more so as she had been consistently annoyed by Andreyev's loud attempts to flirt. "Oh, is he hurt? Can I help?"

"Better stand back, m'lady," advised Banning. She saw the stunner in his hand and the automatic in his waistband. Her lips parted in the large-eyed, snub-nosed face. With the yellow hair that fell softly down to bare shoulders, with a wholly feminine topless shimmergown and a whisper of cosmetics, she was a small walking anachronism.

"What happened?" A shaken courage rallied in her. It was well done, thought the man, considering that she was a child of wealth, never done a day's work in her life, bound for the Jovian Republic as an actual live tourist.

"That's what I'd kind of like to know," he told her. "This character here pulled an equalizer—a gun, I mean—on Engineer Devon. Then I came along and sapped him."

He saw her stiffen. Even aboard the "Thunderbolt", which was not one of the inner-planet luxury liners but a freighter whose few passengers—except her—were bound for Ganymede on business . . . even here there were dimly lit corners and piped music and the majesty of the stars. Banning had noticed how much she and Devon had been together. Therefore he said kindly: "Oh, Luke wasn't hurt. I sent him for help. Must say it's taking him one hell of a time, too. Did the stewards crawl into the fire chamber for a nap?"

She smiled uncertainly. "What do you think the trouble is,

Captain? Did Mr. Andreyev, ah—"

"Slip a cog?" Banning scowled. In his preoccupation he forgot that the rising incidence of nonsanity on Earth made the subject unfit for general conversation. "I doubt it. He came aboard with these toys, remember. I wonder, though. Now that the topic has come up, we do have a rum lot of passengers."

Devon was legitimate enough, his mind continued: a genuine Engineer, nursemaiding the terraforming equipment which was the "Thunderbolt's" prime cargo, the great machines which the Order would use to make Europa habitable.

And Cleonie must be an authentic tourist. (Since he regarded her as a woman, which he did not the crop-headed, tight-lipped, sad-clad creature that was today's typical Western Terrestrial female, Banning thought of her by her first name.) On the other hand—

Andreyev was not a simple Union bureaucrat, sent to negotiate a trade agreement; or, if he was, he was also much more. And how about the big fellow, Robert Falken, allegedly a nucleonic technie offered a job on Callisto? He didn't say much at table, kept to himself, but Banning knew a hard, tough man when he saw one. And Morgan Gentry, astronaut, who said the Republic had hired him to pilot intersatellite shuttles —undoubtedly a trained spaceman, but what was he besides that? And the exchange professor of advanced symbolics, dome-headed little Gomez, was he really bound for a position at the new University of X?

The girl's voice interrupted his reverie: "Captain Banning . . . what *could* be the matter with the passengers? They're all Westerners, aren't they?"

He could still be shocked, just a little bit every now and then. He hesitated a second before realizing that she had spoken not in ill will but from blank naïveté. "What has that got to do with it?" he said. "You don't really think, do you, Miss, that the conflict on Earth is a simple question of Oriental Kali worshippers versus a puritanical protechnological Occident?" He paused for breath, then ploughed on: "Why, the Kali people are only one branch of the Ramakrishian Eclectics, and there are plenty of Asians who stand by population control and Technic civilization—I have a couple in my own crew— and there are Americans who worship the Destroyer as fervently as any Ganges River farmer—and the Husseinite Moslems are closer to you, Miss Rogers, than you are to the New Christendom—"

He broke off, shaking his head. It was too big to be neatly summarized, the schism which threatened to rip Earth apart. He might have said it boiled down to the fact that technology had failed to solve problems which *must* be solved; but he didn't want to phrase it thus, because it would sound antiscientific, and he wasn't.

Thank all kindly gods that there were men on other planets now! The harvest of all the patient centuries since Galileo would not be entirely lost, whatever happened to Earth.

Andreyev pulled himself up till he rested on his hands, head dangling between his shoulders. He groaned.

"I wonder how much of that is put on," mused Banning. "I did a well-calibrated job of slugging him. He shouldn't be too badly concussed." He gave Cleonie a beady look. "Maybe we ought to haul him into a cabin at that. Don't want to rattle any other cash customers, do we? Where are they all, anyway?"

"I'm not sure. I just left my cabin—" She stopped.

Someone came running from aft. The curvature of the hall, which was wrapped around the inner skin of the ship, made it impossible to see more than about forty metres. Banning shifted his gun, warily.

It was the large square-faced man, Falken, who burst into view. "Captain!" he shouted. The metal that enclosed all of them gave his tone a faint, unhuman resonance. "Captain, what happened?"

"How do *you* know about it, son?"

"A . . . eh . . . Engineer Devon—" Falken jogged to a halt, a metre away. "He told me—"

"Told you? Well, did he now?" Banning's grey gaze narrowed. Suddenly the needler in his hand leaped up and found an aim. "Hold it. Hold it there, pardner, and reach."

Falken flushed red. "What the ruination do you mean?"

"I mean that if you even look like you're going after a gun, I'll put you to sleep," said Banning. "Then if it turns out you only intended to offer me a peanut butter sandwich, I'll beg your humble pardon. But something sure smells here."

Falken backed away. "All right, all right, I'll go," he snarled. "I just wanted to help."

Cleonie screamed.

As Andreyev's burly form tackled him by the ankles and he went down, Banning knew a moment of rage at himself. He had been civilized too long . . . inexcusably careless of him—'Sbones and teeth!

He hit the deck with the other man on top. The red face glared murder. Andreyev yanked at the gun in Banning's kilt with one hand, his other grabbed the arm holding the stun pistol.

Banning brought his hard forehead up, into Andreyev's mouth. The fellow screamed. His fingers released the stunner. At that moment Falken joined the fight snatching the sleep weapon before Banning could get it into action.

The skipper reached up with an efficiently unsportsmanlike thumb. He had not quite gouged out Andreyev's eye when the man bellowed and tried to scramble free. Banning rolled away. Falken fired at him. An anaesthetic dart broke near Banning's nose, and he caught a whiff of vapour.

For a moment, while the universe waltzed around him, Banning accomplished nothing more than to reel to his feet. Falken sidestepped the weeping Andreyev, shoved the captain back against the wall, and yanked the automatic from his waistband.

Cleonie came from behind and threw her arms around Falken's neck.

He shouted, bent his back, and tossed her from him. But it had been enough of a distraction. Banning aimed a kick for the solar plexus. Both guns went on a spin from Falken's hands.

Banning's sole had encountered hard muscle. Falken recovered fast enough to make a jump for the nearest weapon. Banning put a large foot on it. "Oh, no, you don't," he growled.

Falken sprang at him. It was not the first time Banning had been in a party which got rough, and he did not waste energy on fisticuffs. His hands snapped forward, open, the edge of a horny palm driving into Falken's larynx. There was a snapping noise.

Falken fell backwards, over Andreyev, who still whimpered and dabbed at his injured eye. Banning stooped for the gun.

A bullet smashed down the corridor, ricocheted, and whined around his ears. Gentry came into view, with the drop on him.

"Oh, oh," said Banning. "School's out." He scooped up Cleonie and scampered back into the companionway.

Up the stairwell! His weight lessened with every jump as he got closer to the ship's axis of spin.

Passing C-deck, he collided with Charles Wayne. The young second mate had obviously been yanked from sleep by the racket. He was pulling on his gold-collared blue uniform jacket as he entered the companionway. "Follow me!" puffed Banning.

Gentry appeared at the foot of the stairs. The automatic in his grasp found an aim on the captain's stomach. "Stay there!" he rapped. "Raise your hands!"

Banning threw himself and Cleonie backwards, into C-deck corridor. The bullet snapped viciously past Wayne's head. "Come on, I told you!" gasped Banning. "Get her to the bridge!"

Wayne looked altogether bewildered, but any spaceman learns to react fast. He slung the girl over his shoulder and dashed down the hall towards an alternate stairwell.

Banning followed. He heard Gentry's shoes clang on metal, up the steps after him. As he ran, he groped after his pipe lighter, got it out, and thumbed the switch.

There were rails and stanchions along the wall, for use in null-gravity. Aided by his lessened weight, Banning swarmed ape fashion up the nearest and waved his flame beneath a small circle in the ceiling.

Then down again, towards the stair! Gentry burst into the hall and fired. Coriolis force deflected the bullet, it fanned the captain's cheek. The next one would be more carefully aimed.

The ceiling thermocouple reacted to heat, flashed a signal, and put the C-deck fire extinguisher system into action with a lather of plastifoam. Gentry's second shot flew off to nowhere. Thereafter he struggled with the stuff while Banning scampered up the stairs.

The bridge was a bubble in the ship's nose, precisely centred on the axis of rotation. There was virtually no weight, only a wilderness of gleaming consoles and the great viewscreen ablaze with its simulacrum of the sky.

Cleonie hung on to a stanchion, torn and shaken by the wretchedness of sudden, unaccustomed free fall. Tetsuo Tokugawa, the first mate, whose watch this was, floated next to her, offering an antidizzy pill. Wayne crouched by the door, wild-eyed. "What's going on, sir?" he croaked.

"I'm curious to know myself," panted Banning. "But it's all hell let out for noon."

Tokugawa gave him a despairing look. "Can you stuff this pill down her throat, skipper?" he begged. "I've seen people toss their dinner in null-gee."

"Uh, yeah, it is rather urgent." Banning hooked a knee around a stanchion, took the girl's head in one hand, and administered the medicine veterinary fashion. Meanwhile he clipped forth his story.

Tokugawa whistled. "What the destruction is this?" he said. "Mutiny?"

"If passengers can mutiny . . . neat point of law, that. Be quiet." Banning cocked his head and listened. There was no sound from the passages beyond the open door. He closed and bolted it.

Wayne looked sick. He wasn't a bad young fellow, thought the captain, but he was brought up in the puritan reaction of today's Western peoples. He was less afraid of danger now, than stunned by a kick to his sense of propriety. Tokugawa was more reliable, being Lunar City bred, with all the Lunar colonist's cat-footed cosmopolitanism.

"What are we going to *do*?" rasped the second mate.

"Find out things," grunted Banning. He soared across to the intercom cabinet, entered it, and flicked switches. The first thing he wanted was information about the ship. If that failed them, it would be a long walk home.

The "Thunderbolt" was a steelloy spheroid, flattened along the axis of the drive-tubes whose skeletal structure jutted like an ancient oil derrick from the stern. She was a big ship: her major diameter more than three hundred metres; she was a powerful ship: not required to drift along a Hohmann ellipse, but moving at a speed which took her on a hyperbolic orbit—from Earth Station Prime to the Jovian System in less than a month! But she had her limitations.

She was not intended to enter an atmosphere, but orbited and let shuttleboats bring or remove her cargo. This was less because of the great mass of her double hull—that wasn't too important, when you put atomic nuclei to work for you—than because of the design itself. To build up her fantastic velocities, she must spurt out ions at nearly the speed of light: which required immensely long accelerating tubes, open to the vacuum of space. They would arc over and burn out if air surrounded the charged rings.

She carried no lifeboat. If you abandon ship at hyperbolic speeds, a small craft doesn't have engine enough to decelerate you before running out of reaction mass. Here, in the big cold darkness beyond Mars, there was no escaping this vessel.

Banning tuned in the screen before him. It gave two-way visual contact between a few key points, in case of emergency. "And if this ain't an emergency," he muttered, "it'll do till one comes along."

First, the biotic plant, armoured at the heart of the ship. He breathed a gusty sigh. No one had tampered with that—air and water were still being renewed.

Next, the control gyros. The screen showed him their housing, like the pillars of some heathen temple. In the free fall at the ship's axis a dead man drifted past them. The slow air currents turned him over and over. When his gaping face nudged the screen pickup, Banning recognized Tietjens, one of the two stewards. He had been shot through the head, and there was a grisly little cloud of red and grey floating around him.

Banning's lips grew thin. "I was supposed to look after you," he mumbled. "I'm sorry, Joppe."

He switched to the engine room. His view was directed towards the main control board, also in the axial null-gee state. The face that looked back at him, framed by the tall machines, belonged to Professor Gomez.

Banning sucked in a breath. "What are you doing there?" he said.

"Oh . . . it's you, Captain. I rather expected you to peer in." The little man shoved himself forward with a groundlubber's awkwardness, but he was calm, not spacesick at all. "Quite a job you did on Falken. He's dead."

"Too bad you weren't in on that party," said Banning. "How are the other boys? Mine, I mean."

"The red-haired man—he was on watch here when I came —I am afraid I found it necessary to terminate him."

"Tietjens and O'Farrell," said Banning, very slowly. "Just shot down, huh? Who else?"

"No one yet. It's your fault, Captain. You precipitated this affair before we were ready; we had to act in haste. Our original plan did not involve harming any person." The shrivelled face grew thoughtful. "We have them all prisoners, except for you there on the bridge. I advise you to surrender peacefully."

"What's the big idea?" growled Banning. "What do you want?"

"We are taking over this ship."

"Are you crazy? Do you know what sort of job it is to handle her—do you know how much kinetic energy she's got, right now?"

"It is unfortunate that Falken died," said Gomez tonelessly. "He was to have been our engineer. But I daresay Andreyev can take his place, with some help from me—I know a bit about nucleonic controls. Gentry, of course, is a trained astrogator."

"But who are you?" shouted Banning. He had the eerie feeling that the whole world had gone gibbering insane around him. "What are you doing this for?"

"It is not essential for you to know that," said Gomez. "If you surrender now, you will receive good treatment and be released as soon as possible. Otherwise we shall probably have to shoot you. Remember, we have all the guns."

Banning told him what he could do with his guns and cut the circuit. Switching on the public-address mike, he barked a summary of the situation for the benefit of any crewmen who might be at liberty. Then, spinning out of the booth, he told the others in a few harsh words how it stood.

Cleonie's face had got back a little colour. Now, between the floating gold locks of hair, it was again drained of blood. But he admired the game way she asked him: "What can we do?"

"Depends on the situation, m'lady," he replied. "We don't know for sure . . . let's see, another steward, two engineers, and a deckhand . . . we don't know if all four of the crewmen still alive are prisoners or not. I'm afraid, though, that they really are."

"Luke," she whispered. "You sent him off—"

Banning nodded. Even in this moment, he read an anguish in her eyes and knew pity for her. "I'm afraid Luke has been clobbered," he said. "Not permanently, though, I hope."

Wayne's gaze was blank and lost. "But what are they *doing*?" he stammered. "Are they . . . ps-ps-psy-chotic?"

"No such luck," said Banning. "This was a pretty well-laid plan. At the proper time, they'd have pulled guns on us and locked us away—or maybe shot us. Luke happened to . . . I don't know what, but it alarmed Andreyev, who stuck him up. Then I horned in. I sent Luke after help. Not suspecting the other passengers, he must have told Tietjens in the presence of another member of this gang. So poor old Joppe got shot, but apparently Luke was just herded off. Then the whole gang was alerted, and Gomez went to take over the engine room while Falken and Gentry came after me." He nodded heavily. "A fast, smooth operation, in spite of our having thrown 'em off balance. No, they're sane, for all practical purposes."

He waited a moment, gathering his thoughts, then:

"The remaining four crewmen would all have been in their quarters, off duty. The situation as she now stands depends on whether Gentry broke off from chasing me in time to surprise them in that one place. I wish I'd got on the mike faster."

Suddenly he grinned. "Tetsuo," he rapped, "stop the ship's rotation. Pronto!"

The mate blinked, then laughed—a short rough bark in his gullet—and leaped for the controls. "Hang on!" said Banning.

"What . . . what do you plan to do, sir?" asked Wayne.

"Put this whole tub into null-gee. It'll equalize matters a bit."

"I don't understand."

"No, you've never seen a weightless free-for-all, have you? Too bad. There's an art to it. A trained man with his hands can make a monkey of a groundlubber with a gun."

It was hard to tell whether Wayne was more deeply shocked at the mutiny or at learning that his captain had actually been in vulgar brawls. "Cheer up, son," said Banning. "You, too, Cleonie. You both looked like vulcanized oatmeal."

There was a brief thrumming. The tangential jets blew a puff of chemical vapour and brought the spin of the ship to a halt. For a moment, the astro screen went crazy, still compensating for a rotation which had ceased, then the cold image of the constellations steadied.

"O.K.," said Banning. "We've got to move fast. Tetsuo, come with me. Charlie, Cleonie, guard the bridge. Lock the door behind us, and don't open it for anyone whose voice you find unmusical. If our boys do show up, tell 'em to wait here."

"Where are you going?" breathed the girl shakenly.

"Out to kill a few people," said Banning with undiminished good cheer.

He led the way, in a long soaring glide through the door. "Up" and "down" had become meaningless; there was only this maze of halls, rooms, and stairwells. His skin prickled with the thought that an armed man might be waiting in any cross-corridor. The silence of the ship drew his nerves taut as wires. He pulled himself along by the rails, hand over hand, accelerating till the doorways blurred past him.

The galley was on B-deck, just "above" passenger country. When Banning opened the door, an unfastened kettle drifted out and gonged on his head. A rack held the usual kitchen assortment of knives. He stuck a few in his waistband, giving the two longest to himself and Tokugawa. "Now I don't feel so nude," he remarked.

"What's next?" whispered the mate.

"If our lads are being kept prisoner, it's probably in crew territory. Let's try—"

The spacemen's own cabins were on this level; they did not require the full Earth-value of spin-gravity given the passengers on A-deck. Banning slipped with a caution that rose exponentially towards the area he always thought of as the forecastle.

He need not have been quite so careful. Andreyev waited with a pistol outside a cabin door, but Andreyev had been unprepared for a sudden chance to no-weight. His misery was not active, but it showed.

Banning launched himself.

Andreyev's abused senses reacted slowly. He looked around, saw the hurtling form, and yelled. Almost instinctively, he whipped his gun about and fired. It was nearly point-blank, but he missed. He could not help missing when the recoil sent him flying backwards with plenty of English.

He struck the farther wall, scrabbled wildly, bounced off it, and pinwheeled to the ceiling. Banning grinned, changed course with a thrust of leg against floor, and closed in. Andreyev fired again. It was a bomb-burst roar in that narrow space. The bullet tore Banning's sleeve. Recoil jammed Andreyev against the ceiling. As he rebounded, it was on to his enemy's knife.

The captain smiled sleepily, grabbed Andreyev's tunic with

his free hand, and completed the job.

Tokugawa dodged a rush of blood. He looked sick. "What did you do that for?" he choked.

"Tietjens and O'Farrell," said Banning. The archaic greenish light faded from his eyes, and he added in a flat tone: "Let's get that door open."

Fists were hammering on it. The thin metal dented beneath the blows but held firm. "Stand aside!" yelled Tokugawa. "I'm going to shoot the lock off—can't find the key, no time—" He picked Andreyev's gun from the air, put the muzzle to the barrier, and fired. He was also thrown back by reaction but knew how to control such forces.

Luke Devon flung the door open. The Engineer looked as bleak as Banning had ever known a man to be. Behind him crowded the others, Nielsen, Bahadur, Castro, Vladimirovitch. Packing five men into a cubbyhole meant for one had in itself been a pretty good way to immobilize them.

Their voices surfed around the captain. "Shut up!" he bawled. "We got work to do!"

"Who else is involved in this?" demanded Devon. Gentry killed Tietjens and took me prisoner . . . herded all of us in here, with Andreyev to help . . . but who else is there to fight?"

"Gentry and Gomez," said Banning. "Falken is dog's meat. We still hold the bridge, and we outnumber 'em now—but they've got the engine room *and* all the guns but one." He passed out knives. "Let's get out of here. We've made enough racket to wake the Old Martians. I don't want Gentry to come pot-hunting."

The men streamed behind him as he dived along another stairwell, towards the bowels of the ship. He wanted to post a guard over the gyros and biotics. But he had not got to them when the spiteful crack of an automatic toned between metal walls.

His hands closed on the rail, slamming him to a halt that skinned his palms. "Hold it," he said, very softly. "That could only have come from the bridge."

If we can shoot a door open, I reckon Gentry can, too.

There was only one approach to the bridge, a short passage-way on which several companionways converged. To either side of this corridor were the captain's and mate's cabins at the far end was the bridge entrance.

Banning came whizzing out of a stairwell. He didn't stop, but glided on into the one opposite. A bullet smashed where he had been.

His brain held the glimpsed image: the door open, Gentry braced in it with his feet on one jamb and his back against the other. That way, he could cover Wayne and Cleonie—if they were still alive—and the approach as well. The recoil of his fire wouldn't bother him at all.

Banning's followers milled about like the debris of a ship burst open. He waited till Gentry's voice reached out:

"So you have all your men back, Captain . . . and therefore a gun, I presume? Nice work. But stay where you are. I'll shoot the first head that pokes around a corner. I know how to use a gun in null-gee, and I've got Wayne and Rogers for hostages. Want to parley?"

Banning stole a glimpse at Devon. The Engineer's nostrils were pinched and bloodless. It was he who answered:

"What are you after?"

"I think you know, Luke," said Gentry.

"Yes," said Devon. "I believe I do."

"Then you're also aware that anything goes. I won't hesitate to shoot Rogers—or dive the ship into the sun before the Guard gets its claws on us! It would be better if you gave up."

There was another stillness. The breathing of his men, of himself, sounded hoarse in Banning's ears. Little drops of sweat pearled off their skin, glistened in the fluorotube light, and danced away on air currents.

He cocked a brow at Devon. The Engineer nodded. "It's correct enough, skipper," he said. "We're up against fanatics."

"We could rush him," hissed Banning. "Lose a man or two, maybe, but—"

"No," said Devon. "There's Cleonie to think about." A curious mask of peace dropped over his bony face. "Let me talk to him. Maybe we can arrange something. You be ready to act as . . . as indicated."

He said, aloud, that he would parley. "Good," grunted Gentry. "Come out slow, and hang on to the rail with both your hands where I can see them." Devon's long legs moved out of Banning's view. "That's close enough. Stop." *He must still be three or four metres from the door*, thought the captain, and moved up to the corner of the stairwell,

It came to him, with a sudden chill, what Devon must be planning. The Rostomily clan had always been that sort. His scalp prickled, but he dared not speak. All he could do was take a few knives from the nearest men.

"Luke." That was Cleonie's voice, a whisper from the bridge. "Luke, be careful."

"Oh, yes." The Engineer laughed. It had an oddly tender note.

"Just what happened to kick off this landslide, anyway?" asked Gentry.

"'Thou hast the most unsavoury similes,'" said Devon.

"What?"

The roar which followed must have jerked all of Gentry's remaining attention to him as Devon launched himself into space.

The gun crashed. Banning heard the bullet smack home. Devon's body turned end over end, tumbling backwards down the hall.

Banning was already around the corner. He did not fire at Gentry; it would have taken a whole fatal second to brace himself properly against a wall.

He threw knives.

The recoil was almost negligible; his body twisted back and forth as his arms moved, but he was used to that. It took only a wink to stick four blades in Gentry.

The spaceman screamed, hawked blood, and scrabbled after the gun that had slipped from his fingers. Tokugawa came flying, hit him with one shoulder. They thudded to the floor. The mate wrapped his legs about Gentry's and administered an expert foul blow to the neck.

Cleonie struggled from the bridge towards Devon. Banning was already there, holding the grey form between his knees while he examined the wound. The girl bumped into them. *How is he?* Banning had heard that raw tone, half shriek, often and often before this day—when women saw the blood of their men.

He nodded. "Could be worse, I reckon. The slug seems to've hit a rib and stopped. Shock knocked him out, but . . . well, a bullet never does as much harm in free fall, the target bounces away from it easier." He swatted at the little red globules in the air. "Damn!"

Wayne emerged, green-faced. "This man . . . shot the door open when we wouldn't let him in," he rattled. "We hadn't any weapon . . . he threatened Miss Rogers—"

"O.K., never mind the breast-beating. Next time remember to stand beside the door and grab when the enemy comes through. Now, I assume you have the medical skills required for your certificate. Get Luke to sick bay and patch him up. Nielsen, help Mr. Wayne. Gentry still alive?"

"He won't be if he doesn't get some first aid quick," said Tokugawa. "You gashed him good." He whistled in awe. "Don't you ever simply *stun* your enemies, boss?"

"Take him along too, Mr. Wayne, but Devon gets priority. Bahadur, break out the vacuum sweeper and get this blood sucked up before it fouls everything. Tetsuo . . . uh, Mr. Tokugawa, go watch the after bulkhead in case Gomez tries to break out. Vladimirovitch, tag along with him. Castro, stick around here."

"Can I help?" asked Cleonie. Her lips struggled for firmness.

"Go to sick bay," nodded Banning. "Maybe they can use you."

He darted into the bridge and checked controls. Everything was still off—good. Gomez couldn't start the engines without rigging a bypass circuit. However, he had plenty of ancillary machines, generators and pumps and whatnot, at his disposal down there. The captain entered the intercom cabinet and switched on the engine room screen.

Gomez's pinched face had taken on a stiffened wildness. "For your information, friend," said Banning, "we just mopped up Andreyev and Gentry. That leaves you alone. Come on out of there, the show's over."

"No," said Gomez. His voice was dull, abnormally calm. It gave Banning a creepy sensation.

"Don't you believe me? I can haul the bodies here if you want."

"Oh, yes, I will take your word." Gomez's mouth twisted. "Then perhaps you will do me the same honour. It is still you who must surrender to me."

Banning waited for a long few seconds.

"I am here in the engine room," said Gomez. "I am alone. I have locked the outer doors: emergency seal, you'll have to burn your way through, and that takes hours. There will be plenty of time for me to disable the propulsion system."

Banning was not a timid man, but his palms were suddenly wet, and he fumbled a thick dry tongue before he could shape words:

"You'd die, too."

"I am quite prepared for that."

"But you wouldn't have accomplished anything! You'd just have wrecked the ship and killed several people."

"I would have kept this affair from being reported to the Union," said Gomez. "The very fact of our attempt is more of a hint than we can afford to let the Guard have."

"What are you doing all this *for?*" howled the captain.

The face in the screen grew altogether unhuman. It was a face Banning knew—millennia of slaughterhouse history knew it—the face of embodied Purpose.

"It is not necessary for you to be told the details," clipped Gomez. "However, perhaps you will understand that the present government's spineless toleration of the Kali menace in the East and the moral decay in the West has to be ended if civilization is to survive."

"I see," said Banning, as gently as if he spoke in the presence of a ticking bomb. "And since toleration is built into Union law—"

"Exactly. I do not say anything against the Uniters. But times have changed. If Fourre were alive today, he would agree that action is necessary."

"It's always convenient to use a dead man for a character witness, isn't it?"

"What?"

"Never mind." Banning nodded to himself. "Don't do anything radical yet, Gomez. I'll have to think about this."

"I shall give you exactly one hour," said the desiccated voice. "Thereafter I shall begin work. I am not an engineer myself, but I think I can disable something—I have studied a trifle about nucleonics. You may call me when you are ready to surrender. At the first suspicion of misbehaviour, I will, of course, wreck the propulsion system immediately."

Gomez turned away.

Banning sat for a while, his mind curiously empty. Then he shoved across to the control board, alerted the crew, and started the rotation again. You might as well have some weight.

"Keep an eye on the screen," he said as he left the main pilot chair. "Call me on the intercom if anything develops. I'll be in sick bay."

"Sir?" Castro gaped at him.

"Appropriate spot," said Banning. "Velocity is equivalent to temperature, isn't it? If so, then we all have a fever which is quite likely to kill us."

Devon lay stretched and stripped on the operating table. Wayne had just removed the bullet with surgical pincers. Now he clamped the wound and began stitching. Nielsen was controlling the sterilizers, both UV and sonic, while Cleonie stood by with bowl and sponges. They all looked up, as if from a dream, when Banning entered. The tools of surgery might be developed today to a point where this was an operation simple enough for a spaceman's meditechnic training; but there was a man on the table who might have died, and only slowly did their minds break away from his heartbeat.

"How is he?" asked the captain.

"Not too bad, sir, considering." Given this job, urgent and specific, Wayne was competent enough; he spoke steadily. "I daresay he presented his chest on purpose when he attacked, knowing the bones had a good chance of acting as armour. There's a broken rib and some torn muscle, of course, but nothing that won't heal."

"Gentry?"

"Conked out five minutes ago, sir," said Nielsen. "I stuck him in the icebox. Maybe they've got revivification equipment on Ganymede."

"Woudn't make much difference," said Banning. "The forebrain would be too far gone by the time we arrived—no personality survival to speak of." He shuddered a little. Clean death was one thing; this was another matter, one which he had never quite got used to. "Luke, though," he went on quickly, "can he stand being brought to consciousness? Right away?"

"No!" Almost, Cleonie lifted her basin to brain him.

"Shut up." He turned his back on her. "It'd be a poor kindness to let him sleep comfy now and starve to death later, maybe, out beyond Pluto. Well, Mr. Wayne?"

"Hm-m-m . . . I don't like it, sir. But if you say so, I guess

I can manage it. Local anaesthesia for the wound and a shot of mild stimulant; oxygen and neoplasma, just in case— Yes, I don't imagine a few minutes' conversation would hurt him permanently."

"Good. Carry on." Banning fumbled after his pipe, remembered that he had dropped it somewhere in all the hullabaloo, and swore.

"What did you say?" asked Nielsen.

"Never mind," said Banning. True, women were supposed to be treated like men these days, but he had old-fashioned ideas. It was useful to know a few earthy languages unfamiliar to anyone else.

Cleonie laid a hand on his arm. "Captain," she said. Her eyes were shadowed, with weariness and with—compassion? "Captain, is it necessary to wake him? He's been hurt so much—for our sakes."

"He may have the only information to save our lives," answered Banning patiently.

The intercom cleared its throat: "Sir . . . Castro on bridge —he's unbolting the main mass-tank access port."

Wayne turned white as he laboured. He understood.

Banning nodded. "I thought so. Did you ask him what he was up to? He promised us an hour."

"Yes, sir. He said we'd get it, too, but . . . but he wanted to be ready, in case—"

"Smart boy. It'll take him awhile to get to the flush valves; they're quite well locked away and shielded. Then the pump has to have time. We might have burned our way in to him by then."

"Maybe we should do it, sir. Now!"

"Maybe. It'll be a race between his wrenches and our torches. I'll let you know. Stand by."

Banning turned back to Devon, gnawing his lip. The Engineer was stirring to wakefulness. As he watched, the captain saw the eyes blink palely open, saw colour creep into the face and the mouth tighten behind the transparent oxygen mask.

Cleonie moved towards the table. "Luke—"

Devon smiled at her, a sudden human warmth in this cold room of machines. Gently, Banning shoved her aside. "You'll get your innings later, girl," he said. Bending over the Engineer:

"Hello, buster. You're going to be O.K. Can you tell me some things in a hell of a hurry?"

"I can try—" It was the merest flutter of air.

Banning began to talk. Devon lay back, breathing deeply and making some curious gestures with his hands. He'd had Tighe System training, then—total integration—good! He *would* be able to hang on to his consciousness, even call up new strength from hidden cellular reserves.

"We clobbered all the gang except Gomez, who seems to be the kingpin. He's holed up in the engine room, threatens to wreck us all unless we surrender to him inside an hour. Does he mean it?"

"Yes. Oh, yes." Devon nodded faintly.

"Who is this outfit? What do they want?"

"Fanatic group . . . quasi-religious . . . powerful, large membership furnishes plenty of money . . . but the real operations are secret, a few men—"

"I think I know who you mean. The Western Reformists, huh?"

Devon nodded again. The pulse that flickered in his throat seemed to strengthen.

Banning spent a bleak moment of review. In recent years, he had stayed off Earth as much as possible; when there, he had not troubled himself with political details, for he recognized all the signs of a civilization going under. It had seemed more worthwhile to give his attention to the Venusian ranch he had bought, against the day of genocide and the night of ignorance and tyranny to follow. However, he did understand that the antitechnic Oriental cult of Kali had created its own opposite pole in the West. And the prim grim Reformists might well try to forestall their enemies by a coup.

"Sort of like the Nazis versus the Communists, back in Germany in the 1920s," he muttered.

"The who?" said Nielsen.

"No matter. It's six of one and half a dozen of the other. Let me see, Luke." Banning took a turn around the room. "In order to overthrow constitutional government and impose their will on Earth, the Reformists would have to kill quite a few hundred millions of people, especially in Asia. That means nuclear bombardment, preferably from space. Am I right?"

"Yes—" said Devon. His voice gained resonance as he went

on. "They have a base, somewhere in the asteroid belt. They hope to build it up to a fortress, with a fleet of ships, arsenal, military corps . . . the works. It's a very long-range thing, of course, but the public aspect of their party is going to need lots of time anyway, to condition enough citizens towards the idea of— Well. At present their base doesn't amount to much. They can't just buy ships, the registry would give them away . . . they have to build . . . they need at least one big supply ship, secretly owned and operated, before they can start serious work at all."

"And we're elected," said Devon. "Yeah. I can even see why. Not only is this a fast ship with a large capacity, but our present cargo, the terraforming stuff, would be valuable to them in itself . . . Uh-huh. Their idea was to take over this clunk, bring her in to their base—and the 'Thunderbolt' becomes another ship which just plain vanished mysteriously."

Devon nodded.

"I scarcely imagine they'd have kept us alive, under the circumstances," went on Banning.

"No."

"How do you know all this?"

"The Order . . . We stay out of politics . . . officially . . . but we have our Intelligence arm and use it quietly." So that was why he'd been reluctant to explain Andreyev's actions! "We knew, in a general way, what the situation was. Of course, we didn't know *this* ship, on this particular voyage, was slated for capture."

"That's fairly obvious. You recognized Andreyev?"

"Yes. Former Engineer, under another name—expelled for . . . good reasons. Surgical changes made, but the overall gestalt bothered me. All of a sudden, I thought I knew who he was. Like a meddling fool, I tried a key word on him. Yes, he reacted, by pulling a gun on me! Later on—again, like an idiot—I didn't think Gentry might be his partner, so I told Tietjens what had happened while Gentry was there." Devon sighed. "Old Rostomily would disown me."

"You weren't trained for secret service work, yourself," said Banning. "All right, Luke. One more question. Gomez wants us to surrender to him. I presume this means we'll let ourselves be locked away except for one or two who slow down the ship while he holds a gun on 'em. After we've decelerated to a point where a boat from the Reformist asteroid can match velocities, he'll radio and—Hell! What I'm getting at is, would our lives be spared afterwards?"

"I doubt it," said the Engineer.

"Oh my darling—" As he closed his eyes, Cleonie came to his side. Their hands groped together.

Banning swung away. "Thanks, Luke," he said. "I didn't know if I had the right to risk lives for the sake of this ship, but now I see there's no risk at all. We haven't got a thing to lose. Cleonie, can you take care of our boy here?"

"Yes," she whispered, enormous-eyed. "If there's no emergency."

"There shouldn't be. They fabricated him out of teflon and rattlesnake leather. O.K., then, you be his nurse. You might also whomp up some coffee and sandwiches. The rest of the crew meet me at the repair equipment lockers, aft section . . . no, you stay put, Castro. We're going to burn our way in to friend Gomez."

"But he . . . he'll dump the reaction mass!" gasped Wayne.

"Maybe we can get at him before he gets at the tanks," said Banning. "A man might try."

"No—look, sir. I know how long it takes to operate the main flush system. Even allowing for Gomez being alone and untrained, he can do it before we can get through the after bulkhead. We haven't a chance that way!"

"What do you recommend, Mr. Wayne?" asked Banning slowly.

"That we give in to him, sir."

"And be shot down out of hand when his pals board the ship?"

"No, sir. There'll be seven of us to one of Gomez before that happens. We have a faint hope of being able to jump him—"

"A very faint hope indeed," said Banning. "He's no amateur. And if we don't succeed, not only will we die, but that gang of hellhounds will have got the start it wants. Whereas, if we burn through to Gomez but fail to stop him disabling the ship . . . well, it'll only be us who die, now. Not a hundred million people twenty or thirty years from now."

Is this the truth? Do you really believe one man can delay the Norns? What is your choice, Captain? By legal definition,

*you are omnipotent and omniscient while the ship is under
way. What shall be done, Oh god of the ships?*

Banning groaned. *Per Jovem*, it was too much to ask of a
man!

And then he stiffened.

"What is it, sir?" Nielsen looked alarmed.

"By Jupiter," said Banning. "Well, by Jupiter!"

"What?"

"Never mind. Come on. We're going to smoke Gomez out
of there!"

The last stubborn metal glared white, ran molten down the
gouge already carved, and froze in gobbets. Bahadur shut off
the electric torch, shoved the mask away from his dark tur-
banned face, and said: "All right, sir."

Banning stepped carefully over the heavy torch cables. His
gang had attacked the bulkhead from a point near the skin of
the ship, for the sake of both surprise and weight. "How's the
situation inside?" he asked the air.

The intercom replied from the bridge, where Castro huddled
over the telescreen that showed him Gomez at work. "Pump
still going sir. I guess he really means business."

"We've got this much luck," said Banning, "that he isn't an
engineer himself. You'd have had those tanks flushed out half
an hour ago."

He stood for another instant, gathering strength and will.
His mind pawed over the facts again.

The outer plates of the ship would stop a fair-sized meteor,
even at hyperbolic relative velocity: it would explode into
vapour, leaving a miniature Moon crater. Anything which might
happen to break through that would lose energy to the self-
sealer between the hulls; at last it would encounter the inner
skin, which could stand well over a hundred atmospheres of
pressure by itself. It was not a common accident for a modern
spaceship to be punctured.

But the after bulkhead was meant to contain stray radiation,
or even a minor explosion, if the nuclear energies which drove
the ship should get out of hand. It was scarcely weaker than
the double hull. The torches had required hours to carve a
hole in it. There would have been little or no saving of time by
cutting through the great double door at the axis of the ship,
which Gomez had locked; nor did Banning want to injure

massive pieces of precision machinery. The mere bulkhead would be a lot easier to repair afterwards—if there was an afterwards.

Darkness yawned before him. He hefted the gun in his hand. "All right, Vladimirovitch, let's go," he said. "If we're not back in ten minutes, remember, let Wayne and Bahadur follow."

He had overruled Tokugawa's anguished protests and ordered the first mate to stay behind under all circumstances. The Lunarite alone had the piloting skill to pull off the crazy stunt which was their final hope. He and Nielsen were making a racket at the other end of the bulkhead, a diversion for Gomez's benefit.

Banning slipped through the hole. It was pitchy beyond, a small outer room where no one had turned on the lights. He wondered if Gomez waited just beyond the door with a bullet for the first belly to come through.

He'd find out pretty quick.

The door, which led into the main control chamber, was a thin piece of metal. Rotation made it lie above Banning's head. He scampered up the ladder. His hand closed on the catch, he turned it with an enormous caution—flung the door open and jumped through.

The fluoros made a relentless blaze of light. Near the middle of that steel cave, floating before an opened panel, he saw Gomez. So the hell-bound Roundhead hadn't heard them breaking in!

He did now. He whirled, clumsily, and scrabbled for the gun in his belt. Banning fired. His bullet missed, wailed and gonged around the great chamber. Gomez shot back. Recoil tore him from the stanchion he held, sent him drifting towards the wall.

Banning scrambled in pursuit, over the spidery network of ladders and handholds. His weight dropped with each leap closer to the axis; he fought down the characteristic Coriolis vertigo. Gomez spiralled away from him, struck a control chair, clawed himself to a stop, and crouched in it.

Banning grew aware of the emergency pump. It throbbed and sang in the metal stillness around him, and every surge meant lost mass . . . like the red spurting from a slashed artery. The flush system was rarely used—only if the reaction mass got

contaminated, or for some such reason. Gomez had found a
new reason, thought Banning grimly. To lose a ship and murder
a crew.

"Turn that thing off, Vlad," he said between his teeth.

"Stay where you are!" screamed Gomez. "I'll shoot! I will!"

"Get going!" roared the captain.

Vladimirovitch hauled himself towards the cutoff switch.
Gomez flipped his pistol to full automatic and began firing.

He didn't hit anything of value in the few seconds granted
him. In a ship rotating in free fall, the pattern of forces operating on a bullet is so complicated that practical ballistics must
be learned all over again. But that hose of lead was bound to
kill someone, by sheer chance and ricochet, unless—

Banning clutched himself to a rod, aimed, and fired.

On the second shot, Gomez jerked. The pistol jarred from his
hand, he slumped back into the chair and lay still.

Banning hurried towards him. It would be worthwhile taking
Gomez alive, to interrogate and— No. As he reached the man,
he saw the life draining out of him. A shot through the heart
is not invariably fatal, but this time it was.

The pump clashed to silence.

Banning whirled about. "Well?" His shout was raw. "How
much did we lose?"

"Quite a bit, sir." Vladimirovitch squinted at the gauges.
His words came out jerkily. "Too much, I'm afraid."

Banning went to join him, leaving Gomez to die alone.

They met in the dining saloon: seven hale men, an invalid,
and a woman. For a moment they could only stare at the
death in each other's eyes.

"Break out the Scotch, Nielsen," said Banning at last. He
took forth his pipe and began loading it. A grin creased his
mouth. "If your faces get any longer, people, you'll be tripping
over your own jawbones."

Cleonie, seated at the head of the couch on which Devon
lay, ruffled the Engineer's hair. Her gaze was blind with sorrow.
"Do you expect us to be happy, after all that killing?" she
asked.

"We were lucky," shrugged Banning. "We lost two good men,
yes. But all the ungodly are dead."

"That's not so good a thing," said Devon. "I'd like to have them narcoed, find out where their asteroid is and—" He paused. "Wait. Gentry's still in the freeze, isn't he? If he was revived at Ganymede, maybe his brain wouldn't be too deteriorated for a deep-memory probe, at least."

"Nix," said Banning. "The stiffs are all to be jettisoned. We've got to lighten ship. If your Order's Intelligence men—or the Guard's, for that matter—are any good, they'll be able to trace back people like our late playfellows and rope in their buddies."

Cleonie shivered. "Please!"

"Sorry." Banning lit his pipe and took a long drag. "It is kind of morbid, isn't it? O.K. then, let's concentrate on the problem of survival. The question is how to use the inadequate amount of reaction mass left in the tanks."

"I'm afraid I don't quite understand," said the girl.

· She looked more puzzled than frightened. Banning liked her all the more for that. Devon was a lucky thus-and-so, if they lived . . . though she deserved better than an Engineer, always skiting through space and pledged to contract no formal marriage till he retired from field service.

"It's simple enough," he told her. "We're on a hyperbolic orbit. That means we're moving with a speed greater than escape velocity for the Solar System. If we don't slow down quite a bit, we'll just keep on going; and no matter how we ration it, there's only a few weeks' worth of food aboard and no suspended-animation stuff."

"Can't we radio for help?"

"We're out of our own radio range to anywhere."

"But won't they miss us—send high-acceleration ships after us? They can compute our orbit, can't they?"

"Not that closely. Too much error creeps in when the path gets as monstrous long as ours would be before we could possibly be overhauled. It'd be remarkable if the Guard ship came as close to us as five million kilometres, which is no use at all." Banning wagged his pipestem at her. "It's up to us alone. We have a velocity of some hundreds of kilometres per second to kill. We don't have reaction mass enough to do it."

Nielsen came in with bottles and glasses. He went around doing the honours while Devon said: "Excuse me, Captain, I assume this has occurred to you, but after all, it's momentum which is the significant quantity, not speed *per se*. If we jettison everything which isn't absolutely essential, cargo, furnishings, even the inner walls and floors—"

"Tet and I figured on that," answered Banning. "You remember just now I said we had to lighten ship. We even assumed stripping off the outer hull and taking a chance on meteors. It's quite feasible, you know. Spaceships are designed to come apart fairly easily under the right tools, for replacement work, so if we all sweat at it, I think we can finish peeling her down by the time we have to start decelerating."

Wayne looked at the whisky bottle. He didn't drink; it wasn't considered quite the thing in today's West. But his face grew tighter and tighter, till suddenly he reached out and grabbed the bottle and tilted it to his mouth.

When he was through choking, he said hoarsely: "All right, sir. Why don't you tell them? We still can't lose enough speed."

"I was coming to that," said Banning.

Devon's hand closed on the girl's. "What are the figures?" he asked in a level tone.

"Well," said Banning, "we can enter the Jovian System if we like, but then we'll find ourselves fuelless with a velocity of about fifty kilometres per second relative to the planet."

The Engineer whistled.

"Must we do that, though?" inquired Bahadur. "I mean, sir, well, if we can decelerate that much, can't we get into an elliptic orbit about the sun?"

"'Fraid not. Fifty k.p.s. is still a lot more than solar escape velocity for that region of space."

"But look, sir. If I remember rightly, Jupiter's own escape velocity is well *over* fifty k.p.s. That means the planet itself will be giving us all that speed. If we didn't come near it, we should have mass enough left to throw ourselves into a cometary—"

"Smart boy," said Banning. He blew smoke in the air and hoisted his glass. "We computed that one, too. You're quite right, we can get into a cometary. The very best cometary we can manage will take a few years to bring us back into radio range of anyone—and of course space is so big we'd never be found on such an unpredictable orbit, unless we hollered for help and were heard."

"*Years,*" whispered Cleonie.

The terror which rose in her, then, was not the simple fear of death. It was the sudden understanding of just how big and old this universe which she had so blithely inhabited really was. Banning, who had seen it before, waited sympathetically.

After a minute she straightened herself and met his eyes. "All right, Captain," she said. "Continue the arithmetic lesson. Why can't we simply ask the Jovians to pick us up as we approach their system?"

"You knew there was a catch, eh?" murmured Banning. "It's elementary. The Republic is poor and backward. Their only spacecraft are obsolete intersatellite shuttles, which can't come anywhere near a fifty k.p.s. velocity."

"And we've no means of losing speed, down to something they can match." Wayne dropped his face into his hands.

"I didn't call you here for a weeping contest," said Banning. "We do have one means. It might or might not work—it's never been tried—but Tetsuo here is one hell of a good pilot. He's done some of the cutest braking ellipses you ever saw in your life."

That made them sit up. But Devon shook his head, wryly. "It won't work," he said. "Even after the alleged terraforming, Ganymede hasn't enough atmosphere to—"

"Jupiter has all kinds of atmosphere," said Banning.

The silence that fell was thunderous.

"No," said Wayne at last. He spoke quickly, out of bloodless lips. "It could only work by a fluke. We would lose speed, yes, if friction didn't burn us up . . . finally, on one of those passes, we'd emerge with a sensible linear velocity. But a broken shell like this ship will be after we lighten her—an atmosphere as thick and turbulent as Jupiter's—there wouldn't be enough control. We'd never know precisely what orbit we were going to have on emergence. By the time we'd computed what path it really was and let the Jovians know and their antiquated boats had reached it . . . we'd be back in Jupiter's air on the next spiral!"

"And the upshot would be to crash," said Devon. "Hydrogen and helium at one hundred and forty degrees Absolute. Not very breathable."

"Oh, we'd have spattered on the surface before we had to try breathing that stuff," said Vladimirovitch sarcastically.

"No, we wouldn't either," said Bahadur. "Our inner hull can stand perhaps two hundred atmospheres' pressure. But Jupiter goes up to the tens of thousands. We would be squashed flat long before we reached the surface."

Banning lifted his brows. "You know a better 'ole?" he chal-.
lenged.

"What?" Wayne blinked at him.

"Know anything which gives us a better chance?"

"Yes, I do." The young face stiffened. "Let's get into that
cometary about the sun. When we don't report in, there'll be
Guard ships hunting for us. We have a very small chance of being found. But the chance of being picked up by the Jovians,
while doing those crazy dives, is infinitesimal!"

· "It doesn't look good either way, does it?" said Cleonie. A sad
little smile crossed her lips. "But I'd rather be killed at once,
crushed in a single blow, than . . . watch all of us shrivel and
die, one by one—or draw lots for who's to be eaten next. I'd
rather go out like a human being."

"Same here," nodded Devon.

"Not I!" Wayne stood up. "Captain, I won't have it. You've
no right to . . . to take the smaller chance, the greater hazard,
deliberately, just because it offers a quicker death. No!"

Banning slapped the table with a cannon-crack noise. "Con-
gratulations on getting your master's certificate, Mr. Wayne,"
he growled. "Now sit down."

"No, by the Eternal! I demand—"

"*Sit down!*"

Wayne sat.

"As a matter of fact," continued Banning mildly, "I agree
that the chance of the Jovians rescuing us is negligible. But I
think we have a chance to help ourselves.

"I think maybe we can do what nobody has ever tried before
—enter Jovian sky and live to brag about it."

From afar, as they rushed to their destiny, Jupiter had a
splendour which no other planet, perhaps not the sun itself,
could match. From a cold great star to an amber disc to a swollen
shield banded with storm—the sight caught your heart.

But then you fought it. You got so close that the shield became
a cauldron and ate you down.

The figures spoke a bleak word: the escape velocity of Jupiter
is about fifty-nine kilometres per second. The "Thunderbolt"
had about fifty-two, relative. If she had simply whizzed by
the planet, its gravitation would have slowed her again, and

eventually she would have fallen back into it with a speed that would vapourize her. There was no possibility of the creaking old boats of the satellite colonists getting close to her at any point of such an orbit; they would have needed far more advance warning than a short-range radio could give them.

Instead, Tokugawa used the last reaction mass to aim at the outer fringes of the atmosphere.

The first pass was almost soundless. Only a thin screaming noise, a sense of heat radiated in human faces, a weak tug of deceleration, told how the ship clove air. Then she was out into vacuum again, curving on a long narrow ellipse.

Banning worked his radio, swearing at the Doppler effect. He got the band of Ganymede at last. Beside him, Tokugawa and Wayne peered into the viewscreen, reading stars and moons, while the computer jabbered out an orbit.

"Hello. Hello. Are you there?"

The voice hissed weakly from X Spaceport: "Heh, 'Thun'er-bolt'. Central Astro Control, Ganymede. Harris speakin'. Got y'r path?"

"To a rough approximation," said Banning. "We'd need several more readings to get it exactly, of course. Stand by to record." He took the tape from the computer and read off the figures.

"We've got three boats in y' area," said Harris. "They'll try t' find y'. G'luck."

"Thanks," said Banning. "We could use some."

Tokugawa's small deft fingers completed another calculation. "We'll strike atmosphere again in about fifty hours, skipper," he reported. "That gives the demolition gang plenty of time to work."

Banning twisted his head around. There was no rear wall now to stop his eyes. Except for the central section, with its vital equipment, little enough remained between the bridge and the after bulkhead. Torches had slashed, wrenches had turned, air locks had spewed out jagged temporary moons for days. The ship had become a hollow shell and a web of bracing.

He felt like a murderer.

Across the diameter of the great spheroid, he saw Devon floating free, ordering the crew into spacesuits. As long as they were in null-gee, the Engineer made an excellent foreman, broken rib and all.

His party was going out to cut loose reactor, fire chamber, ion

tubes, everything aft. Now that the last mass was expended and
nothing remained to drive the ship but the impersonal forces of
celestial mechanics, the engines were so much junk whose
weight could kill them. Never mind the generators—there was
enough energy stored in the capacitor bank to keep the shell
lighted and warmed for weeks. If the Jovians didn't catch them
in space, they might need those weeks, too.

Banning sighed. Since men first steered a scraped-out log or
a wicker basket to sea, it has been an agony for a captain to
lose his ship.

He remembered a submarine once, long ago—it still hurt him
to recall, though it hadn't been his fault. Of course, he'd gotten
the idea which might save all their lives now because he knew
a trifle about submarines . . . or should the Montgolfiers get the
credit, or Archimedes?

Cleonie floated towards him. She had gotten quite deft in
free fall during the time before deceleration in which they
orbited towards Jupiter, when spin had been cancelled to speed
the work of jettisoning. "May I bother you?" she asked.

"Of course." Banning took out his pipe. She cheered him up.
"Though the presence of a beautiful girl is not a bother. By
definition."

She smiled, wearily, and brushed a strand of loose hair from
her eyes. It made a halo about her worn face. "I feel so useless,"
she said.

"Nonsense. Keep the meals coming, and you're plenty of use.
Tietjens and Nielsen were awful belly robbers."

"I wondered—" A flush crossed her cheeks. "I do so want to
understand Luke's work."

"Sure." Banning opened his tobacco pouch and began stuffing
the pipe, not an easy thing to do in free fall. "What's the
question?"

"Only . . . we hit the air going so fast—faster than meteors
usually hit Earth, wasn't it? Why didn't we burn up?"

"Meteors don't exactly burn. They volatilize. All we did was
skim some very thin air. We didn't convert enough velocity into
heat to worry about. A lot of what we did convert was carried
away by the air itself."

"But still—I've never heard of braking ellipses being used when
the speed is as high as ours."

Banning clicked his lighter, held it "above" the bowl, and drew hard. "In actual fact," he said, "I don't think it could be done in Earth or Venus atmosphere. But Jupiter has about ten times the gravitational potential, therefore the air thins out with height correspondingly more slowly. In other words, we've got a deeper layer of thin air to brake us. It's all right. We'll have to make quite a few passes—we'll be at this for days, if we aren't rescued—but it can be done."

He got his pipe started. There was a trick to smoking in free fall. The air-circulating blowers, which kept you from smothering in your own breath, didn't much help as small an object as a pipe. But he needed this comfort. Badly.

Many hours later, using orbital figures modified by further observation, a shuttleboat from Ganymede came near enough to locate the "Thunderbolt" on radar. After manoeuvring around so much, it didn't have reaction mass enough to match velocities. For about a second it passed so close that Devon's crew, working out on the hull, could see it—as if they were the damned in hell watching one of the elect fly past.

The shuttleboat radioed for a vessel with fuller tanks. One came. It zeroed in—and decelerated like a startled mustang. The "Thunderbolt" had already fallen deeper into the enormous Jovian gravity field than the boat's engines could rise.

The drifting ship vanished from sight, into the great face of the planet. High clouds veiled it from telescopes—clouds of free radicals, such as could not have existed for a moment under humanly endurable conditions. Jupiter is more alien than men can really imagine.

Her orbit on re-emergence was not so very much different. But the boats which had almost reached her had been forced to move elsewhere; they could not simply hang there, in that intense field. So the "Thunderbolt" made another long, lonesome pass. By the time it was over, Ganymede was in an unfavourable position, and Callisto had never been in a good one. Therefore the ship entered Jupiter's atmosphere for a third time, unattended.

On the next emergence into vacuum, her orbit had shortened and skewed considerably. The rate at which air drag operated was increasing; each plunge went deeper beneath the poison clouds, each swing through clear space took less time. However, there was hope. The Ganymedeans were finally organizing themselves. They computed an excellent estimate of what the fourth free orbit would be and planted well-fuelled boats strategically close at the right times.

Only—the "Thunderbolt" did not come anywhere near the predicted path.

It was pure bad luck. Devon's crew, working whenever the ship was in vacuum, had almost cut away the after section. This last plunge into stiffening air resistance finished the job. Forces of drag and reaction, a shape suddenly altered, whipped the "Thunderbolt" wildly through the stratosphere. She broke free at last, on a drastically different orbit.

But then, it had been unusual good luck which brought the Jovians so close to her in the first place. Probabilities were merely reasserting themselves.

The radio said in a weak, fading voice: "Missed y' 'gain. Do' know 'f we c'n come near, nex' time. Y'r period's gettin' very short."

"Maybe you shouldn't risk it." Banning sighed. He had hoped for more, but if the gods had decided his ship was to plunge irretrievably into Jupiter, he had to accept the fact. "We'll be all right, I reckon."

Outside, the air roared hollowly. Pressures incomparably greater than those in Earth's deepest oceans waited below.

On his final pass into any approximation of clear space—the stars were already hazed—Banning radioed: "This will be the last message, except for a ten-minute signal on the same band when we come to rest. Assuming we're alive! We've got to save capacitors. It'll be some time before help arrives. When it does, call me. I'll respond if we've survived, and thereafter emit a steady tone by which we can be located. Is that clear?"

"Clear. I read y'. Luck, spaceman . . . over an' out."

Watching the mists thicken in the viewscreen, Banning added figures in his head for the hundredth time.

His schedule called for him to report at Phobos in fifteen days. When he didn't, the Guard would send a high-acceleration ship to find out what had gone wrong. Allow a few days for that. Another week for it to return to Mars with a report of the facts. Mars would call Luna on the radio beam—that, at least, would be quick—and the Guard, or possibly the Engineers, would go to work at once.

The Engineers had ships meant to enter atmosphere: powerful, but slow. Such a vessel could be carried piggyback by a fast ion-dive craft of the Guard. Modifications could be made en route. But the trip would still require a couple of weeks, pessimistically reckoned.

Say, then, six weeks maximum until help arrived. Certainly no less than four, no matter what speeds could be developed by these latest models.

Well, the "Thunderbolt" had supplies and energy for more than six weeks. That long a time under two-plus gees was not going to be fun, though gravanol injections would prevent physiological damage. And the winds were going to buffet them around. That should be endurable, though; they'd be above the region of vertical currents, in what you might call the Jovian stratosphere—

A red fog passed before the screen.

Luke Devon, strapped into a chair like everyone else, called across the empty ship: "If I'd only known this was going to happen—what a chance for research! I do have a few instruments, but it'll be crude as hell."

"Personally," said Banning, "I saved out a deck of cards and some poker chips. But I hardly think you'll have much time for research—in Jovian atmospherics, anyway."

He could imagine Cleonie blushing. He was sorry to embarrass her, he really did like that girl. but the ragged laugh he got from the others was worth it. While men could laugh, especially at jokes as bad as his, they could endure.

Down and down the ship went. Once, caught in a savage gust, she turned over. If everything hadn't been fastened down, there could have been an awful mess. The distribution of mass was such that the hulk would always right itself, but ... yes, reflected Banning, they'd all have to wear some kind of harness attached to the interior braces. It could be improvised.

The wind that boomed beyond the hull faded its organ note, just a trifle.

"We're slowing down," said Tokugawa.

And later, looking up from the radaltimeter: "We've stopped."

"End of the line." Banning stretched. He felt bone-crushingly tired. "Nothing much we can do now. Let's all strap into our bunks and sleep for a week."

His Jovian weight dragged at him. But they were all alive.

And the ship might be hollowed out, but she still held food and drink, tools and materials, games and books—what was needed to keep them sane as well as breathing in the time they must wait.

His calculations were verified. A hollow steelloy shell, three hundred odd metres in diameter, could carry more than a hundred thousand tons, besides its own mass, and still have a net specific gravity of less than 0.03. Now the Jovian air has an average molecular weight of about 3.3, so after due allowance for temperature and a few other items, the result was derived that at such a thickness its pressure is an endurable one hundred atmospheres.

Like an oil drop in a densitometer, like a free balloon over eighteenth-century France, like a small defiant bubble in the sky, the "Thunderbolt" floated.

THE SENSITIVE MAN

I

THE MERMAID TAVERN had been elaborately decorated: great blocks of hewn coral for pillars and booths, stripers and swordfish on the walls, murals of Neptune and his court—including an outsize animated picture of a mermaid ballet, quite an eye-catcher. But the broad quartz windows showed merely a shifting greenish-blue of seawater, and the only live fish visible were in an aquarium across from the bar. Pacific Colony lacked the grotesque loveliness of the Florida and Cuba settlements. Here they were somehow a working city, even in their recreations.

The sensitive man paused for a moment in the foyer, sweeping the big circular room with a hurried glance. Less than half the tables were filled. This was an hour of interregnum, while the twelve-to-eighteen-hundred shift was still at work and the others had long finished their more expensive amusements. There would always be a few around, of course. Dalgetty typed them as he watched.

A party of engineers, probably arguing about the compression strength of the latest submarine tank, to judge from the bored expressions of the three or four rec girls who had joined them. A biochemist, who seemed to have forgotten his plankton and seaweed for the time being and to have focused his mind on the pretty young clerk with him. A couple of hardhand caissoniers, settling down to some serious drinking.

A maintenance man, a computerman, a tank pilot, a diver, a sea rancher, a bevy of stenographers, a bunch of very obvious tourists, more chemists and metallurgists—the sensitive man dismissed them all. There were others he couldn't classify with any decent probability, but after a second's hesitation he decided to ignore them too. That left only the group with Thomas Bancroft.

They were sitting in one of the coral grottoes, a cave of darkness to ordinary vision. Dalgetty had to squint to see in, and the muted light of the tavern was a harsh glare when his pupils were so distended. But, yes—it was Bancroft, all right, and there was an empty booth adjoining his.

Dalgetty relaxed his eyes to normal perception. Even in the short moment of dilation the fluoros had given him a headache. He blocked it off from consciousness and started across the floor.

A hostess stopped him with a touch on the arm as he was about to enter the vacant cavern. She was young, an iridescent mantrap in her brief uniform. With all the money flowing into Pacific Colony, they could afford decorative help here.

"I'm sorry, sir," she said. "Those are kept for parties. Would you like a table?"

"I'm a party," he answered, "or can soon become one." He moved aside a trifle, so that none of the Bancroft group should happen to look out and see him. "If you could arrange some company for me . . ." He fumbled out a C-note, wondering just how such things could be done gracefully.

"Why, of course, sir." She took it with a smoothness he envied and handed him a stunning smile in return. "Just make yourself comfortable."

Dalgetty stepped into the grotto with a fast movement. This wasn't going to be simple. The rough red walls closed in on top of him, forming a space big enough for twenty people or so. A few strategically placed fluoros gave an eerie undersea light, just enough to see by—but no one could look in. A heavy curtain could be drawn if one wanted to be absolutely secluded. Privacy— *uh*-huh!

He sat down at the driftwood table and leaned back against the coral. Closing his eyes, he made an effort of will. His nerves were already keyed up to such a tautness that it seemed they must break, and it took only seconds to twist his mind along the paths required.

The noise of the tavern rose from a tiny mumble to a clattering surf to a huge and saw-edged wave. Voices dinned in his head, shrill and deep, hard and soft, a senseless stream of talking jumbled together into words, words, words. Somebody dropped a glass, and it was like a bomb going off.

Dalgetty winced, straining his ear against the grotto side. Surely enough of their speech would come to him, even through all that rock! The noise level was high, but the human mind, if trained in concentration, is an efficient filter. The outside racket receded from Dalgetty's awareness, and slowly he gathered in the trickle of sound.

First man: "—no matter. What can they do?"

Second man: "Complain to the government. Do you want the FBI on our trail? I don't."

First man: "Take it easy. They haven't yet done so, and it's been a good week now since—"

Second man: "How do you know they haven't?"

Third man—heavy, authoritative voice. Yes, Dalgetty remembered it now from TV speeches—it was Bancroft himself: "*I* know. I've got enough connections to be sure of that."

Second man: "Okay, so they haven't reported it. But why not?"

Bancroft: "You know why. They don't want the government mixing into this any more than we do."

Woman: "Well, then, are they just going to sit and take it? No, they'll find some way to—"

"HELLO, THERE, MISTER!!!"

Dalgetty jumped and whirled around. His heart began to race until he felt his ribs tremble, and he cursed his own tension.

"WHY, WHAT'S THE MATTER, MISTER? YOU LOOK—"

Effort again, forcing the volume down, grasping the thunderous heart in fingers of command and dragging it towards rest. He focused his eyes on the girl who had entered. It was the rec girl, the one he had asked for because he had to sit in this booth.

Her voice was speaking on an endurable level now. Another pretty little bit of fluff. He smiled shakily. "Sit down, sweet.

I'm sorry. My nerves are shot. What'll you have?"

"A daiquiri, please." She smiled and placed herself beside him. He dialled on the dispenser—the cocktail for her, a scotch and soda for himself.

"You're new here," she said. "Have you just been hired, or are you a visitor?" Again the smile. "My name's Glenna."

"Call me Joe," said Dalgetty. His first name was actually Simon. "No, I'll only be here a short while."

"Where you from?" she asked. "I'm clear from New Jersey myself."

"Proving that nobody is ever born in California." He grinned. The control was asserting itself, his racing emotions were checked, and he could think clearly again. "I'm—uh—just a floater. Don't have any real address right now."

The dispenser ejected the drinks on a tray and flashed the charge—$20. Not bad, considering everything. He gave the machine a fifty and it made change, a five-buck coin and a bill.

"Well," said Glenna, "here's to you."

"And you." He touched glasses, wondering how to say what he had to say. Damn it, he couldn't sit here just talking or necking, he'd come to listen but . . . A sardonic montage of all the detective shows he had ever seen winked through his mind. The amateur who rushes in and solves the case, *heigh-ho*. He had never appreciated all the detail involved till now.

There was hesitation in him. He decided that a straightforward approach was his best bet. Deliberately then he created a cool confidence. Subconsciously he feared this girl, alien as she was to his class. All right, force the reaction to the surface, recognize it, suppress it. Under the table his hands moved in the intricate symbolic pattern which aided such emotion-harnessing.

"Glenna," he said. "I'm afraid I'll be rather dull company. The fact is I'm doing some research in psychology, learning how to concentrate under different conditions. I wanted to try it in a place like this, you understand." He slipped out a 2-C bill and laid it before her. "If you'd just sit here quietly. It won't be for more than an hour, I guess."

"Huh!" Her brows lifted. Then, with a shrug and a wry smile, "Okay, you're paying for it." She took a cigarette from the flat case at her sash, lit it, and relaxed. Dalgetty leaned against the wall and closed his eyes again.

The girl watched him curiously. He was of medium height,

stockily built, inconspicuously dressed in a blue short-sleeved tunic, grey slacks, and sandals. His square snub-nosed face was lightly freckled, with hazel eyes and a rather pleasant shy smile. The rusty hair was close-cropped. A young man, she guessed, about twenty-five, quite ordinary and uninteresting, except for the wrestler's muscles and, of course, his behaviour.

Oh, well, it took all kinds.

Dalgetty had a moment of worry. Not because the yarn he had handed her was thin but because it brushed too close to the truth. He thrust the unsureness out of him. Chances were she hadn't understood any of it, wouldn't even mention it. At least not to the people he was hunting.

Or who were hunting him?

Concentration, and the voices slowly came again: "—maybe. But I think they'll be more stubborn than that."

Bancroft: "Yes. The issues are too large for a few lives to matter. Still, Michael Tighe is only human. He'll talk."

The woman: "He can be made to talk, you mean?" She had one of the coldest voices Dalgetty had ever heard.

Bancroft: "Yes. Though I hate to use extreme measures."

Man: "What other possibilities have we got? He won't say anything unless he's forced to. And meanwhile his people will be scouring the planet to find him. They're a shrewd bunch."

Bancroft, sardonically: "What can they do, please? It takes more than an amateur to locate a missing man. It calls for all the resources of a large police organization. And the last thing they want, as I've said before, is to bring the government in on this."

The woman: "I'm not so sure of that, Tom. After all, the Institute is a legal group. It's government sponsored, and its influence is something tremendous. Its graduates—"

Bancroft: "It educates a dozen different kinds of psycho-technicians, yes. It does research. It gives advice. It publishes findings and theories. But believe me, the Psychotechnic Institute is like an iceberg. Its real nature and purpose are hidden way under water. No, it isn't doing anything illegal that I know of. Its aims are so large that they transcend law altogether."

Man: "What aims?"

Bancroft: "I wish I knew. We've only got hints and guesses, you know. One of the reasons we've snatched Tighe is to find out more. I suspect that their real work requires secrecy."

The woman, thoughtfully: "Y-y-yes, I can see how that might be. If the world at large were aware of being—manipulated— then manipulation might become impossible. But just where does Tighe's group want to lead us?"

Bancroft: "I don't know, I tell you. I'm not even sure that they do want to—take over. Something even bigger than that." A sigh. "Let's face it, Tighe is a crusader too. In his own way he's a very sincere idealist. He just happens to have the wrong ideals. That's one reason why I'd hate to see him harmed."

Man: "But if it turns out that we've got to—"

Bancroft: "Why, then we've got to, that's all. But I won't enjoy it."

Man: "Okay, you're the leader, you say when. But I warn you not to wait too long. I tell you, the Institute is more than a collection of unworldly scientists. They've got *someone* out searching for Tighe, and if they should locate him, there could be real trouble."

Bancroft, mildly: "Well, these are troubled times, or will be shortly. We might as well get used to that."

The conversation drifted away into idle chatter. Dalgetty groaned to himself. Not once had they spoken of the place where their prisoner was kept.

All right, little man, what next? Thomas Bancroft was big game. His law firm was famous. He had been in Congress and the Cabinet. Even with the Labour Party in power he was a respected elder statesman. He had friends in government, business, unions, guilds and clubs and leagues from Maine to Hawaii. He had only to say the word, and Dalgetty's teeth would be kicked in some dark night. Or, if he proved squeamish, Dalgetty might find himself arrested on a charge like conspiracy and tied up in court for the next six months.

By listening in he had confirmed the suspicion of Ulrich at the Institute that Thomas Bancroft was Tighe's kidnapper—but that was no help. If he went to the police with that story, they would (a) laugh, long and loud—(b) lock him up for psychiatric investigation—(c) worst of all, pass the story on to Bancroft, who would thereby know what the Institute's children could do and would take appropriate countermeasures.

II

Of course, this was just the beginning. The trail was long. But time was hideously short before they began turning Tighe's brain inside out. And there were wolves along the trail.

For a shivering instant, Simon Dalgetty realized what he had let himself in for.

It seemed like forever before the Bancroft crowd left. Dalgetty's eyes followed them out of the bar—four men and the woman. They were all quiet, mannerly, distinguished-looking, in rich dark slacks. Even the hulking bodyguard was probably a college graduate, Third Class. You wouldn't take them for murderers and kidnappers and the servants of those who would bring back political gangsterism. But then, reflected Dalgetty, they probably didn't think of themselves in that light either.

The enemy—the old and protean enemy, who had been fought down as Fascist, Nazi, Shintoist, Communist, Atomist, Americanist, and God knew what else for a bloody century—had grown craftier with time. Now he could fool even himself.

Dalgetty's senses went back to normal. It was a sudden immense relief to be merely sitting in a dimly lit booth with a pretty girl, to be no more than human for a while. But his sense of mission was still dark within him.

"Sorry I was so long," he said. "Have another drink."

"I just had one." She smiled.

He noticed the $10-figure glowing on the dispenser and fed it two coins. Then, his nerves still vibrating, he dialled another whisky for himself.

"You know those people in the next grotto?" asked Glenna. "I saw you watching them leave."

"Well, I know Mr. Bancroft by reputation," he said. "He lives here, doesn't he?"

"He's got a place over on Gull Station," she said, "but he's not here very much, mostly on the mainland, I guess."

Dalgetty nodded. He had come to Pacific Colony two days before, had been hanging around in the hope of getting close enough to Bancroft to pick up a clue. Now he had done so and his findings were worth little. He had merely confirmed what the Institute already considered highly probable without getting any new information.

He needed to think over his next move. He drained his drink. "I'd better jet off," he said.

"We can have dinner in here if you want," said Glenna.

"Thanks, I'm not hungry." That was true enough. The nervous tension incidental to the use of his powers raised the devil with appetite. Nor could he be too lavish with his funds. "Maybe later."

"Okay, Joe, I might be seeing you." She smiled. "You're a funny one. But kind of nice." Her lips brushed his, and then she got up and left. Dalgetty went out the door and punched for a topside elevator.

It took him past many levels. The tavern was under the station's caissons near the main anchor cable, looking out into deep water. Above it were storehouses, machine rooms, kitchens, all the paraphernalia of modern existence. He stepped out of a kiosk on to an upper deck, thirty feet above the surface. Nobody else was there, and he walked over to the railing and leaned on it, looking across the water and savouring loneliness.

Below him the tiers dropped away to the main deck, flowing lines and curves, broad sheets of clear plastic, animated signs, the grass and flowerbeds of a small park, people walking swiftly or idly. The huge gyro-stabilized bulk did not move noticeably to the long Pacific swell. Pelican Station was the colony's "downtown", its shops and theatres and restaurants, service and entertainment.

Around it the water was indigo blue in the evening light, streaked with arabesques of foam, and he could hear waves rumble against the sheer walls. Overhead the sky was tall with a few clouds in the west turning aureate. The hovering gulls seemed cast in gold. A haziness in the darkened east betokened the southern California coastline. He breathed deeply, letting nerves and muscles and viscera relax, shutting off his mind and turning for a while into an organism that merely lived and was glad to live.

Dalgetty's view in all directions was cut off by the other stations, the rising streamlined hulks which were Pacific Colony. A few airy flex-strung bridges had been completed to link them, but there was still an extensive boat traffic. To the south he could see a blackness on the water that was a sea ranch. His trained memory told him, in answer to a fleeting question, that according to the latest figures, eighteen-point-three per cent of the world's food supply was now being derived from modified strains of seaweed. The percentage would increase rapidly, he knew.

Elsewhere were mineral-extracting plants, fishery bases, experimental and pure research stations. Below the floating city, digging into the continental shelf, was the underwater settlement —oil wells to supplement the industrial synthesizing process, mining, exploration in tanks to find new resources, a slow growth outward as men learned how to go deeper into cold and darkness and pressure. It was expensive, but an overcrowded world had little choice.

Venus was already visible, low and pure on the dusking horizon. Dalgetty breathed the wet pungent sea air into his lungs and thought with some pity of the men out there—and on the Moon, on Mars, between worlds. They were doing a huge and heartbreaking job; but he wondered if it were bigger and more meaningful than this work here in Earth's oceans.

Or a few pages of scribbled equations, tossed into a desk drawer at the Institute. Enough. Dalgetty brought his mind to heel like a harshly trained dog. He was also here to work.

The forces he must encounter seemed monstrous. He was one man, alone against he knew not what kind of organization. He had to rescue one other man before—well, before history was changed and spun off on the wrong course, the long downward path. He had his knowledge and abilities, but they wouldn't stop a bullet. Nor did they include education for this kind of warfare. War that was not war, politics that was not politics but a handful of scrawled equations and a bookful of slowly gathered data and a brainful of dreams.

Bancroft had Tighe—somewhere. The Institute could not ask the government for help, even if to a large degree the Institute was the government. It could, perhaps, send Dalgetty a few men, but it had no goon squads. And time was like a hound on his heels.

The sensitive man turned, suddenly aware of someone else. This was a middle-aged fellow, gaunt and grey-haired, with an intellectual cast of feature. He leaned on the rail and said quietly, "Nice evening, isn't it?"

"Yes," said Dalgetty. "Very nice."

"It gives me a feeling of real accomplishment, this place," said the stranger.

"How so?" asked Dalgetty, not unwilling to make conversation.

The man looked out over the sea and spoke softly as if to himself. "I'm fifty years old. I was born during World War Three and grew up with the famines and the mass insanities that followed. I saw fighting myself in Asia. I worried about a senselessly expanding population pressing on senselessly diminished resources. I saw an America that seemed equally divided between decadence and madness.

"And yet I can stand now and watch a world where we've got a functioning United Nations, where population increase is levelling off and democratic government spreading to country after country, where we're conquering the seas and even going out to other planets. Things have changed since I was a boy, but on the whole it's been for the better."

"Ah," said Dalgetty, "a kindred spirit. Though I'm afraid it's not quite that simple."

The man arched his brows. "So you vote Conservative?"

"The Labour Party *is* conservative," said Dalgetty. "As proof of which it's in coalition with the Republicans and the Neofederalists as well as some splinter groups. No, I don't care if it stays in, or if the Conservatives prosper, or the Liberals take over. The question is—who shall control the group in power?"

"Its membership, I suppose," said the man.

"But just who is its membership? You know as well as I do that the great failing of the American people has always been their lack of interest in politics."

"What? Why, they vote, don't they? What was the last percentage?"

"Eight-eight-point-three-seven. Sure they vote—once the ticket has been presented to them. But how many of them have anything to do with nominating the candidates or writing the platforms? How many will actually take time out to *work* at it—or even to write their Congressmen? 'Ward heeler' is still a term of contempt.

"All too often in our history the vote has been simply a matter of choosing between two well-oiled machines. A sufficiently clever and determined group can take over a party, keep the name and the slogans, and in a few years do a complete behind-the-scenes *volte-face*." Dalgetty's words came fast; this was one facet of a task to which he had given his life.

"Two machines," said the stranger, "or four or five as we've got now, are at least better than one."

"Not if the same crowd controls all of them," Dalgetty said grimly.

"But—"

"'If you can't lick 'em, join 'em.' Better yet, join all sides. Then you *can't* lose."

"I don't think that's happened yet," said the man.

"No, it hasn't," said Dalgetty, "not in the United States, though in some other countries—never mind. It's still in process of happening, that's all. The lines today are drawn not by nations or parties, but by—philosophies, if you wish. Two views of man's destiny cutting across all national political, racial, and religious lines."

"And what are those two views?" asked the stranger quietly.

"You might call them libertarian and totalitarian, though the latter don't necessarily think of themselves as such. The peak of rampant individualism was reached in the nineteenth century, legally speaking. Though, in point of fact, social pressure and custom were more straitjacketing than most people today realize.

"In the twentieth century that social rigidity—in manners, morals, habits of thought—broke down. The emancipation of women, for instance, or the easy divorce or the laws about privacy. But at the same time legal control began tightening up again. Government took over more and more functions, taxes got steeper, the individual's life got more and more bound by regulations saying 'thou shalt' and 'thou shalt not'.

"Well, it looks as if war is going out as an institution. That takes off a lot of pressure. Such hampering restrictions as conscription to fight or work, or rationing, have been removed. What we're slowly attaining is a society where the individual has maximum freedom, both from law *and* custom. It's perhaps farthest advanced in America, Canada, and Brazil, but it's growing the world over.

"But there are elements which don't like the consequences of genuine libertarianism. And the new science of human behaviour, mass and individual, is achieving rigorous formulation. It's becoming the most powerful tool man has ever had—for whoever controls the human mind will also control all that man can do. That science can be used by anyone, mind you. If you'll read between the lines, you'll see what a hidden struggle is shaping up for control of it as soon as it reaches maturity and empirical usability."

"Ah, yes," said the man. "The Psychotechnic Institute."

Dalgetty nodded, wondering why he had jumped into such a lecture. Well, the more people who had some idea of the truth the better—though it wouldn't do for them to know the whole truth either. Not yet.

"The Institute trains so many for governmental posts and does so much advisory work," said the man, "that sometimes it looks almost as if it were quietly taking over the whole show."

Dalgetty shivered a little in the sunset breeze and wished he'd brought his cloak. He thought wearily, *Here it is again. Here is the story they are spreading, not in blatant accusations, not all at once, but slowly and subtly, a whisper here, a hint there, a slanted news story, a supposedly dispassionate article ... Oh, yes, they know their applied semantics.*

"Too many people fear such an outcome," he declared. "It just isn't true. The Institute is a private research organization with a Federal grant. Its records are open to anyone."

"All the records?" The man's face was vague in the gathering twilight.

Dalgetty thought he could make out a sceptically lifted brow. He didn't reply directly but said, "There's a foggy notion in the public mind that a group equipped with a complete science of man—which the Institute hasn't got by a long shot—could 'take over' at once and, by manipulations of some unspecified but frightfully subtle sort, rule the world. The theory is that if you know just what buttons to push and so on, men will do precisely as you wish without knowing that they're being guided. The theory happens to be pure jetwash."

"Oh, I don't know," said the man. "In general terms it sounds pretty plausible."

Dalgetty shook his head. "Suppose I were an engineer," he said, "and suppose I saw an avalanche coming down on me. I might know exactly what to do to stop it—where to plant my dynamite, where to build my concrete wall, and so on. Only the knowledge wouldn't help me. I'd have neither the time nor the strength to use it.

"The situation is similar with regard to human dynamics, both mass and individual. It takes months or years to change a man's convictions, and when you have hundreds of millions of men . . ." He shrugged. "Social currents are too large for all but the slightest, most gradual control. In fact, perhaps the most valuable results obtained to date are not those which show what can be done but what cannot."

"You speak with the voice of authority," said the man.

"I'm a psychologist," said Dalgetty truthfully enough. He didn't add that he was also a subject, observer, and guinea pig in one. "And I'm afraid I talk too much. Go from bad to voice."

"Ouch," said the man. He leaned his back against the rail and his shadowy hand extended a pack. "Smoke?"

"No, thanks, I don't."

"You're a rarity." The brief lighter-flare etched the stranger's face against the dusk.

"I've found other ways of relaxing."

"Good for you. By the way, I'm a professor myself. English Lit at Colorado."

"Afraid I'm rather a roughneck in that respect," said Dalgetty. For a moment he had a sense of loss. His thought processes had become too far removed from the ordinary human for him to find much in fiction or poetry. But music, sculpture, painting—there was something else. He looked over the broad glimmering water, at the stations dark against the first stars, and savoured the many symmetries and harmonies with a real pleasure. You needed senses like his before you could know what a lovely world this was.

"I'm on vacation now," said the man. Dalgetty did not reply in kind. After a moment—"You are too, I suppose?"

Dalgetty felt a slight shock. A personal question from a stranger—well, you didn't expect otherwise from someone like the girl Glenna, but a professor should be better conditioned to privacy customs.

"Yes," he said shortly. "Just visiting."

"By the way, my name is Tyler, Harmon Tyler."

"Joe Thomson." Dalgetty shook hands with him.

"We might continue our conversation if you're going to be around for a while," said Tyler. "You raised some interesting points."

Dalgetty considered. It would be worthwhile staying as long as Bancroft did, in the hope of learning some more. "I may be here a couple of days yet," he said.

"Good," said Tyler. He looked up at the sky. It was beginning to fill with stars. The deck was still empty. It ran around the dim upthrusting bulk of a weather-observation tower which was turned over to its automatics for the night, and there was no one else to be seen. A few fluoros cast wan puddles of luminance on the plastic flooring.

Glancing at his watch, Tyler said casually, "It's about nineteen-thirty hours now. If you don't mind waiting till twenty hundred, I can show you something interesting."

"What's that?"

"Ah, you'll be surprised." Tyler chuckled. "Not many people know about it. Now, getting back to that point you raised earlier . . ."

The half hour passed swiftly. Dalgetty did most of the talking.

"—and mass action. Look, to a rather crude first approxima-tion, a state of semantic equilibrium on a world-wide scale, which of course has never existed, would be represented by an equation of the form—"

"Excuse me." Tyler consulted the shining dial again. "If you don't mind stopping for a few minutes I'll show you that odd sight I was talking about."

"Eh? Oh—oh, sure."

Tyler threw away his cigarette. It was a tiny meteor in the gloom. He took Dalgetty's arm. They walked slowly around the weather tower.

The men came from the opposite side and met them halfway. Dalgetty had hardly seen them before he felt the sting in his chest.

A needle gun!

The world roared about him. He took a step forward, trying to scream, but his throat locked. The deck lifted up and hit him, and his mind whirled towards darkness.

From somewhere, will rose within him, trained reflexes worked, he summoned all that was left of his draining strength and fought the anaesthetic. His wrestling with it was a groping in fog. Again and again he spiralled into unconsciousness and rose strangling. Dimly, through nightmare, he was aware of being carried. Once someone stopped the group in a corridor and asked what was wrong. The answer seemed to come from immensely far away. "I dunno. He passed out—just like that. We're taking him to a doctor."

There was a century spent going down some elevator. The

boathouse walls trembled liquidly around him. He was carried aboard a large vessel; it was not visible through the grey mist. Some dulled portion of himself thought that this was obviously a private boathouse, since no one was trying to stop—trying to stop—trying to stop . . .

Then the night came.

III

He woke slowly, with a dry retch, and blinked his eyes open. Noise of air, he was flying, it must have been a triphibian they took him on to. He tried to force recovery, but his mind was still too paralysed.

"Here. Drink this."

Dalgetty took the glass and gulped thirstily. It was coolness and steadiness spreading through him. The vibrato within him faded, and the headache dulled enough to be endurable. Slowly he looked around, and felt the first crawl of panic.

No! He suppressed the emotion with an almost physical thrust. Now was the time for calm and quick wit and—

A big man near him nodded and stuck his head out the door. "He's okay now, I guess," he called. "Want to talk to him?"

Dalgetty's eyes roved the compartment. It was a rear cabin in a large airboat, luxuriously furnished with reclining seats and an inlaid table. A broad window looked out on the stars.

Caught! It was pure bitterness, an impotent rage at himself. *Walked right into their arms!*

Tyler came into the room, followed by a pair of burly stone-faced men. He smiled. "Sorry," he murmured, "but you're playing out of your league, you know."

"Yeah." Dalgetty shook his head. Wryness twisted his mouth. "I don't league it much either."

Tyler grinned. It was a sympathetic expression. "You punsters are incurable," he said. "I'm glad you're taking it so well. We don't intend any harm to you."

Scepticism was dark in Dalgetty, but he managed to relax. "How'd you get on to me?" he asked.

"Oh, various ways. You were pretty clumsy, I'm afraid." Tyler sat down across the table. The guards remained standing. "We were sure the Institute would attempt a counterblow, and we've studied it and its personnel thoroughly. You were recognized,

Dalgetty—and you're known to be very close to Tighe. So you walked after us without even a face-mask . . .

"At any rate, you were noticed hanging around the colony. We checked back on your movements. One of the rec girls had some interesting things to tell of you. We decided you'd better be questioned. I sounded you out as much as a casual acquaintance could and then took you to the rendezvous." Tyler spread his hands. "That's all."

Dalgetty sighed, and his shoulders slumped under a sudden enormous burden of discouragement. Yes, they were right. He was out of his orbit. "Well," he said, "what now?"

"Now we have you *and* Tighe," said the other. He took out a cigarette. "I hope you're somewhat more willing to talk than he is."

"Suppose I'm not?"

"Understand this," Tyler frowned. "There are reasons for going slow with Tighe. He has hostage value, for one thing. But you're nobody. And while we aren't monsters, I for one have little sympathy to spare for your kind of fanatic."

"Now there," said Dalgetty with a lift of sardonicism, "is an interesting example of semantic evolution. This being, on the whole, an easygoing tolerant period, the word 'fanatic' has come to be simply an epithet—a fellow on the other side."

"That will do," snapped Tyler. "You won't be allowed to stall. We want a lot of questions answered." He ticked the points off on his fingers. "What are the Institute's ultimate aims? How is it going about attaining them? How far has it got? Precisely what has it learned, in a scientific way, that it hasn't published? How much does it know about us?" He smiled thinly. "You've always been close to Tighe. He raised you, didn't he? You should know just as much as he."

Yes, thought Dalgetty, *Tighe raised me. He was all the father I ever had, really. I was an orphan, and he took me in, and he was good.*

Sharp in his mind rose the image of the old house. It had lain on broad wooded grounds in the fair hills of Maine, with a little river running down to a bay winged with sailboats. There had been neighbours—quiet-spoken folk with something more real about them than most of today's rootless world knew. And there had been many visitors, men and women with minds like flickering sword blades.

He had grown up among intellects aimed at the future. He and Tighe had travelled widely. They had often been in the huge pylon of the main Institute building. They had gone over to Tighe's native England once a year at least. But always the old house had been dear to them.

It stood on a ridge, long and low and weathered grey like a part of the earth. By day it had rested in a green sun-dazzle of trees or a glistening purity of snow. By night you heard the boards creaking and the lonesome sound of wind talking down the chimney. Yes, it had been good.

And there had been the wonder of it. He loved his training. The horizonless world within himself was a glorious thing to explore. And that had oriented him outward to the real world—he had felt wind and rain and sunlight, the pride of high buildings and the surge of a galloping horse, thresh of waves and laughter of women and smooth mysterious purr of great machines, with a fullness that made him pity those deaf and dumb and blind around him.

Oh yes, he loved those things. He was in love with the whole turning planet and the big skies overhead. It was a world of light and strength and swift winds, and it would be bitter to leave it. But Tighe was locked in darkness.

He said slowly, "All we ever were was a research and educational centre, a sort of informal university specializing in the scientific study of man. We're not any kind of political organization. You'd be surprised how much we differ in our individual opinions."

"What of it?" shrugged Tyler. "This is something larger than politics. Your work, if fully developed, would change our whole society, perhaps the whole nature of man. We *know* you've learned more things than you've made public. Therefore you're reserving that information for uses of your own."

"And you want it for your purposes?"

"Yes," said Tyler. After a moment, "I despise melodrama, but if you don't co-operate, you're going to get the works. And we've got Tighe too, never forget that. One of you ought to break down if he watches the other being questioned."

We're going to the same place! We're going to Tighe!

The effort to hold face and voice steady was monstrous. "Just where are we bound?"

"An island. We should be there soon. I'll be going back

again myself, but Mr. Bancroft is coming shortly. That should convince you just how important this is to us."

Dalgetty nodded. "Can I think it over for a while? It isn't an easy decision for me."

"Sure. I hope you decide right."

Tyler got up and left with his guards. The big man who had handed him the drink earlier sat where he had been all the time. Slowly the psychologist began to tighten himself. The faint drone of turbines and whistles of jets and sundered air began to enlarge.

"Where are we going?" he asked.

"CAN'T TELL YOU THAT. SHUDDUP, WILL YOU?"

"But surely . . ."

The guard didn't answer. But he was thinking. *Ree-villa-ghee-gay-doe—never could p'rnounce that damn Spig name . . . cripes, what a God-forsaken hole! . . . Mebbe I can work a trip over to Mexico . . . That little gal in Guada . . .*

Dalgetty concentrated. Revilla—he had it now. Islas de Revilla-gigedo, a small group some 350 or 400 miles off the Mexican coast, little visited, with very few inhabitants. His eidetic memory went to work, conjuring an image of a large-scale map he had once studied. Closing his eyes he laid off the exact distance, latitude and longitude, individual islands.

Wait, there was one a little farther west, belonging to the group. And he rifled through all the facts he had ever learned pertaining to Bancroft. Wait now, Bertrand Meade, who seemed to be the kingpin of the whole movement—yes, Meade owned that tiny island.

So that's where we're going! He sank back, letting weariness overrun him. It would be a while yet before they arrived.

Dalgetty sighed and looked out at the stars. Why had men arranged such clumsy constellations when the total pattern of the sky was a big and lovely harmony? He knew his personal danger would be enormous once he was on the ground. Torture, mutilation, even death.

Dalgetty closed his eyes again. Almost at once he was asleep.

IV

They landed on a small field while it was still dark. Hustled out into a glare of lights, Dalgetty did not have much chance to study his surroundings. There were men standing on guard with magnum rifles, tough-looking professional goons in loose grey uniforms. Dalgetty followed obediently across the concrete, along a walk, and through a garden to the looming curved bulk of a house.

He paused just a second as the door opened for them and stood looking out into darkness. The sea rolled and hissed there on a wide beach. He caught the clean salt smell of it and filled his lungs. It might be the last time he ever breathed such air.

"Get along with you." An arm jerked him into motion again.

Down a bare coldly lit hallway, down an escalator, into the guts of the island. Another door, a room beyond it, an ungentle shove. The door clashed to behind him.

Dalgetty looked around. The cell was small, bleakly furnished with bunk, toilet, and washstand, had a ventilator grille in one wall. Nothing else. He tried listening with maximum sensitivity, but he caught only remote confused murmurs.

Dad! he thought. *You're here somewhere too.*

He flopped on the bunk and spent a moment analysing the aesthetics of the layout. It had a certain pleasing severity, the unconscious balance of complete functionalism. Soon Dalgetty went back to sleep.

A guard with a breakfast tray woke him. Dalgetty tried to read the man's thoughts, but there weren't any to speak of. He ate ravenously under a gun muzzle, gave the tray back, and returned to sleep. It was the same at lunchtime.

His time-sense told him that it was 1435 hours when he was roused again. There were three men this time, husky specimens. "Come on," said one of them. "Never saw such a guy for pounding his ear."

Dalgetty stood up, running a hand through his hair. The red bristles were scratchy on his palm. It was a cover-up, a substitute symbol to bring his nervous system back under full control. The process felt as if he were being tumbled through a huge gulf.

"Just how many of your fellows are there here?" he asked.

"Enough. Now get going!"

He caught the whisper of thought—*fifty of us guards, is it? Yeah, fifty, I guess.*

Fifty! Dalgetty felt taut as he walked out between two of them. Fifty goons. And they were trained, he knew that. The Institute had learned that Bertrand Meade's private army was well drilled. Nothing obtrusive about it—officially they were only servants and bodyguards—but they knew how to shoot.

And he was alone in midocean with them. He was alone, and no one knew where he was, and anything could be done to him. He felt cold, walking down the corridor.

There was a room beyond with benches and a desk. One of the guards gestured to a chair at one end. "Sit," he grunted.

Dalgetty submitted. The straps went around his wrists and ankles, holding him to the arms and legs of the heavy chair. Another buckled about his waist. He looked down and saw that the chair was bolted to the floor. One of the guards crossed to the desk and started up a tape recorder.

A door opened in the far end of the room. Thomas Bancroft came in. He was a big man, fleshy but in well-scrubbed health, his clothes designed with quiet good taste. The head was white-maned, leonine, with handsome florid features and sharp blue eyes. He smiled ever so faintly and sat down behind the desk.

The woman was with him—Dalgetty looked harder at her. She was new to him. She was medium tall, a little on the compact side, her blonde hair cut too short, no makeup on her broad Slavic features. Young, in hard condition, moving with a firm masculine stride. With those tilted grey eyes, that delicately curved nose and a wide sullen mouth, she could have been a beauty had she wanted to be.

One of the modern type, thought Dalgetty. *A flesh-and-blood machine, trying to outmale men, frustrated and unhappy without knowing it, and all the more bitter for that.*

Briefly there was sorrow in him, an enormous pity for the millions of mankind. They did not know themselves, they fought themselves like wild beasts, tied up in knots, locked in nightmare. Man could be so much if he had the chance.

He glanced at Bancroft. "I know you," he said, "but I'm afraid the lady has the advantage of me."

"My secretary and general assistant, Miss Casimir." The politician's voice was sonorous, a beautifully controlled instrument. He leaned across the desk. The recorder by his elbow whirred in the flat soundproofed stillness.

"Mr. Dalgetty," he said, "I want you to understand that we aren't fiends. Some things are too important for ordinary rules, though. Wars have been fought over them in the past and may well be fought again. It will be easier for all concerned if you co-operate with us now. No one need ever know that you have done so."

"Suppose I answer your questions," said Dalgetty. "How do you know I'll be telling the truth?"

"Neoscopolamine, of course. I don't think you've been immunized. It confuses the mind too much for us to interrogate you about these complex matters under its influence, but we will surely find out if you have been answering our present questions correctly."

"And what then? Do you just let me go?"

Bancroft shrugged. "Why shouldn't we? We may have to keep you here for a while, but soon you will have ceased to matter and can safely be released."

Dalgetty considered. Not even he could do much against truth drugs. And there were still more radical procedures, prefrontal lobotomy for instance. He shivered. The leatherite straps felt damp against his thin clothing.

He looked at Bancroft. "What do you really want?" he asked. "Why are you working for Bertrand Meade?"

Bancroft's heavy mouth lifted in a smile. "I thought you were supposed to answer the questions," he said.

"Whether I do or not depends on whose questions they are," said Dalgetty. *Stall for time! Put it off, the moment of terror, put it off!* "Frankly, what I know of Meade doesn't make me friendly. But I could be wrong."

"Mr. Meade is a distinguished executive."

"Uh-huh. He's also the power behind a hell of a lot of political figures, including you. He's the real boss of the Actionist movement."

"What do you know of that?" asked the woman sharply.

"It's a complicated story," said Dalgetty, "but essentially Actionism is a—a *Weltanschauung*. We're still recovering from the World Wars and their aftermath. People everywhere are swinging away from great vague capitalized Causes towards a cooler and clearer view of life.

"It's analogous to the eighteenth-century Enlightenment, which also followed a period of turmoil between conflicting fanaticisms. A belief in reason is growing up even in the popular mind, a spirit of moderation and tolerance. There's a wait-and-see attitude towards everything, including the sciences and particularly the new half-finished science of psychodynamics. The world wants to rest for a while.

"Well, such a state of mind has its own drawbacks. It produces wonderful structures of thought, but they've something cold about them. There is so little real passion, so much caution—the arts, for instance, are becoming ever more stylized. Old symbols like religion and the sovereign state and a particular form of government, for which men once died, are openly jeered at. We can formulate the semantic condition at the Institute in a very neat equation.

"And you don't like it. Your kind of man needs something big. And mere concrete bigness isn't enough. You could give your lives to the sciences or to interplanetary colonization or to social correction, as many people are cheerfully doing—but those aren't for you. Down underneath, you miss the universal father-image.

"You want an almighty Church or an almighty State or an almighty *anything*, a huge misty symbol which demands everything you've got and gives in return only a feeling of belonging." Dalgetty's voice was harsh. "In short, you can't stand on your own psychic feet. You can't face the truth that man is a lonely creature and that his purpose must come from within himself."

Bancroft scowled. "I didn't come here to be lectured," he said.

"Have it your way," answered Dalgetty. "I thought you wanted to know what I knew of Actionism. That's it in unprecise verbal language. Essentially you want to be a Leader in a Cause. Your men, such as aren't merely hired, want to be Followers. Only there isn't a Cause around, these days, except the common-sense one of improving human life."

The woman, Casimir, leaned over the desk. She bore a curious intensity in her eyes. "You just pointed out the drawbacks yourself," she said. "This *is* a decadent period."

"No," said Dalgetty. "Unless you insist on loaded connotations. It's a necessary period of rest. Recoil time for a whole society—well, it all works out nicely in Tighe's formulation. The present state of affairs should continue for about seventy-five years, we feel at the Institute. In that time, reason can—we hope—be so firmly implanted in the basic structure of society that when the next great wave of passion comes, it won't turn men against each other.

"The present is, well, analytic. While we catch our breath we can begin to understand ourselves. When the next synthetic—or creative or crusading period, if you wish—comes, it will be saner than all which have gone before. And man can't afford to go insane again. Not in the same world as the lithium bomb."

Bancroft nodded. "And you in the Institute are trying to control this process," he said. "You're trying to stretch out the period of—damn it, of decadence! Oh, I've studied the modern school system too, Dalgetty. I know how subtly the rising generation is being indoctrinated—through policies formulated by *your* men in the government."

"Indoctrinated? Trained, I would say. Trained in self-restraint and critical thinking." Dalgetty grinned with one side of his mouth. "Well, we aren't here to argue generalities. Specifically, Meade feels he has a mission. He is the natural leader of America—ultimately, through the U.N., in which we are still powerful, the world. He wants to restore what he calls 'ancestral virtues'—you see, I've listened to his speeches and yours, Bancroft.

"These virtues consist of obedience, physical *and* mental, to 'constituted authority'—of 'dynamism', which operationally speaking means people ought to jump when he gives an order—of . . . Oh, why go on? It's the old story. Power hunger, the recreation of the Absolute State, this time on a planetary scale.

"With psychological appeals to some and with promises of reward to others, he's built up quite a following. But he's shrewd enough to know that he can't just stage a revolution. He has to make people want him. He has to reverse the social current until it swings back to authoritarianism—with him riding the crest.

"And that of course is where the Institute comes in. Yes, we have developed theories which make at least a beginning at explaining the facts of history. It was a matter not so much of gathering data as of inventing a rigorous self-correcting symbology, and our paramathematics seems to be just that. We haven't published all of our findings, because of the uses to which they could be put. If you know exactly how to go about it, you can shape world society into almost any image you want —in fifty years or less! You want that knowledge of ours for your purposes."

Dalgetty fell silent. There was a long quietness. His own breathing seemed unnaturally loud.

"All right." Bancroft nodded again, slowly. "You haven't told us anything we don't know."

"I'm well aware of that," said Dalgetty.

"Your phrasing was rather unfriendly," said Bancroft. "What you don't appreciate is the revolting stagnation and cynicism of this age."

"Now you're using the loaded words," said Dalgetty. "Facts just *are*. There's no use passing moral judgments on reality; the only thing you can do is try to change it."

"Yes," said Bancroft. "All right then, we're trying. Do you want to help us?"

"You could beat the hell out of me," said Dalgetty, "but it wouldn't teach you a science that it takes years to learn."

"No, but we'd know just what you have and where to find it. We have some good brains on our side. Given your data and equations, they can figure it out." The pale eyes grew wholly chill. "You don't seem to appreciate your situation. You're a prisoner, understand?"

Dalgetty braced his muscles. He didn't reply.

Bancroft sighed. "Bring him in," he said.

One of the guards went out. Dalgetty's heart stumbled. *Dad,* he thought. It was anguish in him. Casimir walked over to stand in front of him. Her eyes searched his.

"Don't be a fool," she said. "It hurts worse than you know. Tell us."

He looked up at her. *I'm afraid,* he thought. *God knows I'm afraid.* His own sweat was acrid in his nostrils. "No," he said.

"I tell you they'll do everything!" She had a nice voice, low and soft, but it roughened now. Her face was colourless with strain. "Go on, man, don't condemn yourself to—mindlessness!"

There was something strange here. Dalgetty's senses began to reach out. She was leaning close, and he knew the signs of horror, even if she tried to hide them. *She's not so hard as she makes out—but then why is she with them?*

He threw a bluff. "I know who you are," he said. "Shall I tell your friends?"

"No, you don't!" She stepped back, rigid, and his whetted senses caught the fear-smell. In a moment there was control, and she said, "All right then, have it your way."

And underneath, the thought, slowed by the gluiness of panic. *Does he know I'm FBI?*

FBI! He jerked against the straps. Ye gods!

Calmness returned to him as she walked to her chief, but his mind whirred. Yes, why not? Institute men had little connection with the Federal detectives, who, since the abolition of a discredited Security, had resumed a broad function. They might easily have become dubious about Bertrand Meade on their own, have planted operatives with him. They had women among them too, and a woman was always less conspicuous than a man.

He felt a chill. The last thing he wanted was a Federal agent here.

The door opened again. A quartet of guards brought in Michael Tighe. The Briton halted, staring before him. *"Simon!"* It was a harsh sound, full of pain.

"Have they hurt you, Dad?" asked Dalgetty very gently.

"No, no—not till now." The grey head shook. "But you . . ."

"Take it easy, Dad," said Dalgetty.

The guards hustled Tighe over to a front-row bench and sat him down. Old man and young locked eyes across the bare space.

Tighe spoke to him in the hidden way. *What are you going to do? I can't sit and let them—*

Dalgetty could not reply unheard, but he shook his head. "I'll be okay," he answered aloud.

Do you think you can make a break? I'll try to help you.

"No," said Dalgetty. "Whatever happens, you lie low. That's an order."

He blocked off sensitivity as Bancroft snapped, "Enough. One of you is going to yield. If Dr. Tighe won't, then we'll work on him and see if Mr. Dalgetty can hold out."

He waved his hand as he took out a cigar. Two of the goons stepped up to the chair. They had rubberite hoses in their hands.

The first blow thudded against Dalgetty's ribs. He didn't feel it—he had thrown up a nerve bloc—but it rattled his teeth together. And while he was insensitive he'd be unable to listen in on . . .

Another thud, and another. Dalgetty clenched his fists. What to do, what to do? He looked over to the desk. Bancroft was smoking and watching as dispassionately as if it were some mildly interesting experiment. Casimir had turned her back.

"Something funny here, chief." One of the goons straightened. "I don't think he's feeling nothing."

"Doped?" Bancroft frowned. "No, that's hardly possible." He

rubbed his chin, regarding Dalgetty with wondering eyes. Casimir wheeled around to stare. Sweat filmed Michael Tighe's face, glistening in the chill white light.

"He can still be hurt," said the guard.

Bancroft winced. "I don't like outright mutilation," he said. "But still—I've warned you Dalgetty."

"*Get out, Simon*," whispered Tighe. "*Get out of here.*"

Dalgetty's red head lifted. Decision crystallized within him. He would be no use to anyone with broken arms, a crushed foot, an eye knocked out, seared lungs— and Casimir was FBI, she might be able to do something at this end in spite of all.

He tested the straps. A quarter inch of leatherite—he could snap them, but would he break his bones doing it?

Only one way to find out, he thought bleakly.

"I'll get a blowtorch," said one of the guards in the rear of the room. His face was wholly impassive. Most of these goons must be moronic, thought Dalgetty. Most of the guards in the twentieth-century extermination camps had been. No inconvenient empathy with the human flesh they broke and flayed and burned.

He gathered himself. This time it was rage, a cloud of fury rising in his mind, a ragged red haze across his vision. That they would *dare!*

He snarled as the strength surged up in him. He didn't even feel the straps as they popped across. The same movement hurtled him across the room towards the door.

Someone yelled. A guard leaped in his path, a giant of a man. Dalgetty's fist sprang before him, there was a cracking sound, and the goon's head snapped back against his own spine. Dalgetty was already past him. The door was shut in his face. Wood crashed as he went through it.

A bullet wailed after him. He dodged down the corridor, up the nearest steps, the walls blurred with his own speed. Another slug smacked into the panelling beside him. He rounded a corner, saw a window, and covered his eyes with an arm as he leaped.

The plastic was tough, but a hundred and seventy pounds hit it at fifteen feet per second. Dalgetty went through!

Sunlight flamed in his eyes as he hit the ground. Rolling over and bouncing to his feet, he set out across lawn and garden. As he ran his vision swept the landscape. In that state of fear and wrath, he could not command much thought, but his memory stored the data for re-examination.

V

The house was a rambling two-story affair, all curves and planes between palm trees, the island sloping swiftly from its front to a beach and dock. On one side was the airfield, on another the guard barracks. To the rear, in the direction of Dalgetty's movement, the ground became rough and wild, stones and sand and saw grass and clumps of eucalyptus, climbing upwards for a good two miles. On every side, he could see the infinite blue sparkle of ocean. Where could he hide?

He didn't notice the vicious cholla through which he raced, and the dry gulping of his lungs was something dreadfully remote. But when a bullet went past one ear, he heard that and drew more speed from some unknown depth. A glance behind revealed his pursuers boiling out of the house, men in grey with the hot sunlight blinking off their guns.

He ducked around a thicket, flopped, and belly-crawled over a rise of land. On the farther side, he straightened again and ran up the long slope. Another slug and another. They were almost a mile behind now, but their guns had a long reach. He bent low, zigzagging as he ran. The bullets kicked up spurts of sand around him.

A six-foot bluff loomed in his path, black volcanic rock shining like wet glass. He hit it at full speed. He almost *walked* up its face and in the instant when his momentum was gone caught a root and yanked himself to the top. Again he was out of their sight. He sprang around another hulk of stone and skidded to a halt. At his feet, a sheer cliff dropped nearly a hundred feet to a white smother of surf.

Dalgetty gulped air, working his lungs like a bellows. A long jump down, he thought dizzily. If he didn't crack his skull open on a reef, he might well be clawed under by the sea. But there was no other place for him to go.

He made a swift estimate. He had run the upward two miles in a little over nine minutes, surely a record for such terrain. It would take the pursuit another ten or fifteen to reach him. But he couldn't double back without being seen, and this time they'd be close enough to fill him with lead.

Okay, son, he told himself, *You're going to duck now, in more than one sense.*

His light waterproof clothes, tattered by the island growth, would be no hindrance down there, but he took off his sandals and stuck them in his belt pouch. Praise all gods, the physical side of his training had included water sports. He moved along the cliff edge, looking for a place to dive. The wind whined at his feet.

There—down there. No visible rocks, though the surf boiled and smoked. He willed full energy back into himself, bent his knees, jackknifed into the sky.

The sea was a hammer blow against his body. He came up threshing and tumbling, gasped a mouthful of air that was half salt spray, was pulled under again. A rock scraped his ribs. He took long strokes, always upwards to the blind white shimmer of light. He got to the crest of one wave and rode it in, surfing over a razorback reef.

Shallow water. Blinded by the steady rain of salt mist, deafened by the roar and crash of the sea, he groped towards shore. A narrow pebbly beach ran along the foot of the cliff. He moved along it, hunting a place to hide.

There—a seaworn cave, some ten feet inward, with a yard or so of fairly quiet water covering its bottom. He splashed inside and lay down, exhaustion clamping a hand on him.

It was noisy. The hollow resonance of sound filled the cave like the inside of a drum, but he didn't notice. He lay on the rocks and sand, his mind spiralling towards unconsciousness, and let his body make its own recovery.

Presently he regained awareness and looked about him. The cave was dim, with only a filtered greenish light to pick out black walls and slowly swirling water. Nobody could see much below the surface—good. He studied himself. Lacerated clothes, bruised flesh, and a long bleeding gash in one side. That was not good. A stain of blood on the water would give him away like a shout.

Grimacing, he pressed the edges of the wound together and willed that the bleeding stop. By the time a good enough clot was formed for him to relax his concentration, the guards were scrambling down to find him. He didn't have many minutes left. Now he had to do the opposite of energizing. He had to slow metabolism down, ease his heartbeat, lower his body temperature, dull his racing brain.

He began to move his hands, swaying back and forth, muttering the autohypnotic formulas. His incantations, Tighe had called them. But they were only stylized gestures leading to conditioned reflexes deep in the medulla. *Now I lay me down to sleep* . . .

Heavy, heavy—his eyelids were drooping, the wet walls receding into a great darkness, a hand cradling his head. The noise of surf dimmed, became a rustle, the skirts of the mother he had never known, came in to bid him good night. Coolness stole over him like veils dropping one by one inside his head. There was winter outside, and his bed was snug.

When Dalgetty heard the nearing rattle of boots—just barely through the ocean and his own drowsiness—he almost forgot what he had to do. No, yes, now he knew. Take several long, deep breaths, oxygenate the bloodstream, then fill the lungs once and slide down under the surface.

He lay there in darkness, hardly conscious of the voices, dimly perceived.

"A cave here—a place for him to hide."

"Nah, I don't see nothing."

Scrunch of feet on stone. "Ouch! Stubbed my damn toe. Nah, it's a closed cave. He ain't in here."

"Hm? Look at this, then. Bloodstains on this rock, right? He's *been* here, at least."

"Under water?" Rifle butts probed but could not sound the inlet.

The woman's voice. "If he is hiding down below, he'll have to come up for air."

"When? We gotta search this whole damn beach. Here, I'll just give the water a burst."

Casimir, sharply— "Don't be a fool. You won't even know if you hit him. Nobody can hold his breath more than three minutes."

"Yeah, that's right, Joe. How long we been in here?"

"One minute, I guess. Give him a couple more. Cripes! D'ja see how he ran? He ain't human!"

"He's killable, though. Me, I think he's just rolling around in the surf out there. This could be fish blood. A shark chased another fish in here and bit it."

Casimir: "Or, if his body drifted in, it's safely under. Got a cigarette?"

"Here y'are, miss. But say, I never thought to ask. How come you came with us?"

Casimir: "I'm as good a shot as you are, buster, and I want to be sure this job's done right."

Pause.

Casimir: "Almost five minutes. If he can come up now, he's a seal. Especially with his body ogygen-starved after all that running."

In the slowness of Dalgetty's brain, there was a chill wonder about the woman. He had read her thought, she was FBI, but she seemed strangely eager to hunt him down.

"Okay, let's get outta here." ·

Casimir: "You go on. I'll wait here just in case and come up to the house pretty soon. I'm tired of following you around."

"Okay. Let's go, Joe."

It was another four minutes or so before the pain and tension in his lungs became unendurable. Dalgetty knew he would be helpless as he rose, still in his semihibernating state, but his body was shrieking for air. Slowly he broke the surface.

The woman gasped. Then the automatic jumped into her hand and levelled between his eyes. "All right, friend. Come on out." Her voice was very low and shook a trifle, but there was grimness in it.

Dalgetty climbed on to the ledge beside her and sat with his legs dangling, hunched in the misery of returning strength. When full wakefulness was achieved, he looked at her and found she had moved to the farther end of the cave.

"Don't try to jump," she said. Her eyes caught the vague light in a wide glimmer, half frightened. "I don't know what to make of you."

Dalgetty drew a long breath and sat upright, bracing himself on the cold slippery stone. "I know who you are," he said.

"Who, then?" she challenged.

"You're an FBI agent planted on Bancroft."

Her gaze narrowed, her lips compressed. "What makes you think so?"

"Never mind—you are. That gives me a certain hold on you, whatever your purposes."

The blonde head nodded. "I wondered about that. That

remark you made to me down in the cell suggested—well, I couldn't take chances. Especially when you showed you were something extraordinary by snapping those straps and bursting the door open. I came along with the search party in hope of finding you."

He had to admire the quick mind behind the wide smooth brow. "You damn near did—for them," he accused her.

"I couldn't do anything suspicious," she answered. "But I figured you hadn't leaped off the cliff in sheer desperation. You must have had some hiding place in mind, and under water seemed the most probable. In view of what you'd already done, I was pretty sure you could hold your breath abnormally long." Her smile was a little shaky. "Though I didn't think it would be *inhumanly* long."

"You've got brains," he said, "but how much heart?"

"What do you mean?"

"I mean, are you going to throw Dr. Tighe and me to the wolves now? Or will you help us?"

"That depends," she answered slowly. "What are you here for?"

His mouth twisted ruefully. "I'm not here on purpose at all," Dalgetty confessed. "I was just trying to get a clue to Dr. Tighe's whereabouts. They outsmarted me and brought me here. Now I *have* to rescue him." His eyes held hers. "Kidnapping is a Federal offence. It's your duty to help me."

"I may have higher duties," she countered. Leaning forward, tautly, "But how do you expect to do this?"

"I'm damned if I know," Dalgetty looked moodily out at the beach and the waves and the smoking spindrift. "But that gun of yours would be a big help."

She stood for a moment, scowling with thought. "If I don't come back soon, they'll be out hunting for me."

"We've got to find another hiding place," he agreed. "Then they will assume I survived after all and grabbed you. They'll be scouring the whole island for us. If we haven't been located before dark, they'll be spread thin enough to give us a chance."

"It makes more sense for me to go back now," she said. "Then I can be on the inside to help you."

He shook his head. "Uh-uh. Quit making like a stereoshow detective. If you leave me your gun, claiming you lost it, that's sure to bring suspicion on you, the way they're excited right now. If you don't, I'll still be on the outside and unarmed—and what could you do, one woman alone in that nest? Now we're two with a shooting iron between us. I think that's a better bet."

After a while, she nodded. "Okay, you win. Assuming"—the half-lowered gun was raised again with a jerking motion—"that I will aid you. Who are you? *What* are you, Dalgetty?"

He shrugged. "Let's say I'm Dr. Tighe's assistant and have some unusual powers. You know the Institute well enough to realize this isn't just a feud between two gangster groups."

"I wonder . . ." Suddenly she clashed the automatic back into its holster. "All right. For the time being only, though!"

Relief was a wave rushing through him. "Thank you," he whispered. Then, "Where can we go?"

"I've been swimming around here in the quieter spots," she said. "I know a place. Wait here."

She stepped across the cave and peered out its mouth. Someone must have hailed her, for she waved back. She stood leaning against the rock, and Dalgetty saw how the seaspray gleamed in her hair. After a long five minutes, she turned to him again.

"All right," she said. "The last one just went up the path. Let's go." They walked along the beach. It trembled underfoot with the rage of the sea. There was a grinding under the snort and roar of surf, as if the world's teeth ate rock.

The beach curved inward, forming a small bay sheltered by outlying skerries. A narrow path ran upwards from it, but it was towards the sea that the woman gestured. "Out there," she said. "Follow me." She took off her shoes as he had done and checked her holster: the gun was waterproof, but it wouldn't do to have it fall out. She waded into the sea and struck out with a powerful crawl.

VI

They climbed up on one of the hogback rocks some ten yards from shore. This one rose a good dozen feet above the surface. It was cleft in the middle, forming a little hollow hidden from land and water alike. They crawled into this and sat down, breathing hard. The sea was loud at their backs, and the air felt cold on their wet skins.

Dalgetty leaned back against the smooth stone, looking at

the woman, who was unemotionally counting how many clips she had in her pouch. The thin drenched tunic and slacks showed a very nice figure. "What's your name?" he asked.

"Casimir," she answered, without looking up.

"First name, I mean. Mine is Simon."

"Elena, if you must know. Four packs, a hundred rounds plus ten in the chamber now. If we have to shoot them all, we'd better be good. These aren't magnums, so you have to hit a man just right to put him out of action."

"Well," shrugged Dalgetty, "we'll just have to lumber along as best we can. I oak we don't make ashes of ourselves."

"Oh, *no!*" He couldn't tell whether it was appreciation or dismay. "At a time like this, too."

"It doesn't make me very popular," he agreed. "Everybody says to elm with me. But, as they say in France, ve are alo-o-one now, mon cherry, and tree's a crowd."

"Don't get ideas," she snapped.

"Oh, I'll get plenty of ideas, though I admit this isn't the place to carry them out." Dalgetty folded his arms behind his head and blinked up at the sky. "Man, could I use a nice tall mint julep right now."

Elena frowned. "If you're trying to convince me you're just a simple American boy, you might as well quit," she said thinly. "That sort of—of emotional control, in a situation like this, only makes you less human."

Dalgetty swore at himself. She was too damn quick, that was all. And her intelligence might be enough for her to learn . . .

Will I have to kill her?

He drove the thought from him. He could overcome his own conditioning about anything, including murder, if he wanted to, but he'd never want to. No, that was out. "How did you get here?" he asked. "How much does the FBI know?"

"Why should I tell you?"

"Well, it'd be nice to know if we can expect reinforcements."

"We can't." Her voice was bleak. "I might as well let you know. The Institute could find out anyway through its government connections—the damned octopus!" She looked into the sky. Dalgetty's gaze followed the curve of her high cheekbones. Unusual face—you didn't often see such an oddly pleasing arrangement. The slight departure from symmetry . . .

"We've wondered about Bertrand Meade for some time, as every thinking person has," she began tonelessly. "It's too bad there are so few thinking people in the country."

"Something the Institute is trying to correct," Dalgetty put in.

Elena ignored him. "It was finally decided to work agents into his various organizations. I've been with Thomas Bancroft for about two years now. My background was carefully faked, and I'm a useful assistant. But even so, it was only a short while back that I got sufficiently into his confidence to be given some inkling of what's going on. As far as I know, no other FBI operative has learned as much."

"And what have you found out?"

"Essentially the same things you were describing in the cell, plus more details on the actual work they're doing. Apparently the Institute was on to Meade's plans long before we were. It doesn't speak well for your purposes, whatever they are, that you haven't asked us for help before this.

"The decision to kidnap Dr. Tighe was taken only a couple of weeks ago. I haven't had a chance to communicate with my associates in the force. There's always someone around, watching. The setup's well arranged, so that even those not under suspicion don't have much chance to work unobserved, once they've got high enough to know anything important. Everybody spies on everybody else and submits periodic reports."

She gave him a harsh look. "So here I am. No official person knows my whereabouts, and if I should disappear, it would be called a deplorable accident. Nothing could be proved, and I doubt if the FBI would ever get another chance to do any effective spying."

"But you have proof enough for a raid," he ventured.

"No, we haven't. Up till the time I was told Dr. Tighe was going to be snatched, I didn't know for certain that anything illegal was going on. There's nothing in the law against like-minded people knowing each other and having a sort of club. Even if they hire tough characters and arm them, the law can't protest. The Act of Nineteen Ninety-nine effectively forbids private armies, but it would be hard to prove Meade has one."

"He doesn't really," said Dalgetty. "Those goons aren't much more than what they claim to be—bodyguards. This whole fight is primarily on a—a mental level."

"So I gather. And can a free country forbid debate or propaganda? Not to mention that Meade's people include some powerful men in the government itself. If I could get away from here alive, we'd be able to hang a kidnapping charge on Thomas Bancroft, with assorted charges of threat, mayhem, and conspiracy, but it wouldn't touch the main group." Her fists clenched. "It's like fighting shadows."

"'You war against the sunset-glow. The judgment follows fast, my lord!'" quoted Dalgetty. *Heriot's Ford* was one of the few poems he liked. "Getting Bancroft out of the way would be something," he added. "The way to fight Meade is not to attack him physically but to change the conditions under which he must work."

"Change them to what?" Her eyes challenged his. He noticed that there were small gold flecks in the grey. "What does the Institute want?"

"A sane world," he replied.

"I've wondered," she said. "Maybe Bancroft is more nearly right than you. Maybe I should be on his side after all."

"I take it you favour libertarian government," he said. "In the past, it's always broken down sooner or later, and the main reason has been that there aren't enough people with the intelligence, alertness, and toughness to resist the inevitable encroachments of power on liberty.

"The Institute is trying to do two things—create such a citizenry and simultaneously to build up a society which itself produces men of that kind and reinforces those traits in them. It can be done, given time. Under ideal conditions, we estimate it would take about three hundred years for the whole world. Actually, it'll take longer."

"But just what kind of person is needed?" Elena asked coldly. "Who decides it? *You* do. You're just the same as all other reformers, including Meade—hell-bent to change the whole human race over to your particular ideal, whether they like it or not."

"Oh, they'll like it," he smiled. "That's part of the process."

"It's a worse tyranny than whips and barbed wire," she snapped.

"You've never experienced those, then."

"You *have* got that knowledge," she accused. "You have the

data and the equations to be—sociological engineers."

"In theory," he said. "In practice, it isn't that easy. The social forces are so great that—well, we could be overwhelmed before accomplishing anything. And there are plenty of things we still don't know. It will take decades, perhaps centuries, to work out a complete dynamics of man. We're one step beyond the politician's rule of thumb, but not up to the point where we can use slide rules. We have to feel our way."

"Nevertheless," she said, "you've got the beginnings of a knowledge which reveals the true structure of society and the processes that make it. Given that knowledge, man could in time build his own world order the way he desired it, a stable culture that wouldn't know the horrors of oppression or collapse. But you've hidden away the very fact that such information exists. You're using it in secret."

"Because we have to," Dalgetty said. "If it were generally known that we're putting pressure on here and there and giving advice slanted just the way we desire, the whole thing would blow up in our faces. People don't like being shoved around."

"And still you're doing it!" One hand dropped to her gun. "You, a clique of maybe a hundred men . . ."

"More than that. You'd be surprised how many are with us."

"You've decided you are the almighty arbiters. Your superior wisdom is going to lead poor blind mankind up the road to heaven. I say it's down the road to hell! The last century saw the dictatorship of the elite and the dictatorship of the proletariat. This one seems to be birthing the dictatorship of the intellectuals. I don't like any of them!"

"Look, Elena." Dalgetty leaned on one elbow and faced her. "It isn't that simple. All right, we've got some special knowledge. When we first realized we were getting somewhere in our research, we had to decide whether to make our results public or merely to give out selected, less important findings. Don't you see, no matter what we did, it would have been us, the few men, who decided? Even destroying all our information would have been a decision."

His voice grew more urgent. "So we made what I think was the right choice. History shows as conclusively as our own equations that freedom is not a 'natural' condition of man. It's a metastable state at best, all too likely to collapse into tyranny. The tyranny can be imposed from outside by the better-

organized armies of a conqueror, or it can come from within—
through the will of the people themselves, surrendering their
rights to the father-image, the almighty leader, the absolute
state.

"What use does Bertrand Meade want to make of our findings if he can get them? To bring about the end of freedom
by working on the people till they themselves desire it. And
the damnable part of it is that Meade's goal is much more
easily attained than ours.

"So suppose we made our knowledge public. Suppose we
educated anyone who desired it in our techniques. Can't you
see what would happen? Can't you see the struggle that would
be waged for control of the human mind? It could start as
innocuously as a businessman planning a more effective adver-
tising campaign. It would end in a welter of propaganda,
counter-propaganda, social and economic manipulations, corrup-
tion, competition for the key offices—and so, ultimately, there
would be violence.

"All the psychodynamic tensors ever written down won't stop
a machine gun. Violence riding over a society thrown into
chaos, enforced peace—and the peacemakers, perhaps with the
best will in the world, using the Institute techniques to restore
order. Then one step leads to another, power gets more and
more centralized, and it isn't long before you have the total
state back again. Only this total state could *never* be over-
thrown!"

Elena Casimir bit her lip. A stray breeze slid down the rock
wall and rumpled her bright hair. After a long while she said,
"Maybe you're right. But America today has, on the whole, a
good government. You could let them know."

"Too risky. Sooner or later, someone, probably with very
idealistic motives, would force the whole thing into the open.
So we're keeping hidden even the fact that our most important
equations exist—which is why we didn't ask for help when
Meade's detectives finally learned what they did."

"How do you know your precious Institute won't become just
such an oligarchy as you describe?"

"I don't," he replied, "but it's improbable. You see, the recruits
who are eventually taught everything we know are pretty thoroughly indoctrinated with our own present-day beliefs. And
we've learned enough individual psych to do some real indoc-

trinating! They'll pass it on to the next generation, and so on.

"Meanwhile, we hope the social structure and the mental climate is being modified in such a way that eventually it would be very difficult, if not impossible, for anyone to impose absolute control by any means. For, as I said before, even an ultimately developed psychodynamics can't do everything. Ordinary propaganda, for instance, is quite ineffective on people trained in critical thinking.

"When enough people the world over are sane, we can make the knowledge general. Meanwhile, we've got to keep it under wraps and quietly prevent anyone else from learning the same things independently. Most such prevention, by the way, consists merely of recruiting promising researchers into our own ranks."

"The world's too big," she said very softly. "You can't foresee all that'll happen. Too many things could go wrong."

"Maybe. It's a chance we've got to take." His own gaze was sombre.

They sat for a while in stillness. Then she said, "It all sounds very pretty. But—what are you, Dalgetty?"

"Simon," he corrected.

"What are you?" she repeated. "You've done things I wouldn't have believed were possible. *Are you human?*"

"I'm told so." He smiled.

"Yes? I wonder! How is it possible that you—"

He wagged a finger. "Ah-ah! Right of privacy." And with swift seriousness, "You know too much already. I have to assume you can keep it secret all your life."

"That remains to be seen," Elena said, not looking at him.

VII

Sundown burned across the waters, and the island rose like a mountain of night against the darkening sky. Dalgetty stretched cramped muscles and peered over the bay.

In the hours of waiting, there had not been much said between him and the woman. He had dropped a few questions, with the careful casualness of the skilled analyst, and got the expected reactions. He knew a little more about her—a child of the strangling dying cities and shadowy life of the 1980's, forced to armour herself in harshness, finding in the long training for her work and now in the job itself an ideal to substitute for the tenderness she had never known.

He felt pity for her but there was little he could do to help just now. To her own queries he gave guarded replies. It occurred to him briefly that he was, in his way, as lonesome as she. *But of course I don't mind—or do I?*

Mostly they tried to plan their next move. For the time, at least, they were of one purpose. She described the layout of house and grounds and indicated the cell where Michael Tighe was ordinarily kept. But there was not much they could do to think out tactics. "If Bancroft gets alarmed enough," she said, "he'll have Dr. Tighe flown elsewhere."

He agreed. "That's why we'd better hit tonight, before he can get that worried." The thought was pain within him. *Dad, what are they doing to you now?*

"We have also the matter of food and drink." Her voice was husky with thirst and dull with the discouragement of hunger. "We can't stay out here like this much longer." She gave him a strange glance. "Don't you feel weak?"

"Not now," he said. He had blocked off the sensations.

"They—*Simon!*" She grabbed his arm. "A boat—hear?"

The murmur of jets drifted to him through the beating waves. "Yeah. Quick—underneath!"

They scrambled over the hogback and slid down its farther side. The sea clawed at Dalgetty's feet, and foam exploded over his head. He hunched low, throwing one arm about her as she slipped. The airboat murmured overhead, hot gold in the sunset light. Dalgetty crouched, letting the breakers run coldly around him. The ledge where they clung was worn smooth, offered little to hold on to.

The boat circled, its jets thunderous at low speed. *They're worried about her now. They must be sure I'm still alive.*

White water roared above his head. He breathed a hasty gasp of air before the next comber hit him. Their bodies were wholly submerged, their faces shouldn't show in that haze of foam—but the jet was soaring down, and there would be machine guns on it.

Dalgetty's belly muscles stiffened, waiting for the tracers to burn through him.

Elena's body slipped from his grasp and went under. He hung there, not daring to follow. A stolen glance upwards— yes, the jet was out of sight again, moving back towards the field. He dived off the ledge and struck into the waves. The girl's head rose over them as he neared. She twisted from him and made her own way back to the rock. But when they were in the hollow again, her teeth rattled with chill, and she pressed against him for warmth.

"Okay," he said shakily. "Okay, we're all right now. You are hereby entitled to join our Pacific wet-erans' club."

Her laugh was small under the boom of breakers and hiss of scud. "You're trying hard, aren't you?"

"I—*oh*, oh! Get *down!*"

Peering over the edge, Dalgetty saw the men descending the path. They were half a dozen, armed and wary. One had a WT radio unit on his back. In the shadow of the cliff, they were almost invisible as they began prowling the beach.

"Still hunting us!" Her voice was a groan.

"You didn't expect otherwise, did you? I'm just hoping they don't come out here. Does anybody else know of this spot?" He held his lips close to her ear.

"No, I don't believe so," she breathed. "I was the only one who cared to go swimming at this end of the island. But . . ."

Dalgetty waited, grimly. The sun was down at last, the twilight thickening. A few stars twinkled to life in the east. The goons finished their search and settled in a line along the beach.

"Oh-oh," muttered Dalgetty. "I get the idea. Bancroft's had the land beaten for me so thoroughly he's sure I must be somewhere out to sea. If I were he, I'd guess I'd swum far out to be picked up by a waterboat. So—he's guarding every possible approach against a landing party."

"What can we do?" whispered Elena. "Even if we can swim around their radius of sight we can't land just anywhere. Most of the island is vertical cliff. Or can you . . .?"

"No," he said. "Regardless of what you think, I don't have vacuum cups on my feet. But how far does that gun of yours carry?"

She stole a glance over the edge. Night was creeping in. The island was a wall of blackness, and the men at its foot were hidden. "You can't *see!*" she protested.

He squeezed her shoulder. "Oh yes, I can, honey. But whether I'm a good enough shot to . . . We'll have to try it, that's all."

Her face was a white blur, and fear of the unknown put metal in her voice. "Part seal, part cat, part deer, part what else? I don't think you're human, Simon Dalgetty."

He didn't answer. The abnormal voluntary dilation of pupils hurt his eyes.

"What else has Dr. Tighe done?" Her tone was chill in the dark. "You can't study the human mind without studying the body too. What's he done? Are you the mutant they're always speculating about? Did Dr. Tighe create or find homo superior?"

"If I don't plug that radio com-set before they can use it," he said, "I'll be homo-genized."

"You can't laugh it off," she said through taut lips. "If you aren't of our species, I have to assume you're our enemy—till you prove otherwise!" Her fingers closed hard on his arm. "Is that what your little gang at the Institute is doing? Have they decided that mere humanity isn't good enough to be civilized? Are they preparing the way for your kind to take over?"

"Listen," he said wearily. "Right now we're two people, very mortal indeed, being hunted. So shut up!"

He took the pistol from her holster and slipped a full clip into its magazine. His vision was at high sensitivity now, her face showed white against the wet rock, with grey highlights along its strong cheekbones beneath the wide frightened eyes. Beyond the reefs, the sea was gunmetal under the stars, streaked with foam and shadow.

Ahead of him, as he rose to his feet, the line of guards stood out as paler darknesses against the vertiginous island face. They had mounted a heavy machine gun to point seawards and a self-powered spotlight, not turned on, rested nearby. Those two things could be dangerous, but first he had to find the radio set that could call the whole garrison down on them.

There! It was a small hump on the back of one man, near the middle of the beach. He was pacing restlessly up and down with a tommy gun in his hands. Dalgetty raised the pistol with slow hard-held concentration, wishing it were a rifle. *Remember your target practice now, arm loose, fingers extended, don't pull the trigger but squeeze—because you've got to be right the first time!*

He shot. The weapon was a military model, semi-noiseless and with no betraying streak of light. The first bullet spun the goon on his heels and sent him lurching across sand and rock. Dalgetty worked the trigger, spraying around his victim, a storm of lead that *must* ruin the sender.

Chaos on the beach! If that spotlight went on with his eyes at their present sensitivity, he'd be blind for hours. He fired carefully, smashing lens and bulb. The machine gun opened up, stuttering wildly into the dark. If someone elsewhere on the island heard that noise—Dalgetty shot again, dropping the gunner over his weapon.

Bullets spanged around him, probing the darkness. One down, two down, three down. A fourth was running along the upward path. Dalgetty fired and missed, fired and missed, fired and missed. He was getting out of range, carrying the alarm—*there!* He fell slowly, like a jointed doll, rolling down the trail. The two others were dashing for the shelter of a cave, offering no chance to nail them.

Dalgetty scrambled over the rock, splashed into the bay, and struck out for the shore. Shots raked the water. He wondered if they could hear his approach through the sea noise. Soon he'd be close enough for normal night vision. He gave himself wholly to swimming.

His feet touched sand and he waded ashore, the water dragging at him. Crouching, he answered the shots coming from the cave. The shriek and yowl were everywhere around him now. It seemed impossible that they should not hear up above. He tensed his jaws and crawled towards the machine gun. A cold part of him noticed that the fire was in a random pattern. They couldn't see him, then.

The man lying by the gun was still alive but unconscious. That was enough. Dalgetty crouched over the trigger. He had never handled a weapon like this, but it must be ready for action—only minutes ago it had tried to kill him. He sighted on the cave mouth and cut loose.

Recoil made the gun dance till he caught on to the trick of using it. He couldn't see anyone in the cave, but he could bounce lead off its walls. He shot for a full minute before stopping. Then he crawled away at an angle till he reached the cliff. Sliding along this, he approached the entrance and waited. No sound came from inside.

He risked a quick glance. Yes, it had done the job. He felt a little sick.

Elena was climbing out of the water when he returned. There was a strangeness in the look she gave him. "All taken care of?"

she asked tonelessly.

He nodded, remembered she could hardly see the movement, said aloud. "Yes, I think so. Grab some of this hardware and let's get moving."

With his nerves already keyed for night vision it was not difficult to heighten other perceptions and catch her thinking . . . *not human. Why should he mind if he kills human beings when he isn't one himself?*

"But I do mind," he said gently. "I've never killed a man before and I don't like it."

She jerked away from him. It had been a mistake, he realized. "Come on," he said. "Here's your pistol. Better take a tommy gun too if you can handle it."

"Yes," she said. He had lowered his reception again, her voice fell quiet and hard. "Yes, I can use one."

On whom? he wondered. He picked up an automatic rifle from one of the sprawled figures. "Let's go," he said. Turning, he led the way up the path. His spine prickled with the thought of her at his back, keyed to a pitch of near-hysteria.

"We're out to rescue Michael Tighe, remember," he whispered over his shoulder. "I've had no military experience, and I doubt that you've ever done anything like this either, so we'll probably make every mistake in the books. But we've got to get Dr. Tighe."

She didn't answer.

At the top of the path, Dalgetty went down on his stomach again and slithered up over the crest. Slowly he raised his head to peer in front of him. Nothing moved, nothing stirred. He stooped low as he walked forward.

The thickets fenced off vision a few yards ahead. Beyond them, at the end of the slope, he could glimpse lights. Bancroft's place must be one glare of radiance. How to get in there without being seen? He drew Elena close to him. For a moment she stiffened at his touch, then she yielded. "Any ideas?" he asked.

"No," she replied.

"I could play dead," he began tentatively. "You could claim to have been caught by me, to have got your gun back and killed me. They might lose suspicion then and carry me inside."

"You think you could fake *that*?" She pulled away from him again.

"Sure. Make a small cut and force it to bleed enough to look like a bullet wound—which doesn't usually bleed much, anyway. Slow down heartbeat and respiration till their ordinary senses couldn't detect them. Near-total muscular relaxation, including even those unromantic aspects of death which are so rarely mentioned. Oh, yes."

"Now I know you aren't human," she said. There was a shudder in her voice. "Are you a synthetic thing? Did they make you in the laboratory, Dalgetty?"

"I just want your opinion of the idea," he muttered with a flicker of anger.

It must have taken an effort for Elena to wrench clear of her fear for him. But then she shook her head. "Too risky. If I were one of those fellows, with all you've already done to make me wonder about you, the first thing I'd do on finding your supposed corpse would be to put a bullet through its brain—and maybe a stake through its heart. Or can you survive that too?"

"No," he admitted. "All right, it was just a thought. Let's work a bit closer to the house."

They went through brush and grass. It seemed to him that an army would make less noise. Once his straining ears caught a sound of boots, and he yanked Elena into the gloom under a eucalyptus. Two guards tramped by, circling the land on patrol. Their forms loomed huge and black against the stars.

Near the edge of the grounds, Dalgetty and Elena crouched in the long stiff grass and looked at the place they must enter. The man had to lower his visual sensitivity as they approached the light. There were floodlights, harsh on dock, airfield, barracks, and lawn, with parties of guards moving around each section. Light showed in only one window of the house, on the second story. Bancroft must be there, pacing and peering out into the night where his enemy stirred. Had he called by radio for reinforcements?

At least no airboat had arrived or left. Dalgetty knew he would have seen one in the sky. Dr. Tighe was here yet—if he lived.

Decision grew in the man. There was a wild chance. "Are you much of an actress, Elena?" he whispered.

"After two years as a spy I'd better be." Her face bore a hint of puzzlement under the tension as she looked at him. He could guess her thought—*For a superman, he asks some simple-minded questions. But then what is he? Or is he only dissembling?*

He explained his idea. She scowled. "I know it's crazy," he told her, "but have you anything better to offer?"

"No. If you can handle your part . . ."

"And you yours." He gave her a bleak look; but there was an appeal in it. Suddenly his half-glimpsed face looked strangely young and helpless. "I'll be putting my life in your hands. If you don't trust me, you can shoot. But you'll be killing a lot more than me."

"Tell me what you are," she said. "How can I know what the ends of the Institute are when they're using such means as you? Mutant or android or"—she caught her breath—"or actually a creature from outer space, the stars. Simon Dalgetty, what are you?"

"If I answered that," he said with desolation in his voice, "I'd probably be lying anyway. You've got to trust me this far."

She sighed. "All right." He didn't know if she was lying too.

He laid the rifle down and folded his hands on top of his head. She walked behind him, down the slope towards the light, her submachine gun at his back.

As he walked, he was building up a strength and speed no human ought to possess.

One of the sentries pacing through the garden came to a halt. His rifle swung up, and the voice was a hysterical yammer: "Who goes?"

"It's me, Buck," cried Elena. "Don't get trigger-happy. I'm bringing in the prisoner."

"Huh?"

Dalgetty shuffled into the light and stood slumped, letting his jaw hang slack, as if he were near falling with weariness.

"You *got* him!" The goon sprang forward.

"Don't holler," said Elena. "I got this one, all right, but there are others. You keep on your beat. I got his weapons from him. He's harmless now. Is Mr. Bancroft in the house?"

"Yeah, yeah—sure." The heavy face peered at Dalgetty with more than a tinge of fear. "But lemme go along. Yuh know what he done last time."

"Stay on your post!" she snapped. "You've got your orders. I can handle him."

VIII

It might not have worked on most men, but these goons were not very bright. The guard nodded, gulped, and resumed his pacing. Dalgetty walked on up the path towards the house.

A man at the door lifted his rifle. "Halt, there! I'll have to call Mr. Bancroft first." The sentry went inside and thumbed an intercom switch.

Dalgetty, poised in a nervous tautness that could explode into physical strength, felt a clutch of fear. The whole thing was so fiendishly uncertain—anything could happen.

Bancroft's voice drifted out. "That you, Elena? Good work, girl! How'd you do it?" The warmth in his tone, under the excitement, made Dalgetty wonder briefly just what the relationship between those two had been.

"I'll tell you upstairs, Tom," she answered. "This is too big for anyone else to hear. But keep the patrols going. There are more like this creature around the island."

Dalgetty could imagine the primitive shudder in Thomas Bancroft, instinct from ages when the night was prowling terror about a tiny circle of fire. "All right. If you're sure he won't—"

"I've got him well covered."

"I'll send over half a dozen guards just the same. Hold it."

The men came running from barracks, where they must have been waiting for a call to arms, and closed in. It was a ring of tight faces and wary eyes and pointing guns. They feared him, and the fear made them deadly. Elena's countenance was wholly blank.

"Let's go," she said.

A man walked some feet ahead of the prisoner, casting glances behind him all the time. One followed on either side, the rest were at the rear. Elena walked among them, her weapon never wavering from his back. They went down the long hand-some corridor and stood on the purring escalator. Dalgetty's eyes roved with a yearning in them—how much longer, he wondered, would he be able to see anything at all?

The door to Bancroft's study was ajar, and Tighe's voice drifted out. It was a quiet drawl, unshaken despite the blow it must have been to hear of Dalgetty's recapture. Apparently he was continuing a conversation begun earlier:

". . . Science goes back a long way, actually. Francis Bacon speculated about a genuine science of man. Boole did some work along those lines as well as inventing the symbolic logic which was to be such a major tool in solving the problem.

"In the last century, a number of lines of attack were developed. There was already the psychology of Freud and his successors, of course, which gave the first real notion of human semantics. There were the biological, chemical, and physical approaches to man as a mechanism. Comparative historians like Spengler, Pareto, and Toynbee realized that history did not merely happen but had some kind of pattern.

"Cybernetics developed such concepts as homeostasis and feedback, concepts which were applicable to individual man and to society as a whole. Games theory, the principle of least effort, and Haeml's generalized epistemology pointed towards basic laws and the analytical approach.

"The new symbologies in logic and mathematics suggested formulations—for the problem was no longer one of gathering data so much as of finding a rigorous symbolism to handle them and indicate new data. A great deal of the Institute's work has lain simply in collecting and synthesizing all these earlier findings."

Dalgetty felt a rush of admiration. Trapped and helpless among enemies made ruthless by ambition and fear, Michael Tighe could still play with them. He must have been stalling for hours, staving off drugs and torture by revealing first one thing and then another—but subtly, so that his captors probably didn't realize he was only telling them what they could find in any library.

The party entered a large room, furnished with wealth and taste, lined with bookshelves. Dalgetty noticed an intricate Chinese chess set on the desk. So Bancroft or Meade played chess—that was something they had in common, at least, on this night of murder.

Tighe looked up from the armchair. A couple of guards stood behind him, their arms folded, but he ignored them. "Hello, son," he murmured. Pain flickered in his eyes. "Are you all right?"

Dalgetty nodded mutely. There was no way to signal the Englishman, no way to let him hope.

Bancroft stepped over to the door and locked it. He gestured at the guards, who spread themselves around the walls, their guns aimed inward. He was shaking ever so faintly, and his eyes glittered as with fever. "Sit down," he said. *"There!"*

Dalgetty took the indicated armchair. It was deep and soft. It would be hard to spring out of quickly. Elena took a seat opposite him, poised on its edge, the tommy gun in her lap. It was suddenly very still in the room.

Bancroft went over to the desk and fumbled with a humidor. He didn't look up. "So you caught him," he said.

"Yes," replied Elena. "After he caught me first."

"How did you—turn the tables?" Bancroft took out a cigar and bit the end off savagely. "What happened?"

"I was in a cave, resting," she said tonelessly. "He rose out of the water and grabbed me. He'd been hiding underneath longer than anybody would have thought possible. He forced me out to a rock in the bay there—you know it? We hid till sundown, when he opened up on your men on that beach. He killed them all.

"I'd been tied, but I'd managed to rub the strips loose. It was just a piece off his shirt he tied me with. While he was shooting I grabbed a stone and clipped him behind the ear. I dragged him to shore while he was still out, took one of the guns lying there, and marched him here."

"Good work." Bancroft inhaled raggedly. "I'll see that you get a proper bonus for this, Elena. But what else? You said . . ."

"Yes." Her gaze was steady on him. "We talked, out there in the bay. He wanted to convince me I should help him. Tom—he isn't human."

"Eh?" Bancroft's heavy form jerked. With an effort he steadied himself. "What do you mean?"

"That muscular strength and speed and telepathy. He can see in the dark and hold his breath longer than any man. No, he isn't human."

Bancroft looked at Dalgetty's motionless form. The prisoner's eyes clashed with his, and it was he who looked away again. "A telepath, did you say?"

"Yes," she answered. "Do you want to prove it, Dalgetty?"

There was stillness in the room. After a moment Dalgetty spoke. "You were thinking, Bancroft, 'All right, damn you, can you read my mind? Go ahead and try it, and you'll know what I'm thinking about you.' The rest was obscenities."

"A guess," said Bancroft. Sweat trickled down his cheeks. "Just a good guess. Try again."

Another pause, then, "'Ten, nine, seven, A, B, M, Z, Z . . .' Shall I keep on?" Dalgetty asked quietly.

"No," muttered Bancroft. "No, that's enough. What are you?"

"He told me," put in Elena. "You're going to have trouble believing it. I'm not sure if I believe it myself. But he's from another star."

Bancroft opened his lips and shut them again. The massive head shook in denial.

"He is—from Tau Ceti," said Elena. "They're way beyond us. It's the thing people have been speculating about for the last hundred years."

"Longer, my girl," said Tighe. There was no emotion in his face or voice save a dry humour, but Dalgetty knew what a flame must suddenly be leaping up inside him. "Read Voltaire's *Micromégas*."

"I've read such fiction," said Bancroft harshly. "Who hasn't?" All right, why are they here, what do they want?"

"You could say," spoke Dalgetty, "that we favour the Institute."

"But you've been raised from childhood . . ."

"Oh yes. My people have been on Earth a long time. Many of them are born here. Our first spaceship arrived in nineteen sixty-five." He leaned forward in the chair. "I expected Casimir to be reasonable and help me rescue Dr. Tighe. Since she hasn't done so, I must appeal to your own common sense. We have crews on Earth. We know where all our people are at any given time. If necessary, I can die to preserve the secret of our presence, but in that case you will die too, Bancroft. The island will be bombed."

"I . . ." The chief looked out of the window into the enormity of night. "You can't expect me to—to accept this as if . . ."

"I've some things to tell you which may change your mind," said Dalgetty. "They will certainly prove my story. Send your men out, though. This is only for your ears."

"And have you jump me!" snapped Bancroft.

"Casimir can stay," said Dalgetty, "and anyone else you are absolutely certain can keep a secret and control his own greed."

Bancroft paced once around the room. His eyes flickered back and forth over the watching men. Frightened faces, bewildered faces, ambitious faces—it was a hard decision, and Dalgetty knew grimly that his life rested on his and Elena's estimate of Thomas Bancroft's character.

"All right! Dumason, Zimmerman, O'Brien, stay in here. If that bird moves, shoot him. The rest of you wait just outside." They filed out. The door closed behind them. The three guards left posted themselves with smooth efficiency, one at the window and one at either adjoining wall. There was a long quiet.

Elena had to improvise the scheme and think it at Dalgetty. He nodded. Bancroft planted himself before the chair, legs spread wide as if braced for a blow, fists on hips.

"All right," he said. "What do you want to tell me?"

"You've caught me," said Dalgetty, "so I'm prepared to bargain for my life and Dr. Tighe's freedom. Let me show you—" He began to rise, gripping both arms of his chair.

"Stay where you are!" snapped Bancroft, and three guns swivelled around to point at the prisoner. Elena backed away until she stood beside the one near the desk.

"As you will." Dalgetty leaned back again, casually shoving his chair a couple of feet. He was now facing the window and, as far as he could tell, sitting exactly on a line between the man there and the man at the farther wall. "The Union of Tau Ceti is interested in seeing that the right kind of civilizations develop on other planets. You could be of value to us, Thomas Bancroft, if you can be persuaded to our side, and the rewards are considerable." His glance went for a moment to the girl, and she nodded imperceptibly. "For example . . ."

The power rushed up in him. Elena clubbed her gun butt and struck the man next to her behind the ear. In the fractional second before the others could understand and react, Dalgetty was moving.

The impetus which launched him from the chair sent that heavy padded piece of furniture sliding across the floor to hit the man behind him with a muffled thud. His left fist took Bancroft on the jaw as he went by. The guard at the window had no time to swing his gun back from Elena and squeeze the trigger before Dalgetty's hand was on his throat. His neck snapped.

Elena stood over her victim even as he toppled and aimed at the man across the room. The armchair had knocked his rifle aside. "Drop that or I shoot," she said.

Dalgetty snatched up a gun for himself, levelling it at the door. He more than half expected those outside to come rushing in, expected hell would explode. But the thick oak panels must have choked off sound.

Slowly, the man behind the chair let his rifle fall to the floor. His mouth was stretched wide with supernatural fear.

"My God!" Tighe's long form was erect, shaking, his calm broken into horror. "Simon, the risk . . ."

"We didn't have anything to lose, did we?" Dalgetty's voice was thick, but the abnormal energy was receding from him. He felt a surge of weariness and knew that soon the payment must be made for the way he had abused his body. He looked down at the corpse before him. "I didn't mean to do that," he whispered.

Tighe collected himself with an effort of disciplined will and stepped over to Bancroft. "He's alive, at least," he said. "Oh, my God, Simon! You could have been killed so easily."

"I may yet. We aren't out of the woods by any means. Find something to tie those two others up with, will you, Dad?"

The Englishman nodded. Elena's slugged guard was stirring and groaning. Tighe bound and gagged him with strips torn from his tunic. Under the submachine gun, the other submitted meekly enough. Dalgetty rolled them behind a sofa with the one he had slain.

Bancroft was wakening too. Dalgetty located a flask of bourbon and gave it to him. Clearing eyes looked up with the same terror. "Now what?" mumbled Bancroft. "You can't get away—"

"We can damn well try. If it had come to fighting with the rest of your gang, we'd have used you as a hostage, but now there's a neater way. On your feet! Here, straighten your tunic, comb your hair. Okay, you'll do just as you're told, because if anything goes wrong, we'll have nothing at all to lose by shooting you." Dalgetty rapped out his orders.

Bancroft looked at Elena, and there was more than physical hurt in his eyes. "Why did you do it?"

"FBI," she said.

He shook his head, still stunned, and shuffled over to the desk visiphone and called the hangar. "I've got to get to the

9

mainland in a hurry. Have the speedster ready in ten minutes.
No, just the regular pilot, nobody else. I'll have Dalgetty with
me, but it's okay. He's on our side now."

They went out the door. Elena cradled her tommy gun under
one arm. "You can go back to the barracks, boys," said Bancroft wearily to the men outside. "It's all been settled."

A quarter hour later, Bancroft's private jet was in the air.
Five minutes after that, he and the pilot were bound and locked
in a rear compartment. Michael Tighe took the controls. "This
boat has legs," he said. "Nothing can catch us between here
and California."

"All right." Dalgetty's tones were flat with exhaustion. "I'm
going back to rest, Dad." Briefly his hand rested on the older
man's shoulder. "It's good to have you back," he said.

"Thank you, son," said Michael Tighe. "I can't tell you more.
I haven't the words."

IX

Dalgetty found a reclining seat and eased himself into it. One
by one, he began releasing the controls over himself—sensitiv-
ities, nerve blocs, glandular stimulation. Fatigue and pain mounted within him. He looked out at the stars and listened to the
dark whistle of air with merely human senses.

Elena Casimir came to sit beside him, and he realized that his
job wasn't done. He studied the strong lines of her face. She
could be a hard foe but just as stubborn a friend.

"What do you have in mind for Bancroft?" he asked.

"Kidnapping charges for him and that whole gang," she said.
"He won't wriggle out of it, I can guarantee you." Her eyes
rested on him, unsure, a little frightened. "Federal prison psy-
chiatrists have Institute training," she murmured. "You'll see
that his personality is reshaped *your* way, won't you?"

"As far as possible," Simon said. "Though it doesn't matter
much. Bancroft is finished as a factor to be reckoned with. There's
still Bertrand Meade himself, of course. Even if Bancroft made
a full confession, I doubt that we could touch him. But the
Institute has now learned to take precautions against extralegal
methods—and within the framework of the law, we can give him
cards and spades and still defeat him."

"With some help from my department," Elena said. There was

a touch of steel in her voice. "But the whole story of this rescue will have to be played down. It wouldn't do to have too many ideas floating around in the public mind, would it?"

"That's right," he admitted. His head felt heavy, he wanted to rest it on her shoulder and sleep for a century. "It's up to you, really. If you submit the right kind of report to your superiors, it can all be worked out. Everything else will just be detail. But otherwise, you'll ruin everything."

"I don't know." She looked at him for a long while. "I don't know if I should or not. You may be correct about the Institute and the justice of its aims and methods. But how can I be sure, when I don't know what's behind it? How do I know there wasn't more truth than fiction in that Tau Ceti story, that you aren't really the agent of some nonhuman power quietly taking over all our race?"

At another time Dalgetty might have argued, tried to veil it from her, tried to trick her once again. But now he was too weary. There was a great surrender in him. "I'll tell you if you wish," he said, "and after that it's in your hands. You can make us or break us."

"Go on, then." Her tone withdrew into wariness.

"I'm human," he said. "I'm as human as you are. Only I've had rather special training, that's all. It's another discovery of the Institute for which we don't feel the world is ready. It'd be too big a temptation for too many people, to create followers like me." He looked away, into the windy dark. "The scientist is also a member of society and has a responsibility towards it. This—restraint—of ours is one way in which we meet that obligation."

She didn't speak, but suddenly one hand reached over and rested on his. The impulsive gesture brought warmth flooding through him.

"Dad's work was mostly in mass-action psych," he said, making his tone try to cover what he felt, "but he has plenty of associates trying to understand the individual human being as a functioning mechanism. A lot's been learned since Freud, both from the psychiatric and the neurological angle. Ultimately, those two are interchangeable.

"Some thirty years ago, one of the teams which founded the Institute learned enough about the relationship between the conscious, subconscious, and involuntary minds to begin practical tests. Along with a few others, I was a guinea pig. And their theories worked.

"I needn't go into the details of my training. It involved physical exercises, mental practice, some hypnotism, diet, and so on. It went considerably beyond the important Synthesis education, which is the most advanced thing known to the general public. But its aim—only partially realized as yet—its aim was simply to produce the completely integrated human being."

Dalgetty paused. The wind flowed and muttered beyond the wall.

"There is no sharp division between conscious and subconscious or even between those and the centres controlling involuntary functions," he said. "The brain is a continuous structure. Suppose, for instance, that you become aware of a runaway car bearing down on you.

"Your heartbeat speeds up, your adrenalin output increases, your sight sharpens, your sensitivity to pain drops—it's all preparation for fight or flight. Even without obvious physical necessity, the same thing can happen on a lesser scale—for example, when you read an exciting story. And psychotics, especially hysterics, can produce some of the damnedest physiological symptoms you ever saw."

"I begin to understand," she whispered.

"Rage or fear brings abnormal strength and fast reaction. But the psychotic can do more than that. He can show physical symptoms like burns, stigmata or—if female—false pregnancy. Sometimes he becomes wholly insensitive in some part of his body via a nerve bloc. Bleeding can start or stop without apparent cause. He can go into a coma, or he can stay awake for days without getting sleepy. He can—"

"Read minds?" It was a defiance.

"Not that I know of." Simon chuckled. "But human sense organs are amazingly good. It only takes three or four quanta to stimulate the visual purple—a little more, actually, because of absorption by the eyeball itself. There have been hysterics who could hear a watch ticking twenty feet away that the normal person could not hear at one foot. And so on.

"There are excellent reasons why the threshold of perception is relatively high in ordinary people—the stimuli of usual conditions would be blinding and deafening, unendurable, if there weren't a defence." He grimaced. "I *know!*"

"But the telepathy?" Elena persisted.

"It's been done before," he said. "Some apparent cases of mind reading in the last century were shown to be due to extremely acute hearing. Most people subvocalize their surface thoughts. With a little practice, a person who can hear those vibrations can learn to interpret them. That's all." He smiled with one side of his mouth. "If you want to hide your thoughts from me, just break that habit, Elena."

She looked at him with an emotion he could not quite recognize. "I see," she breathed. "And your memory must be perfect too, if you can pull any datum out of the subconscious. And you can—do everything, can't you?"

"No," he said. "I'm only a test case. They've learned a great deal by observing me, but the only thing that makes me unusual is that I have conscious control of certain normally subconscious and involuntary functions. Not all of them, by a long shot. And I don't use that control any more than necessary.

"There are sound biological reasons why man's mind is so divided and plenty of penalties attached to a case like mine. It'll take me a couple of months to get back in shape after this bout. I'm due for a good old-fashioned nervous breakdown, and while it won't last long, it won't be much fun while it does last."

The appeal rose in his eyes as he watched Elena. "All right," he said. "Now you have the story. What are you going to do about it?"

For the first time she gave him a real smile. "Don't worry," she said. "Don't worry, Simon."

"Will you come hold my hand while I'm recuperating?" he asked.

"I'm holding it now, you fool," Elena answered.

Dalgetty chuckled happily. Then he went to sleep.

THE MOONRAKERS

I

THE HUNGRY MAN jumped from his boat and fell into silence. He could hear blood rustle along his veins, air move back through his nostrils, the tiny whirr of a pump sucking it back to the renewal tank. He was aware of tension in his flesh, the angles at which his joints were cocked, the smell of his enclosed self, an emptiness in his stomach—above everything else, that emptiness. But otherwise he was alone, the universe beyond his helmet more hollow than himself. Twelve thousand visible stars, undimmed and unwinking, powdered the black with glory. The Milky Way girdled creation, one frozen waterfall. To his left lay the sun, shrunken but still intolerably bright. It didn't matter. It was all too remote.

He pulled consciousness back to normal, hard practicality. *I'm getting light-headed*, he thought. *Can't afford to. Not yet.* The dead ship swelled in his vision as he neared. Light flamed so harshly off the sternward curve that he must shade that side of his face with a gauntlet. Holes gaped in the great spheroid like mouths. He selected the largest, a shattered viewport, and redirected his path with a short, begrudged jet from his propulsion tubes.

Instruments would have made possible a neater approach. He might have brought his boat nearly alongside the wreck. But he had only the minimum of electronic aids. For the rest, he must rely on the senses and muscles which he, and his fathers before him, had trained to some kind of ultimate.

His mind wandered again for a moment, and he found himself trying to imagine travel on Earth. Or even Mars. Not so much the business of open air, greenery, bigger sun, horizons reaching for miles; he thought he could pretty well visualize that from films he had seen. No, the interplay of vectors. Like running under acceleration the whole time . . . The hull loomed before him, a rounded cliff. He twisted about and struck, boots first. The shock ran through shins to skull. Automatically, circuits embedded in the heavy soles were closed. Charges separated; the "lower" half became positive with respect to the ship. Electrons within her metal swirled to meet him. There was no danger of an arc through that insulation; he was simply held with enough force.

Careful to move just one foot at a time, he walked to the ragged edge of the hole. Sunlight spilled through, casting hard ebon shadows behind equipment and controls. He scowled. Damn! The rocks had really torn this one. She'd need a lot of expensive repair before she was fit to use again—which diminished her salvage value and so, most importantly, his commission.

Unless, of course, her cargo was special. Eagerness tingled in him, driving out languor. He entered.

By the bobbing light-puddle of his flashbeam, he made his way down a gloomy corridor and a black well to the central hold.

It wasn't sealed. Never was, on an unmanned freighter. He opened a door and stepped in among racked crates. His beam sought around, and letters jumped into view:

HESPERIA ELECTRONICS
SCX-107
CONDUCTOR ELEMENTS
2000

He didn't bother with the handling directions that followed. His light sprang from place to place, finding the same words repeated. His heart began to flutter.

"Holy Judas," he mumbled, and he went on in a litany of joy which got louder and more profane by the minute.

This wasn't the entire cargo. Nobody could want so many room-temperature superconductor units at once. But what he had seen made him rich.

He trembled. A wave of weakness passed through him. *Better get back fast. Never mind the rest o' what's aboard. Plenty time to look, later on.*

Whirling, he left the room in such a rush that he pulled both feet free and must drift, sickened by rotational forces, with many curses until he encountered a bulkhead and got a grip. That sobered him. He proceeded cautiously thereafter, out of the ship and back to his boat. What a hell of a thing to kill his stupid self now, in any of the thousand ways that are possible in space—when women and whisky and riot waited for him in the Keep.

Narrow, comfortless, the vessel enclosed him with metal. He cycled through the air lock and removed his spacesuit, extra careful not to touch its frosting chilled surfaces with bare hands. Then he went forward, took his navigational sights, computed his quantities, and sent a maser beam straight across two million empty miles.

"Sadler in salvage boat 'Captain Hook' to Operations Control, the Keep," he intoned. A string of code symbols followed. Chief Kerrigan took no chances. If he wasn't sure that one of his own people were trying to raise his stronghold—well, they might be Martians who had an inkling of its orbit, and he wouldn't reply.

Acknowledgment was slow in coming. Sadler added some rather insulting remarks to his call signal.

"Operations Control, the Keep, receiving Sadler in 'Captain Hook', " broke from the speaker. "Hi, Dave. This is Bob Mackintosh on duty. What's the word? Over."

"I . . . I've got her." The hungry man gulped and mastered his voice. "The Martian. I'm matched to her path, and I've been aboard. Cargo seems in good shape and, uh, valuable. But I'm out o' food and damn near out o' jet mass. You'll have to load some for me on the tug. Come as fast as you can, huh? Over."

Half a minute passed while the beam flew on its way and the answer returned. Sadler floated, listening to a thin hiss that was the background talking of the stars.

"You must've had a long chase, then," Mackintosh said. "Why didn't you let somebody else know who was in a better position to intercept? We were beginnin' to think she'd get clean away from us. Over."

"You know damn well why not," Sadler rapped. "I wasn't about to split my commission with anybody, long's I knew I could overhaul. Now hustle off with your duff, Bob. See that I get the best, 'specially grub. I'll be able to pay for it. Then report to the Chief, and tell the other boys they can shut down their radar sweeps and come home from their orbits. Because she's mine!"

II

Though Syrtis is the biggest and busiest city on Mars, and the capital, it is also the oldest. New skyscrapers gleam for miles around the centre, each set in its own green acres, until southward the town fades into the agricultural lands that ring the equator, northward to untouched deserts of ruddy sand and raw crags. But downtown, most buildings were raised by the pioneers.

Thick walls of grey stone, red-mortared, bulk gracelessly for a few stories and end in flat roofs where flittercraft park. The trappings of modern commercialism look unnatural on such façades.

Their solidity is deceptive. Now that the atmosphere project has been completed, oxygen and water vapour are gnawing away the Martian rock so fast that the narrow, twisted streets are always dusty. This district won't last many more generations.

James Church was glad to be alive while he could still have an office there. He was somewhat of a traditionalist.

He stood at an open window, pipe in mouth, hands behind back, and looked forth while he waited for his visitor. The embrasures showed traces of the fittings which had once kept out gases lethally cold and thin. It also bore energy gun gouges from a later period, when an argument at the Mariner across the street had erupted into Bloody Tenthday.

The Mariner continued in business. People moved in and out of its door, under the corroded simulacrum of the space probe, and Church caught snatches of music, the whine of a lodestar set, even imagined he could hear dice click and roulette wheels turn. But probably the babble of gaily clad pedestrians was too loud. The sun sets late in these latitudes during a summer twice as long as Earth's and Syrtis had got down to the serious matter of amusement while daylight yet remained. Church took a breath of air between puffs. It was cool, there would be frost tonight. Ice-crystal clouds gleamed in a purplish sky. A flight of geese crossed them. *Well, well,* he thought, *so the Ministry of Ecology really is getting somewhere with that scheme. Never expected them to. But they do say the genetic engineers have licked the drift problem. Wonder how. Must read up on it, if I ever get time.*

The intercom on his battered old desk said: "Misser Dobshinsky to see you."

Church crossed the floor. "Come on in," he said. The door heard him and opened. He stood expectant—not anybody's idea of a typical Martian, being short and stocky, grey-haired and quietly dressed, with a comfortable small paunch bulging the front of his pyjamas. Only the sun-darkened skin and the faded blue eyes, crow's footed from a lifetime of squinting across bare dunes, fitted the picture.

Philip Dobshinsky was long and lean and barrel-chested enough to pass. He was also somewhat younger, handsomer, and more colourful in his garments than Church would have looked for in a member of the Interplanetary Shippers' Association. He paused, glanced around the little room cluttered with books and mementos, and registered hesitation. The outer office of Church: Investigators & Guardians was not very impressive either.

"How's your luck?" The detective offered his hand across the desk. "Sit down. Care for a puff?"

"Well—no, thanks, better not right now." Dobshinsky waved aside the proffered cigarette case, though Twin Moons was an expensive tobacco-marijuana blend. "Maybe a drink, if you will do me the service."

"Surely. Scotch? The genuine article, I swear, not that sulphuric acid they make at Devil's Kettle." Church settled into a swivel chair going back to years before the colonists were up to manufacturing loungers and opened a coldbox.

Dobshinsky was nervous. His own seat had trouble adjusting to his contours, the way he shifted about. Church smiled as he busied himself with glasses. "I know," he drawled. "You're wondering how come a supposedly high-powered police agency operates out of such a hole in the wall. Answer's simple: I like it this way. Money spent to impress clients is better spent on good booze and food and pot and girls. Relax, son."

"I am new to these matters," Dobshinsky said. "We all are. I mean, us members of the Association. Our human control problems used to be simple. Thanks." He took his drink. Ice tinkled with the haste of his swallowing.

Church blew smoke and said, "Your call only mentioned you'd like to discuss possible business. But pretty plain, you had the asteroid piracy in mind."

"Well . . . yes." Dobshinsky squared his shoulders. "Hitherto, the Neopinks Agency has done our policing for us, as you must know. They don't seem able to cope with this problem, however. If you can do something—frankly, you can have our contract from then on."

Church held a carefully noncommittal expression. But his pulse accelerated a little, and his gaze strayed to the pictures on his desk. A man with two sons in college, a daughter soon ready for it—with a desire to study at the Beaux Arts in Paris to boot—could find good use for business on that scale. Also, Mary had been talking about a better house in Thaumasia, where they usually moved during the northern hemisphere's winter . . . "Before we say any more," he murmured, "have you considered an appeal to the government?"

"Huh?" Dobshinsky lost awkwardness in startlement. "What can they do?"

"Well, this is a matter affecting the public weal. Not just one bobber gunning for another who's broken hoax limits, but a bunch of insurrectionists turned pirate who're causing serious economic loss."

"To the shippers."

"In the long run, to all Mars. Prices and insurance rates are headed for Andromeda, aren't they? Then too, our whole interplanetary policy is involved."

"But what has the government got in the way of trained, equipped peace officers? They hire that out themselves." Dobshinsky took another long pull at his glass. "Oh, we have approached them. If the navy could clean out the Belt—But no luck. You'll read the details in the confidential summary, if you take the job."

"Thanks for service," Church said. The other man looked puzzled. Church grinned. "I mean for putting the matter so tactfully. You might have said, 'If I get the job.' But let's dig as close to bedrock as we can in an informal talk. You've lost another vessel?"

" 'The Queen of Thyle'," said Dobshinsky through tight lips. "If that means anything to you."

" 'Fraid not." Church, whose profession brought him to every facet of the world, was less narrowly concentrated on minding his own affairs than the average Martian. But hitherto interplanetary shipping had lain outside his purview. The big-money boys took care of their own.

Until lately.

"Our most recent loss, and one of the most serious," Dobshinsky said. "Besides her own value, which runs into seven figures, there was her cargo. Among other things, a gigabuck's worth of computer units for Pallas. And this is less than twenty decadays since the 'Jove' was captured."

Church raised his brows a trifle. "Excuse me," he said, "but are you sure that no acts of God are involved? That is the official claim."

"Morally sure. For instance, the 'Jove' was carrying robot

mining machinery to Ganymede. The Neopinks report, from their branch on Earth, that Supertronics has offered a load of this same stuff at cutthroat prices. They say it's because they've found cheaper production methods; and of course serial numbers and so forth are different; but still, when this sort of thing happens again and again and again—"

"Yes, I see." Church nodded. "I wonder," he mused, half to himself, "why the so-called acts of God are always catastrophes." Briskly: "I gather the 'Jove' herself hasn't turned up?"

"Not yet, anyhow. Maybe she was utterly ruined; or maybe the asterites want to repair her and keep her for their own use; or maybe she's on her way to Luna at this moment, with a crew claiming salvage." The last word was spat out.

"Hm, yeah, this is getting out of phase."

"What do you mean, Misser? It is out of phase! I can show you figures to prove the whole Martian economy is in danger of being wrecked. And Earth sits back, rakes in the loot, and waits to come feast off what's left of us!"

III

Felix Kerrigan, Chief of the Keep, looked at the man before his throne and said: "No."

Nicholas Riskin stiffened. "Now wait a minute—" he began.

"You heard me." Kerrigan's huge right hand made a chopping gesture. "The Rule is the Rule, and I don't compute to break her. Or break faith with my men, come to that." He gestured at Sadler, who stood tall and gaunt on one side, glaring at Riskin. "Dave here found the 'Queen o' Thyle'. His commission is ten per cent of everything she fetches. What kind o' Chief 'ud I be if I diddled him out o' what he's earned?"

"But nobody's proposing to rob him," Riskin protested. He had been educated on Mars, and his enunciation sounded prissy, even to him, amidst the rough asterite dialect. "The Council will pay full value."

"In Free Worlds dollars," Sadler scoffed. "I want Earth dollars that I can spend on Earth goods. What do they make here in the Belt worth tossin' into the sun?"

Riskin moistened his lips and glanced around. He felt very much alone.

The council chamber was larger and more luxurious than most

of the rooms hollowed out of this planetoid. In fact, it was crowded with barbaric opulence. Scarlet tapestries covered the walls, genuine mutiger skins snarled from the floor, the table and chairs were not plastic but massive oak. An archway opened on to the feasting hall, equally magnificent. Thence drifted the sounds of drink and laughter, as the crew of Riskin's ship mingled with the salvagers and their girls. But tautness dwelt here.

Kerrigan sat his nickel-iron high seat like a heathen god. He was, indeed, a throwback to days when Earth herself was young and wild—six feet four and broad to match, his features darkly bearded, his eyes ice-green. Garments added to the effect. Where Sadler wore a noisy coverall and Riskin plain civilian pyjamas, Kerrigan had blue tunic and white trousers, flamboyant with gold. From his officer's cap fluoresced the star of a Chief.

Riskin, who was small and bald, and whose work did not ordinarily demand physical courage, thought about bluster. "Look, you," he could say, "I represent the Council, which represents all of us. Do you think you can make an enemy of every other Chiefdom in the Belt?" But no. Kerrigan might lose his temper. More likely, and worse, he might guffaw. Barring occasional skirmishes, the lords of the asteroids didn't wage war on each other. Resources were lacking to do so; besides, it was safer and far more lucrative to prey on the Martians.

Then too, there was a question of principle, or, perhaps better, of politics. A lord must stand by his followers, if only because otherwise they would pitch him out the air lock and elect someone else. Let matters come to a vote, and Kerrigan's colleagues were apt to decide he had done right.

Wherefore, matters must not come to a vote. Riskin relaxed and donned a smile. It was not insincere. He must try diplomacy, which was his real job anyway.

He made a slight bow to Sadler. "I beg your pardon, Misser," he said. "There was no intention of cheating you. The Council sent me here to make a proposal. You turned it down. Very well, you're within your rights, so let's have no further hard words."

The spaceman shook hands. "Swab-o by me." His temper had subsided as swiftly as it had flared. "You un'erstand, I don't want to hurt the common cause or nothin'. But here, so many years, I been scrapin' along on base pay. Most I ever got was a share now and then, when I detected a wreck same time as somebody else—and always more than one other bobber, too. Now my big chance finally came, and I risked my guts to take it. I won't let go."

"Of course not." Riskin glanced at Kerrigan. "But this does raise certain issues of policy. Might we have a private discussion, sir?"

"Well—" the Chief scowled. He was probably anxious to get into the feasting hall. His current mistress presided over the merrymaking, and they said he was jealous about her. But hospitality was incumbent on him. "Okay, if it don't take too long."

He bounded from the room with muscular strides that Riskin had trouble matching, even in this feeble gravity. Doubtless he spent many more exercise hours per day than were necessary to keep the organism functional.

At the end of a corridor, he opened a door to his private office. Riskin had never been there before and was startled to find bleak efficiency. Though, of course, he reminded himself, a Chief could not be stupid. Nor could an ordinary spaceman. Simple though the asteroid boats were (with no planetary pulls or atmospheres to fight, no radiation screens needed this far from the sun), you didn't survive without a fair knowledge of physics and chemistry. That, however, was about as far as schooling went in the Free Worlds. The Councilman hoped Kerrigan's basically good brain could absorb a rapid lesson in history and economics.

A spaceship's viewport had been set in the outer wall, with a cliff overhang concealing it from above. Like other asterite strongholds, the Keep was camouflaged to look like any of a half million naked worldlets. The scene was breathstopping. Dark metallic stone tumbled to a chopped-off verge. Beyond swarmed the stars.

For a shocking instant, fear went down Riskin's nerves. The Others, the Aliens, the Ones out Yonder—Angrily, he checked his emotions. *Superstition!* he scolded himself. *The modern equivalent of angels, demons, and ghosts, with too many sensational stories and shows about them for too many generations, until their image has become bound in with our most primitive instincts . . . Oh, yes, certainly nonhuman races exist. We've even picked up traces of their radio, their nuclear engine emissions. But no more. They're too far away.*

He bent his attention back to Kerrigan. The Chief didn't take a chair, but motioned Riskin to one. "Speak your piece," he said curtly.

"I'm not sure where to begin," Riskin said. He took out cigars and offered one. Kerrigan shook his head. Tobacco was so scarce that few asterites outside the colonies that Mars retained had formed the habit.

Riskin made a production of lighting his, "Believe me, sir," he said, "the Council Secretariat isn't being arbitrary. We can't be. We know we're just hirelings who're paid to adjudicate disputes and keep abreast of events throughout the Solar System and make policy suggestions for the common cause. But we've given this salvage matter a great deal of serious thought. We'd like to see every capture turned over to a central authority which would then arrange sale and/or distribution of the spoils. Naturally, there would still be incentive payments for the men who do the work. But the present system—well, I'm not sure but what it may bring about the downfall of the Free Worlds."

"Huh?" Kerrigan exclaimed. After a moment: "Okay. Misser, I'm listenin'."

"The picture is rather large," said Riskin, encouraged. "Do you mind if I repeat a number of things you already know? You see, people take for granted the facts they grew up with, and so don't always grasp how those facts are related."

Kerrigan wrestled with his personal desires and won. He folded arms and eased his stance. A dweller in space learns patience.

Riskin blew a smoke ring. "We've always told ourselves that we are simply repeating history," he began. "Mars was colonized by malcontents who wanted freedom from the Incorporated State. They developed an individualistic civilization of their own. To finance the enormous job of making their planet habitable, they pulled the Great Swindle on Earth. I needn't go into its complexities. Let's just say they arranged that enough influential factions in the United Protectorates benefited too. So the *fait accompli* was accepted, albeit with a grudge that hasn't died yet."

"I know that much," Kerrigan growled. "I read a book once in a while."

"Of course. I am simply laying it out on the chart so we can compare our own case. Because that is *not* parallel. It only looks so.

"Consider. With lower gravity and closer proximity to the mineral wealth of the Belt, Mars became the principal shipper. That was partly a matter of necessity. Earth's resources are such that she doesn't need a big merchant fleet. Martian companies can usually underbid hers. So most cargo travels in Martian bottom, most Terrestrial spacecraft are Mars-built, and Mars was the state that colonized the asteroids.

"But life here was hard and harsh. It's still no cushion of fluff-foam. Imagine what it was like in the first decades. Few were willing to come and work if they were doing all right at home. In other words, we are descended from misfits who were descended from other misfits. People like that don't make the best organization men. They tended to strike out on their own as soon as they could afford to. This required too much capital for a single man, though. Hence, little private companies sprang up, each headed by its founder. He necessarily held ship captain's authority over his followers; any other system would have been quick death. There's the origin of the Chiefdoms."

Riskin flicked ash off his cigar. "Don't you see?" he continued. "We brag about being noble democrats who're claiming our due from the tyrants of the mother planet, as their ancestors did from Earth. But the truth is that the Chiefs found themselves too often in conflict with the Bill of Liberties and other fine points of Martian law. They couldn't help that. It was either establish a new kind of civilization, adapted to local conditions, or else go back to working for a company on Pallas or Ceres or wherever.

"So . . . we broke free. Mars didn't like that. But suppression would have been too costly for their taste. Besides, Earth is delighted. She's brought pressure to bear, economic and political. There have been threats of military pressure, too, polite, but nonetheless threats. Mars would lose a war. Hence, she's cut off trade with the Free Worlds, hoping to starve us into submission. We've little to offer Earth, which hasn't merchant ships to spare for us anyway.

"Therefore we've taken to—let's be blunt—to pirating Martian vessels on the asteroid and Jovian routes. We find buyers on Earth; even some on the Martian asteroids, under the rose. With the money we get, we purchase from Earth what we need."

He stopped, out of breath, a little hoarse, and wishing for a drink.

Kerrigan frowned. "I don't see what you're gettin' at," he said, "except what everybody knows."

"Just this," replied Riskin. "Put my banalities together, and you'll see that we've got a revolutionary war on our hands. Nobody gives it that name, and perhaps not many recognize it as such, but the fact is there. If we don't organize to wage it properly, we're going to lose."

"How?" .

"We can't continue forever as we are. Suppose Mars finds countermeasures that we can't evade. We have considered a number of possibilities in the Secretariat. If one of them works, we're back where we started, cut off to die on the vine.

"The worst possibility is that Mars will go ahead and recognize our independence. I'm sure that nothing but exasperation has kept her from doing so thus far. What happens then? The profits are in the bigger asteroids that Mars has kept. We can't support ourselves by ordinary trade—not without a much bigger capital investment than we can make or that Mars or Earth will make for us. We'll face the choice of giving up our way of life and becoming hired hands again . . . or starving.

"We have to take steps against the day."

"Um-m-m." Kerrigan began to pace, an eerie balletlike series of leaps. The constellations glittered behind his head. "I admit I've sometimes wondered—but we don't get a lot of news out here."

Riskin rose and said eagerly: "Thus far, things have simply happened. One event led to another. The Chiefs found they could capture Martian ships; in desperation, they did so; this became an important part of their economy. Your hydroponics plants and protein vats and so forth supply you with food and Lo-Gee pills. You mine the rocks and refine the ores. You produce a certain amount of everything you need. But only a limited amount, because you can count on picking up a vessel worth megabucks every few years. That's why you maintain people like Sadler. Well, what happens if you never get another ship? Are you prepared to find other work for him?"

Kerrigan stopped, lowered his head, and regarded Riskin from beneath tightened brows. "What does the Council suggest?"

"That we use the salvage business for the common cause, as long as we still have it. Under the present system, a capture belongs to the Chiefdom that pulled the stunt off. So, all right, the Chief uses most of his ninety per cent for machines, replacement parts, and similar practical purposes. That strengthens the Free Worlds as a whole and is therefore good. But he also buys luxuries; and the individual salvager is apt to spend his commission on nothing else. That is not good.

"Furthermore"—his cigar stabbed the air—"even in buying the necessities, there is no co-ordination. You acquire a new computer, say. Fine. But Chief Brill over in Dragon's Nest also gets a computer. Duplication. Why doesn't he get an isotope separator instead and trade you alloys for information? You'd both be ahead."

Kerrigan tugged his beard. "Yeah, I see your point. Got to think it over, but maybe you're right. Well, s'pose you are. How do I convince Dave Sadler?"

"I admit we hadn't quite realized the extent of that problem, off in Centralia," Riskin sighed. "It shouldn't be insoluble, though. If the Council Secretariat can have the marketing of captures and can decide on the basis of common cause what goods should go to the Chiefdoms that turn them in—and even supply those places which haven't made a capture for some time —well, we could still pay the regular finders' commissions. They ought to be in local dollars, rather than Earth's or Mars'. The Free Worlds need foreign exchange in the worst way. However . . . hm . . . we could establish a luxury industry and pleasure resort of our own, for the boys to squander their earnings."

Kerrigan was silent awhile, brooding at the viewport. "Maybe," he said at length. "You Councilmen have done a good job so far. We'd never have managed without your direction, your agents on Mars, your wheedlin' us into doin' what's sensible. I'm not dead against you, myself. Some o' the other Chiefs might be."

"If you set an example, with the 'Queen of Thyle'"—Riskin stopped. Kerrigan had swung ominously about. Riskin continued in haste, but smoothly: "Of course, there would be compensations. We don't expect you to be unselfish for nothing. That can be worked out."

"Maybe so." The green eyes narrowed. "Yeah. Just maybe so."

"I can stay here as long as need be, to discuss these questions," Riskin said.

"Good enough." Calculation faded from the baron. He laughed aloud and slapped the smaller man on the back. Riskin rocketed halfway across the chamber. "Oops, sorry. C'mon. We'll talk again after sleep. Right now, we got a feast ready for us."

IV

While he waited in Dobshinsky's sumptuous anteroom, Church made a mental sorting of the secret reports he had studied. The human receptionist was an obstacle to concentration, being quite sumptuous herself. But Church found he could settle for an occasional eye-wandering in that direction. He was a staid man who did not personally use the drugs and girls that custom said he should offer his clients, though that same temperament made him a wolf at the poker table.

The history of asterite buccaneering showed a disturbing pattern, he thought. At first, the matter had been pretty open. Ships vanished, loot appeared in the market. With businessmen as fanatic about privacy as any other Martians, investigators couldn't trace back through commercial channels. But they followed the orbits of the lost vessels, a heartbreakingly long and costly search across so many megamiles. Eventually they recovered certain drifting fragments. These confirmed what undercover agents had learned by other means. Here and there, some asterites had taken their flimsy little boats and lain in wait. Schedules being then a matter of public knowledge, a drone ship's orbit was easily computable. When their prey hove close, they matched velocities, cut their way in with laser torches, disconnected the autopilot, and made off with their prize.

The Martian navy was engaged to go in search of the culprits; this was back before the so-called Independence. A few were summoned to court. The judgments against them may have been the last straw before the Declaration of Hidalgo. The rest could not be found. There was no record of which asteroids they had chosen to live on, among hundreds of thousands.

As part of the starving-out policy, the Association put its orbital drones on to the Earth and Venus runs. From the latter routes, they transferred those more expensive vessels that were capable of travelling the whole way under acceleration. A pirate had no hope of intercepting a quarry which, by the time his radar spotted it, was making scores of miles per second with respect to him.

But ships continued to disappear. More undercover work was done, especially on Earth, which had recognized the asterite nation with haste and glee. So—through spies of their own, the Chiefs had learned what homing signals to use. An autopilot must needs respond to such a beam, follow the looter wherever he wished. Signals were changed. Only a handful of ultimately trusted men now had the needful information.

After a short interval, losses resumed, and this time at a catastrophic rate. A spationaval engineer deduced the cause. Asterite agents in the Martian companies must have substituted course tapes in the "pilots", which then took the ships elsewhere than intended. At least, the theory seemed worth trying. All personnel in all such sections were replaced. Losses stopped.

For a while.

Then, in quick succession, the "Jehu", "Ahab", and "Li'l David" failed to deliver their cargoes. The Neopinks got men in among loading personnel and discovered that time bombs were being planted in the engine rooms. It was a crude method, suggesting desperation. The guilty people were fired, and security precautions were tightened. Again Mars had a respite.

But now—

The inner door opened. A fleshy man stalked out. He managed somehow to look indignant and smug at once. Church recognized but didn't greet him: an attaché of the United Protectorates Embassy.

"Please come in, sir," cooed the receptionist.

Church refrained from the bawdy answer that a younger Martian would probably have made. He was not only middleaged, he was worried. He strode through to the panelled luxury of Dobshinsky's office. As President of Transjovian Portage and secretary of the Association, the man rated an acre or two of mahogany desk and a fiftieth-floor view from the Gratte-Ciel Tower. Church ignored the spectacle of the Grand Aqueduct's triumphal march across painted desert and shook hands absently.

"Be seated," Dobshinsky said. "Apologies, that you had to wait. That damned Earthling just wouldn't go away."

"What'd he want?" Church began stuffing his pipe. "I imagine something relevant to our problem."

"Yes. A 'friendly note of caution'." Dobshinsky bit off the

words as if they were personal enemies. "We're not to arm our ships."

"Eh? How can Earth stop you? I mean they've been able to invoke the Open Space Treaty against us, twisting it around to mean that we can't send the navy against the Free Worlds. But how can that apply to commercial vessels?"

"He said his government would construe the installing of heavy weapons as piracy and take a, quote, very grave view, unquote. I asked him how Earth construes the piracy that has in fact been going on, and he had the degaulle to say it's stopped!"

"Hm-m-m . . . yes, I meant to discuss that angle with you. But short of a declaration of war—and you know public opinion on Earth would have to reach sheer panic before military measures can be considered—short of that, what can they do to keep Association ships unarmed?"

"If nothing else, they can embargo our trade. They do need some goods and services we've been supplying, but they can manage for themselves, and no doubt the asterites would be glad to help out. On the other hand, Mars absolutely has to have trade with Earth. We've come a long way since pioneer times, but we're not yet to the point where we can maintain a complex technology without imports of certain items. Oh, they've got us by the globes, they do." Dobshinsky's hand shook as he reached for a puff to calm himself. "God, I hate Earthlings!"

"Well, now, that may be going a touch too far," Church said mildly. "I've known some decent ones."

"Name 'em. Greasy mass-men! They even think in slogans."

"M-m-m, well, the Incorporated State has naturally produced a, uh, gullible type of citizen. His life's so thoroughly regulated that his main freedom lies in fantasies, which the sensies and the advertisers are quick to supply. Maybe for the average Earthling, those hackneyed old show motifs are more real and meaningful than his own life. Anway, sheep always did stampede easy. That's how come our grandfathers were able to put the Great Swindle over." Church got his pipe under way. "No matter. Our problem is with the Free Worlds."

"Do me the service not to call them that!"

"Why not? What they call themselves. And really, to be quite honest, I'm not unsympathetic with them."

Dobshinsky, feeling better after a drag or two, merely asked, "Indeed? How?"

Church smiled. "Could be my chromosomes. Matheny was a great-uncle of mine, and one of my direct ancestors was in on the Boston Tea Party. Seriously, though, I like to read socio-historical treatises, and I see the asterites and us as being equally victims of a common enough process."

"Which is?"

"The growth of nomadism. On Earth, the ancient nomads were not the progenitors of civilization. They were offshoots of it, weak tribes who'd been forced into lands that nobody else wanted. There they invented special survival techniques. But they were always a fringe people of civilization, dependent on it for a good many necessities." Church shrugged. "To be sure, their Spartan way of life called forth the more grim-jawed virtues. They became warriors *par excellence*, who raided the settled countries and occasionally conquered them. But from a long-range point of view, they couldn't help themselves. Circumstances determined their culture. Same thing with the asterites."

Dobshinsky had been pondering more immediate subjects. "You know," he said, "even if we can't put gun turrets on our ships, I don't see anything to prevent our having some armed men aboard each one."

"To be ripped apart when the meteoroids hit?"

"They'd have heavy shelter. And they'd reap the boarding parties."

"Once or twice. Then the asterites would board with guns of their own. No dice there." Church frowned. "Besides, I hate killing."

"Killing may be necessary. If only Earth weren't—Why can't we put on counterpressure? Refuse delivery of ships under construction for Terrestrial lines . . . that'd hurt the corporations, who'd squeal to their government."

"They sure would," Church agreed. "I must admit, even in his greedy moments, even when he's a high-priced executive, the Earthling is a shortsighted beast. But in this particular case, no, Mars wouldn't get the outplanet exchange that delivery of those ships can earn for us. We'd suffer worst."

His pipestem wagged didactically. "I've drawn a different conclusion from your files than your previous agency did," he said. "Your interview today with the Embassy bobber confirms me.

Matters are rather more serious for us than anyone thinks."

Dobshinsky fell still and alert.

"It does superficially look as if this latest method of piracy is a last-ditch measure," Church said. "The economics is so marginal, we suppose. They have to maintain patrols over enormous volumes of space. When their radar detects a ship, they have to scatter cosmic gravel in quantities which must be fantastic for those wretched little boats they own. They have to hope that the relative rock velocity will knock out the engine so they can match speeds. This doesn't always happen by a long shot. Usually a ship proceeds at acceleration and simply arrives with holes drilled through her. Or, if she is disabled, she and her cargo may well be so damaged that the loot doesn't pay for the operation."

Dobshinsky nodded. "One reason we've given you the contract is that the previous agency predicted, on those grounds, that piracy would soon sputter out. It hasn't."

"Right. There's at least one extremely subtle mind in back of this, and he's pulled off a masterstroke." Church's pipe had gone dead. He rekindled the tobacco.

"You see," he went on, "hitherto it was well established that piracy was involved. Oh, the traces were often concealed by the time the loot reached the market. But enough evidence remained to convict the rest. So anyone on Earth who bought the stuff was receiving stolen goods. You can say what you like about Earthlings, but while they number crooks among them, the average citizen has a far stiffer moral code than you or I or our neighbour down the street. The Earthling gets downright stuffy about some things we take for granted. One reason our ancestors left, of course. But anyhow, this fencing of stolen Martian property could not have gone on much longer. There'd have been too great a public outcry, as the facts inevitably came to light.

"Today, however—why, the asterites claim they're only salvaging vessels wrecked in natural disasters. That's acceptable."

"Yeah!" Dobshinsky jeered. "Overnight, meteoroids become more frequent by several orders of magnitude. We analysed a few, wedged in structural members of ships that did get by, and found traces of human-type organic material. They'd been handled, those rocks! How stupid is even an Earthling required to be?"

"Not too much, really," Church said. "Don't forget, he's a scientific ignoramus. A couple of respected astronomers say the recent trouble must be due to the debris of an extralarge comet family re-entering the Solar System after a million years or so. A chemist adds that organics do occur naturally in cosmic objects, like the carbonaceous chondrites, and your findings merely bear out the old suggestion that complex molecules got formed in the original preplanetary nebula.

"Yes, yes, the common citizen may still harbour a few suspicions. But he's conditioned to believe Authority. He's in no position himself to disprove any of those sonorous pronouncements. Very possibly, he's heard on his favourite religious programme that God is punishing the licentious Martians. And, to be sure, some of the payoff from looting us trickles down to him. All in all, there's nothing anymore to disturb the smooth functioning of his hypocrisy organ.

"That's one reason I believe a powerful mind is behind this wrecking system."

"Can it go on, though?" Dobshinsky wondered. "You said the method was clumsy and expensive."

"It is, too much so for an individual Chief. For everyone who makes a rich haul, a dozen may go broke. But if they spread the expense out among themselves in some fashion . . . and if, very much on the Q.T., Earth's government adds a subsidy, perhaps only in the form of extra-high prices for their 'salvaged goods' . . . you read the hand?"

"Luck, yes," Dobshinsky breathed. He took a long drag on his cigarette.

"I suppose you could try something like, say, going out of the ecliptic plane on your routes," Church suggested.

"For a while, perhaps," Dobshinsky said. "In the long run, no. Too expensive. Between having to send our craft under power through the Belt and having to use Hohmann orbits for the more profitable Earth trade, and losing several vessels a year—we're too close to the red as is."

Church sighed. He had expected that, simply because so obvious a dodge was not already being used by the shippers.

His gaze drifted outward. Orchards stood brave and green on the desert verge. A dust storm marched along the horizon like some great beast, tawny under the sky. *Yes,* he thought, *the badlands are beautiful too. We've built something infinitely*

*precious here on Mars. A man is not only free under the law;
when he wants, he can go to the ultimate freedom, the simple
being alone in wilderness.*

*My grandfathers gave me this. I must not let it be taken from
my grandchildren, before they are even born.*

He shook himself, stared straight at Dobshinsky, and said:
"The problem before us, I think, is to come to grips with whoever's behind the Chiefs. Or come to terms with him. I have the
vague beginnings of a possible answer to the whole mess. But
first we've got to find this man."

"In x billion cubic miles of space?" The other's smile went no
deeper than his lips.

"We have a start. Those double agents on Mars."

"Who are they?" Dobshinsky slumped in his seat. "Sure, plain
to see, at least one of the people who could've programmed those
'pilots' must be guilty. But there were a good three dozen."

"What did you do, besides fire the lot?"

"What else could we do? This isn't Earth, you know! Oh, our
agency did tail them for a while. But nothing suspicious was
noted. We finally decided the man was going to lie low in-
definitely and gave up. Having blacklisted him, we'd drawn
his teeth, so why should he bother with anything else?"

"I am not sure his teeth aren't still in place," Church said.
"In fact, on the basis that the current method of piracy is paying, I suspect he's been making a lunch off us right along. I'm
going to try and find him."

V

Once upon a time, before man set foot on Mars, the twin
moons were the occasion of much romancing. Perhaps a wistful
vestige of this was responsible for later attempts to get some
good out of them. True, from the ground they were hardly
visible to the naked eye, and proposals to beef up their albedo
by plating them with aluminium never got past the facts of
engineering. But no few prospectors lost their shirts—in some
cases, their pants as well—before the knowledge sank in that
neither Phobos nor Deimos is anything but a ten-mile chunk
of valueless rock. For a while after Independence, the Martian
navy thought about establishing a base on one of them. Then
the Constitution was amended to weaken government still fur-

ther, defence passed into the hands of chartered companies, and unsentimental cost accountants showed that you got more detection range and more safety for your investment by just leaving ships in orbit.

An entertainment syndicate built a swank lodge and fun house on Phobos. The view of Mars, gigantic in the spatial sky, was impressive. But any planetside honky-tonk could fake the same effect with a video wall. Quite a few did, and you need buy no ferry tickets to reach them. The syndicate went broke.

Accordingly, there were cheers when several universities and research institutes clubbed together to establish an observatory on the far side of Deimos. The bulk of the outer moon screened interference from the busy Martian radio channels, solar wind was not often strong enough at this distance to bother X-ray and cosmic-ray instruments, the maddeningly cryptic indications of the Ones Out Yonder could be received for half the thirty-hour period, and of course the visible-spectrum seeing was magnificent. For a while, the place was a major tourist attraction, which helped to pay expenses.

Over the years, that dropped off. A rancher, a waterman, an entrepreneur, a conman, a housewife had other things to think about than the latest news of what the quasars were up to. Observatory finances grew a little strained. The board was glad to accept help from some wealthy foundations on Earth. Terrestrial scientists in turn were glad to get temporary appointments to the Deimos staff. The recent diplomatic stress did not affect cordiality. Scientists were above politics.

For that matter, Church reflected, the average Martian was too. There had never been any imperialism in the Belt, simply private companies going there to make a dollar. If those companies were in trouble, that was their hard luck. *Maybe I shouldn't be so smug about Earthling shortsightedness,* he thought. *We're not much better. We do worry over ecology and conservation at home, because we must. But so few of us look beyond. The long-range good of the whole human race demands that it get established in the asteroids now, while the job is still fairly cheap to do, before mineral resources on the planets get so low that we'll have no choice, at a time when the cost will be appalling, socially as well as economically. Only, can you persuade anyone of that? Uh-uh!*

He forced away missionary ardour. The problem on hand was to live through the next few weeks.

The ferry eased into her cradle. Engine roar died off into a ringing silence. Church unharnessed himself and rose. Deimos gravity was so weak that he bounded to the overhead and smacked his pate. Forward in the long, empty cabin—he was the sole passenger in what was otherwise a load of supplies—the co-pilot turned about to grin at him. "I warned you, Dr. Quist," he said. "Better let me give you a hand."

Church fell into his role. Under the life mask, his vocalizer made his voice high and old; but the waspishness was his own doing, and he felt rather proud of it. "I have been here before, young fellow!"

Years had passed since last he wore a disguise. He was still conscious of the artificial flesh clinging to head and hands, slithering as microminiaturized transducers converted the subtle movement of muscles into equivalences which were not identities. But long-earned skills were rapidly reasserting themselves. Bald and stooped, he shuffled down the aisle with convincing unsteadiness.

"Not for some while, you haven't," the co-pilot said. "And you ground-huggers—no disrespect, Pop, but you got to grow up in this kind o' gee-field to handle yourself really well. Take my arm."

"You are an asterite yourself, eh?" Church asked.

"Yes, from Juno. Can't wait to go back, either, but what with the troubles, this is the only work I can get at the moment." The lanky young man floated to join him.

Church wasn't surprised. Those asterites not in rebellion were Martian citizens, as free to move around in Martian territory as anyone else. A good principle, too, even if it had simplified the planting of spies and saboteurs. He uttered a few grumbles but accepted the help.

On his way out, he had a glimpse of the surface: spacefield, a few domes, and some instruments thrusting over the near horizon, black and skeletal against the stars. Then he was in the lock tube, drifting dreamlike from rung to rung until he emerged in the terminal.

A dark-haired, sharp-featured man, also with the asterite look about him, waited. "Dr. Quist," he said, extending his hand with a slightly forced smile. "Welcome."

"Thank you for service," Church said. "You are, ah, Henry Lawrence of the radio division?"

"The same. I computed I'd better show you to your quarters and get you settled. Things must have changed quite a bit since you were here last, what with the new installations. This all your baggage?" He took the foot locker from the co-pilot. Church admired how deftly he handled the considerable mass. Weight might be small, but inertia hadn't lost an ounce.

They started down a ramp, into the bowels of the satellite. Lawrence looked harried. "We're glad to have so distinguished a guest," he said. "But pardon us if we aren't as hospitable as we should be. Our programmes keep us quite busy—my own section the most. Frankly, I don't see what you could learn by coming in person that couldn't just as well be faxed to you at the University."

"Thought I told you on the maser," Church snapped. In the process of getting Quist's co-operation, he had studied the astronomer with care. That old devil didn't consciously trade on his reputation: he took it for granted that he was the dean of his field. "Have to see the equipment in action before I can lay out a feasible programme for you to consider. The write-up in the *Journal* was intolerably vague, sir, intolerably. How'd it ever get by the referee?"

Lawrence presented a sour grin. "Well," he said, "you don't look too closely at gift wrappings. If a foundation on Earth buys you a big new microwave 'scope, and one of the foundation's men wants to add to his list of publications by doing the report —you see?"

Church muttered something. They went on at a rapid pace. The corridors were austere, empty during this work period. A whirr of fans, an odour of probably bad cooking, a faint vibration of life-support machinery were the only signs of man. Cold fluoro light glistened off sweat filmed on Lawrence's forehead. He kept glancing sideways at his companion.

He suspects, Church realized with a jolt.

And then: *Maybe that's best. Time is short. I meant to poke around until I had real proof. But if I take a chance and force the issue—*

"How long have you been here yourself?" he asked.

"A year," Lawrence said. He checked himself. "Half a Mars year, that is."

"So you have spent more time with the Terrestrial calendar than ours, eh? And yet you're an asterite born. Hm. All of a sudden, a new 'scope, and a new staff member to take charge of it. Were you part of the gift wrapping?"

Lawrence stopped. Church had some trouble braking. "Do you complain of my programme, sir?" Lawrence demanded rigidly.

"No, no, no, confound it!" Church stamped his foot, which caused him to bound a trifle. "Merely wondering. Mean to say, with men like Arnolfo and Mihailov—"

"If you have forgotten who I am," Lawrence said, chill, "consult *Who's Who in Science*. My previous position was on Luna at Ley Institute. After a sabbatical leave, I came here as part of the regular exchange programme. This way, if you will do me the service." He started off again.

Fits together, right enough, Church thought. *A clumsy deception by my standards. But Martians aren't hard to hoodwink in those respects. They're so afraid of the state becoming powerful that they don't allow it a really professional counterintelligence corps.*

I could be wrong, though. Let's see how he reacts.

"No offence intended, sir," he said in Quist's tone, which indicated that he didn't really give a damn whether any was taken or not. "One gets overly suspicious in these times, with the rebellion and the piracy. I had stock in Transjovian, which tumbled after the 'Io' was pirated."

Lawrence's face went blank. "What makes you think she was? She never reported in, nothing more."

"Come, now. Come, now. She was right in the middle of that lot whose programme tapes were altered. But shall we discuss more pleasant matters? Where did you go on your sabbatical?"

Lawrence clipped his mouth shut. They reached a door in the residential section, which he opened on to a bleak little room. "Your quarters, sir," he said.

Church's hopes sagged. But when they were both inside, Lawrence closed the door. He stood with his back to it, fists clenched, and asked, "What do you want, anyway?"

The breath gushed from Church. He sat down and fumbled in his old-fashioned tunic for a pipe. "A confidential talk," he answered. "Won't you have a seat, Misser Vaughan? I believe that was your name while you were programming autopilots."

The younger man poised an instant yet, before he lowered himself to the bunk. "Who are you?" he said low.

"My card."

Lawrence/Vaughan read and whistled. "Are you Church in person?"

"Yes."

"But—"

"Why not send one of my operatives? A huskier, less dissipated bobber, to trace every clue and, in the end, take your gun away from you?" Church laughed. Above the hound zeal that throbbed in him, he felt an immense and joyous relaxation. "Why, son, I never imagined you'd be stupid enough to pack one."

Lawrence clutched his own knees. "What do you propose to do?"

"I told you. Talk. Simply talk. Not much else I can do, is there? You're guilty of crimes against private property—nothing else, the narrow way our law defines treason. The courts could force you to make what restitution is in your power. But my clients are a lot more interested in preventing further loss than they are in garnisheeing what pittance you may earn for the rest of your life."

Lawrence looked bewildered. "How did you find me?"

Church extracted a tobacco pouch and got to work. "We had some information on everybody who'd been in a position to fake those tapes," he said. "Not much. Most had changed names and gone into other lines. Common enough practice, if you're under a cloud and live in a labour shortage economy. Some disappeared beyond trace—again, nothing suspicious; well within legal rights. But I computed the rebellion involves better brains than the popular image of a feudal Chief allows for.

"Having got a good agent to Mars—you were smuggled in under cover of that 'sabbatical,' correct?—they wouldn't write you off when your first mission ended. Rather they'd realize that the programme-alteration technique would be discovered by us and prepare a new job for you to step into when that happened. What job could that be? Well, I thought, now that spaceship schedules through the Belt are kept secret, it'd be mighty helpful for your side to know when a vessel is leaving Mars and in what direction. Flash that information to rebel

HQ, and they can notify whatever Chief is in a position to take advantage, and that way cut down the total cost of piracy to where it shows a profit. So-o, what better cover for a radar and a maser than a new 'scope which Earth obligingly bought for Deimos? When I found that a bright young bobber of asterite origin—but with years of residence on Luna behind him, and with a marked resemblance to the vanished Misser Vaughan— had been put in charge, well, the clue seemed worth following up."

"I am a radio astronomer," Lawrence said defensively.

"Sure, you'd have to be, since that's where most of your time must go. Only once in a while do you spot a ship. Even if you could do so oftener, you wouldn't, for fear of tipping your hand." Church lit his pipe and blew a thick cloud. "No hard feelings. You're a patriot and so forth. Mainly, I was after you so as to get a wire into your high command, or whatever you call it."

"What?"

"Look," Church said, "the Martian government is too diffuse and must operate too openly for undercover negotiations. Besides, Earth has tied its hands. Our private companies have no official standing. Nevertheless, they have some proposals to make. You Free Worlders rely on the sheer size of space, the number of uncatalogued asteroids, for an important part of your defence. We can't dicker with your GHQ till we know where it is. Thus far, we don't."

"I don't either," Lawrence said. "If I should be captured—"

"Relax. You aren't. We're simply talking. You must be able to find some places. A stronghold, say. Once I got there and met the Chief, he could ship me to GHQ or have a spokesman come to me. As I said, the whole thing has to be carried out unofficially and hush-hush, which is another reason for this roundabout way of contacting your people. You come along and navigate me. That's all I want from you."

"What do you intend to propose?" Lawrence asked.

"Sorry. Can't tell you that."

Lawrence bristled. "Then why should I cooperate?"

"Because if not," Church said in his mildest voice, "things might get a wee bit rough for you. On the other hand, if you do help out, well, I have quite a large expense account—"

VI

The Martian shipyards made delivery to Earth, and the liner "Atlantis"—freight plus luxury passenger accommodations—embarked on her maiden voyage. She did not make the once popular cruise to the Jovian moons. Though no Terrestrial craft had been lost in the recent difficulties, that could well be due to there being comparatively few of them; so let the Martians, driven by necessity, hazard the Belt run alone, until it was certain that the spate of rockstorms was indeed over. Meanwhile, the "Atlantis" would operate on the Triangle: Luna, Venus, Mars, and home again.

No difficulties were anticipated. Even if the allegations about piracy were true, the United Protectorates stood on excellent terms with the Free Worlds. Besides, underpowered asterite boats could never match velocities with this sleek giant. And however bitterly some of them complained, the Martians dared not so much as break off diplomatic relations.

At most, their casinos and pleasure houses would fleece the tourists during the layover. But that was expected. These were wealthy people, prepared to pay for a good time in a place where Earth's moralistic writ did not run.

The "Atlantis" was two days out, purring along a complex but readily calculable path towards Venus, when her electronics officer detected an object on the radar. He frowned, took distance and vectors, and fed them to a computer. After reading the printout, he made use of other instruments. Then he buzzed the captain.

"Trouble?" asked the voice from the intercom.

"N-no, sir. Not exactly." The officer stared past his desk, out the turret viewports to a sky resplendent with stars. One plate was polarized, making the sun a dull purple disc wreathed with faerie streamers. "Another ship seems to want to rendezvous. Paths intersect with matched velocities in about half an hour. But I can't raise her on the beam and . . . well, she's evidently not under power, because there's no jet radiation."

"Meteoroid?" wondered the captain. "An interstellar object might have a peculiar orbit."

"Be a strange coincidence if it came in precisely right to meet us, sir. Besides, the heavy weather in the Belt seems to have ended. The Martians haven't reported any losses for months. I'd guess this is one of their ships, possibly in trouble. Say their jet mass is low for some reason. They could detect us at a great distance—or even know beforehand just where we'd be, what with all the publicity we've had—and use their last reserves to get into a rendezvous track."

"That doesn't make much sense," argued the captain. "But —very well, we'll hold course. If it is a rock, we'll know in ample time to dodge. I'll be on deck immediately." As an afterthought: "Let's alert the passengers. They'd never forgive us if they missed the fun."

As the moment approached, the main lounge grew crowded and the drink dispensers clicked busily. A young lady hunting for a husband edged close to a distinguished-looking corporation executive who had not mentioned his wife at home. "How thrilling," she declaimed. "Does this happen often in space?"

"Never, that I know of," he answered. "According to the announcements, they aren't communicating. So I guess their radio got knocked out by the same thing that drained their tanks. Only if they had mass enough left to intercept us, they should have been able to limp to Venus or—There she is! Holy Success!"

He did not omit to lay an arm around his companion's waist, nor she to lean against him. But their awareness sprang through the viewport, out among cold constellations. Everyone's did; the babble was choked off. A steward cried, once, "That wasn't built by—" and dared say no more.

The strange vessel swelled in sight with terrifying speed. She was smaller than the "Atlantis", barracuda lean. No jets showed, only a ring of enigmatic cones around the waist. She must have a radiation screen; but why did it glow with a flickering violet luminance?

"Now hear this!" bawled from the annunciator. "Captain Daniels to all passengers. Take acceleration seats. Take acceleration seats at once. We're going into free fall for contact, and we may have to apply thrust without warning. All crew personnel to emergency stations."

The executive and the lady got separated in the scramble to find places and harness in.

On the bridge, the first officer bit his lip. "Should we try to out-accelerate them, sir?"

"I doubt if we can," said the captain harshly. "When they don't need jets. No, we'll match exact velocities and send a gig over. My God! The first ship from Outside!"

And meeting *his* command. With visions of sensie interviews dancing through his head, he issued orders. Engines brawled; forces tugged briefly at human muscles; then there were silence and weightlessness. The two craft ran parallel, some five hundred metres apart.

Until—"Look, she's coming towards us!" the first officer screamed.

Incredibly, with no tiniest spurt of ions, the stranger glided near. *Electrical attraction?* whirled in the captain's mind. *No, with that much voltage, we'd be seeing discharge effects. Magnetism? No, whatever that is made of, ours is nonferrous.*

Gravity control. Faster-than-light travel. I've experienced this moment a thousand times, on a thousand shows—but now it's real.

He heard himself say, in a cracked tone: "We're scarcely the first other race they've met. They must know what they're doing."

A shock and shudder, a metal belling, announced that the ships had come together. From an after viewport, the third officer said that main air locks had touched precisely and clung together, like a kiss.

The aliens came aboard.

They were man-size in their grotesque spacesuits, but the heads that grinned within the helmets were monstrous, and the hands each terminated in four fingers of witchlike length.

They paid scant attention to crewmen's efforts at sign language, merely gestured with ugly guns and rounded everyone efficiently up. Dreadful hours followed while they ransacked the vessel, stem to stern, leaving ruin behind.

Finally some of them came to the lounge where the humans were packed together. They chose two specimens, seemingly at random except that one was a male engineer and one a stewardess, and marched them off. Captain Daniels' horror and pity were tempered by relief that both poor devils happened to be Martian citizens.

Another jolt of reaction told that the visitors had let go.

The officers of the "Atlantis" fought through the mob around them—no easy task, when it was being hysterical in three dimensions. Starboard viewports showed the other craft receding with contemptuous slowness.

Assessment of damage took so much time that the liner was again alone, as far as the naked eye could tell, when the officers conferred.

"They didn't actually steal much," the C.E. reported from his department. "Mostly they took things apart, to learn our technology, I suppose. The fusion reactor hasn't been touched. My gang may be able to repair the jets."

"They made a thorough wreck of my stuff," said the electronics officer. "Not an instrument is functional. Probably didn't want us to call for help." He smiled with a certain bleak pleasure. "But they can't be too familiar with crystal masers, because I can fix that in a couple of hours and beam Venus for help."

Captain Daniels shuddered with the slacking off of tension. "Looks like we escaped easy," he said, "except for that man and woman they took to—to dissect? But what's ahead for the human race?"

He stared out at the stars, the countless lairs of Them. The nightmare of a lifetime's sensie plays ran along every nerve in him, and he couldn't switch off the show.

VII

Felix Kerrigan, Chief of the Keep, struggled out of his life mask. "Why!" he gusted. "I was smotherin' in that thing." He looked around the crowded cabin. Among the lean faces of his men, a few stood out that did not belong. There were the engineer and stewardess from the "Atlantis"; there was Nicholas Riskin of the Council Secretariat; and there was James Church. "Let's get goin'."

"Not yet," Riskin reminded him. "We have to wait till we've drifted so far that none of them will see we really do have jets, under our false hull. Oh, and don't forget to leave that pretty field fluorescence on."

"Hoo, what jets we got!" Dave Sadler said admiringly. He had never ridden in a Martian-built cruiseboat before.

He racked his spacesuit. In spite of appearance, it was a beautiful piece of work. Good engineers had helped design it, as well as one of the best costumers on Mars. Too bad it must be destroyed. "Damnation," he complained, "you should'a let us loot. That hulk was loaded!"

"And what would happen to the illusion of interstellar invaders when your plunder hit the market?" Church drawled.

Riskin frowned. "To be honest," he said, "I don't see where that makes any difference. I told you before, we went along with you in this because you made it a condition of supplying the Free Worlds, as well as our suspending salvage operations. But now what? Surely you don't think this fantastic ploy will really come off!"

"But I do," Church said. "So do some damn competent psycho-sociologists we consulted. Remember, this isn't going to be the only evidence. Traces of nonhuman camps have been planted here and there; Martians will report similar raids on their ships; and after an Earth vessel had such an experience, well, not many Earthlings will figure us for liars."

"Even so—plain common sense—".

"That's not too ordinary a commodity on Earth. You know what a gullible lot they are there, how liable to panic. And then there's that ingrained awe and fear of the Others, way down on the unconscious level where reason doesn't operate." A thought struck Church. He swore at himself for not having checked the matter personally; but with so much else to do, it had slipped his mind. "You did remove those superconductor rings built into her hull, didn't you?"

"Yeah, sure," Kerrigan grunted. "Made it look like we'd stripped the bulkheads down at that point to study the wiring, just like you briefed us to do."

"Good. Any proof that our 'gravity drive' was plain old high-powered magnetic attraction would hash the whole project."

"What *are* they going to think?" Riskin worried.

"They'll think a hundred different things," Church shrugged. "Certain Martians and asterites, especially, will consider this may have been a hoax. But they're scarcely going to see the motive, and anyhow, who dares take the chance it's not for real? Surely not Earth. There's going to be one sky-raising public clamour on Earth for defence. Which, of course, will please the corporations that stand to make big money off defence contracts."

Riskin regarded him narrowly. "I'm still not entirely sure what your motive is," he said.

"Why, to get you asterites off our necks," Church laughed. "We've been paying you Danegeld these past months to leave us alone, but we can't subsidize you forever."

He went into more detail when he reported to Dobshinsky. That was in his own office, which he knew for certain wasn't bugged.

He leaned back till his swivel chair creaked, cocked feet on desk, and chuckled around his pipe. "According to the latest news," he said, "the operation has gone over like a rocket. Rumour is that the Terrestrial Embassy is now pressuring you to arm your ships."

"True," Dobshinsky said. "Ridiculous."

"No, no. You must, to stay in character and maintain the war fever. You can afford the cost. You're not being plundered anymore, and the tribute to the Free Worlds will shortly begin being phased out. Mainly, though, you'll have more shipping than you can handle."

"What with the space defences that are planned? Yes, I suppose so."

"And the Asteroid Belt the most obvious region to fortify," Church added—unnecessarily, in view of the multitudinous discussions that had gone before, but he felt entitled to gloat. "So Mars and the Free Worlds generously permit Earth to use existing settlements as industrial and military bases. In the end, they'll inherit the goodies that get constructed.

"Meanwhile, money pours in—so much that the asterites can buy whatever they need, no further reason for piracy. And the surplus will go to trade between them and us, because public opinion in both our states is cool towards the great invasion scare and neither government is going to spend much on war material."

Dobshinsky frowned. "I don't like this," he said. "Oh, I argued for your scheme with the Association because I couldn't see any alternative, but still, now that we're committed—Do you plan to let those bastards go scot-free?"

"The asterites, you mean? Why not, in the short run? You know very well you can't conquer them by force. So let's make friends. I'm sure you don't give any more of a spit than me whether they fly our flag or their own."

"No, of course not," Dobshinsky said. "Nonetheless—"

"And remember," Church interrupted, "we've doomed them culturally. The defence boom will bring large-scale industrialization to them. I think that's a good thing for the human race as a whole. Man needs to plant himself firmly out there. But feudalism and nomadism can't coexist with massive industry. Those Chiefs who don't manage to set themselves up as heads of companies will be squeezed out and abandoned by their own people. Good luck, man, how much revenge do you want?"

"How long can the illusion last, though?" Dobshinsky fretted.

"Long enough," Church said. "The hundred or so people who know anything about our Boston Tea Party were carefully picked, and they're scattered far and wide. Oh, perhaps eventually the lid will blow off. If not, the scare will still peter out in time; everyone'll decide this was just an isolated gang of bandits. But, by then, the process will have gone irrevocably far. There'll be too big an investment in the Belt to abandon."

"Suppose the truth does become known?"

"Why, in that case, you need only remind the Solar System that the 'Atlantis' was worked over by Free Worlders. If Earth didn't object when we were on the receiving end of that, Earth will scarcely have much of a backblast coming in this instance.

"No, we have ample justification. Besides—"

Church rose and walked to the window. Night had fallen, with the pyrotechnic swiftness of Mars. Above all the neon glitter stood a sky very nearly as splendid as the one in space.

"It's barely possible," he said in a low voice, "that while the hooraw goes on, humans will find a way themselves to reach the stars."

STARFOG

"FROM ANOTHER UNIVERSE. Where space is a shining cloud, two hundred light-years across, roiled by the red stars that number in the many thousands, and where the brighter suns are troubled and cast forth great flames. Your spaces are dark and lonely."

Daven Laure stopped the recording and asked for an official translation. A part of *Jaccavrie*'s computer scanned the molecules of a plugged-in memory cylinder, identified the passage, and flashed the Serievan text on to a reader screen. Another part contained the multitudinous tasks of planetary approach. Still other parts waited for the man's bidding, whatever he might want next. A Ranger of the Commonalty travelled in a very special ship.

And even so, every year, a certain number did not come home from their missions.

Laure nodded to himself. Yes, he'd understood the woman's voice correctly. Or, at least, he interpreted her sentences approximately the same way as did the semanticist who had interviewed her and her fellows. And this particular statement was as difficult, as ambiguous as any which they had made. Therefore: (a) Probably the linguistic computer on Serieve had done a good job of unravelling their basic language. (b) It had accurately encoded its findings—vocabulary, grammar, tentative reconstruction of the underlying world-view—in the cylinders which a courier had brought to Sector HQ. (c) The re-encoding, into his own neurones, which Laure underwent on his way here, had taken well. He had a working knowledge of the tongue which —among how many others?—was spoken on Kirkasant.

"Wherever that may be," he muttered.

The ship weighed his words for a nanosecond or two, decided no answer was called for, and made none.

Restless, Laure got to his feet and prowled from the study cabin, down a corridor to the bridge. It was so called largely by courtesy. *Jaccavrie* navigated, piloted, landed, lifted, maintained, and, if need be, repaired and fought herself. But the projectors here offered a full outside view. At the moment, the bulkheads seemed cramped and barren. Laure ordered the simulacrum activated.

The bridge vanished from his eyes. Had it not been for the G-field underfoot, he might have imagined himself floating in space. A crystal night enclosed him, unwinking stars scattered like jewels, the frosty glitter of the Milky Way. Large and near, its radiance stopped down to preserve his retinas, burned the yellow sun of Serieve. The plane itself was a growing crescent, blue banded with white, rimmed by a violet sky. A moon stood opposite, worn golden coin.

But Laure's gaze strayed beyond, towards the deeps and then, as if in search of comfort, the other way, towards Old Earth. There was no comfort, though. They still named her Home, but she lay in the spiral arm behind this one, and Laure had never seen her. He had never met anyone who had. None of his ancestors had, for longer than their family chronicles ran. Home was a half-remembered myth; reality was here, these stars on the fringes of this civilization.

Serieve lay near the edge of the known. Kirkasant lay somewhere beyond.

"Surely not outside of spacetime," Laure said.

"If you've begun thinking aloud, you'd like to discuss it," *Jaccavrie* said.

He had followed custom in telling the ship to use a female voice and, when practical, idiomatic language. The computer had soon learned precisely what pattern suited him best. That was not identical with what he liked best; such could have got disturbing on a long cruise. He found himself more engaged, inwardly, with the husky contralto that had spoken in strong rhythms out of the recorder than he was with the mezzo-soprano that now reached his ears.

"Well . . . maybe so," he said. "But you already know everything in the material we have aboard."

"You need to set your thoughts in order. You've spent most of our transit time acquiring the language."

"All right, then, let's run barefoot through the obvious." Laure paced a turn around the invisible deck. He felt its hardness, the vibration back through his sandals, he sensed the almost subliminal beat of driving energies, he caught a piny whiff of air as the ventilators shifted to another part of their odour-temperature-ionization cycle; but still the stars blazed about him, and their silence seemed to enter his bones. Abruptly, harshly, he said: "Turn that show off."

The ship obeyed. "Would you like a planetary scene?" she asked. "You haven't yet looked at those tapes from the elf castles on Jair that you bought—"

"Not now." Laure flung himself into a chair web and regarded the prosaic metal, instruments, manual override controls that surrounded him. "This will do."

"Are you feeling well? Why not go in the diagnoser and let

me check you out? We've time before we arrive."

The tone was anxious. Laure didn't believe that emotion was put on. He refrained from anthropomorphizing his computer, just as he did those nonhuman sophonts he encountered. At the same time, he didn't go along with the school of thought which claimed that human-sensibility terms were absolutely meaningless in such connections. An alien brain, or a cybernetic one like *Jaccavrie*'s, could think; it was aware, it had conation. Therefore it had analogies to his.

Quite a few Rangers were eremitic types, sane enough but basically schizoid. That was their way of standing the gaff. It was normal for them to think of their ships as elaborate tools. Daven Laure, who was young and outgoing, naturally thought of his as a friend.

"No, I'm all right," he said. "A bit nervous, nothing else. This could turn out to be the biggest thing I . . . you and I have tackled yet. Maybe one of the biggest anyone has, at least on this frontier. I'd've been glad to have an older man or two along." He shrugged. "None available. Our service should increase its personnel, even if it means raising dues. We're spread much too thin across—how many stars?"

"The last report in my files estimated ten million planets with a significant number of Commonalty members on them. As for how many more there may be with which these have reasonably regular contact—"

"Oh, for everything's sake, come off it!" Laure actually laughed, and wondered if the ship had planned things that way. But, regardless, he could begin to talk of this as a problem rather than a mystery.

"Let me recapitulate," he said, "and you tell me if I'm misinterpreting matters. A ship comes to Serieve, allegedly from far away. It's like nothing anybody has ever seen, unless in historical works. (They haven't got the references on Serieve to check that out, so we're bringing some from HQ.) Hyperdrive, gravity control, electronics, yes, but everything crude, archaic, bare-bones. Fission instead of fusion power, for example . . . and human piloting!

"That is, the crew seem to be human. We have no record of their anthropometric type, but they don't look as odd as people do after several generations on some planets I could name. And the linguistic computer, once they get the idea that it's there to decipher their language and start cooperating with it, says their speech appears to have remote affinities with a few that we know, like ancient Anglic. Preliminary semantic analysis suggests their abstractions and constructs aren't quite like ours, but do fall well inside the human psych range. All in all, then, you'd assume they're explorers from distant parts."

"Except for the primitive ship," *Jaccavrie* chimed in. "One wouldn't expect such technological backwardness in any group which had maintained any contact, however tenuous, with the general mass of the different human civilizations. Nor would such a slow, underequipped vessel pass through them without stopping, to fetch up in this border region."

"Right. So . . . if it isn't a fake . . . their gear bears out a part of their story. Kirkasant is an exceedingly old colony . . . yonder." Laure pointed towards unseen stars. "Well out in the Dragon's Head sector, where we're barely beginning to explore. Somehow, somebody got that far, and in the earliest days of interstellar travel. They settled down on a planet and lost the trick of making spaceships. Only lately have they regained it."

"And come back, looking for the companionship of their own kind." Laure had a brief, irrational vision of *Jaccavrie* nodding. Her tone was so thoughtful. She would be a big, calm, dark-haired woman, handsome in middle age though getting somewhat plump . . . "What the crew themselves have said, as communication got established, seems to bear out this idea. Beneath a great many confused mythological motifs, I also get the impression of an epic. voyage, by a defeated people who ran as far as they could."

"But Kirkasant!" Laure protested. "The whole situation they describe. It's impossible."

"Might not that Vandage be mistaken? I mean, we know so little. The Kirkasanters keep talking about a weird home environment. Ours appears to have stunned and bewildered them. They simply groped on through space till they happened to find Serieve. Thus might their own theory, that somehow they blundered in from an altogether different continuum, might it not conceivably be right?"

"Hm-m-m. I guess you didn't see Vandange's accompanying letter. No, you haven't, it wouldn't've been plugged into your memory. Anyway, he claims his assistants examined that ship down to the bolt heads. And they found nothing, no mechanism, no peculiarity, whose function and behaviour weren't obvious. He really gets indignant. Says the notion of interspace-time transference is mathematically absurd. I don't have quite his faith in mathematics, myself, but I must admit he has one common-sense point. If a ship could somehow flip from one entire cosmos to another ... why, in five thousand years of interstellar travel, haven't we got some record of it happening?"

"Perhaps the ships to which it occurs never come back."

"Perhaps. Or perhaps the whole argument is due to misunderstanding. We don't have any good grasp of the Kirkasanter language. Or maybe it's a hoax. That's Vandange's opinion. He claims there's no such region as they say they come from. Not anywhere. Neither astronomers nor explorers have ever found anything like a . . . a space like a shining fog, crowded with stars—"

"But why should these wayfarers tell a falsehood?" *Jaccavrie* sounded honestly puzzled.

"I don't know. Nobody does. That's why the Serievan government decided it'd better ask for a Ranger."

Laure jumped up and started pacing again. He was a tall young man, with the characteristic beardlessness, fair hair and complexion, slightly slanted blue eyes of the Fireland mountaineers on New Vixen. But since he had trained at Starborough, which is on Aladir not far from Irontower City, he affected a fashionably simple grey tunic and blue hose. The silver comet of his calling blazoned his left breast.

"I don't know," he repeated. There rose in him a consciousness of that immensity which crouched beyond this hull. "Maybe they are telling the sober truth. We don't dare not know."

When a few score million people have an entire habitable world to themselves, they do not often build high. That comes later, along with formal wilderness preservation, disapproval of fecundity, and inducements to emigrate. Pioneer towns tend to be low and rambling. (Or so it is in that civilization wherein the Commonalty operates. We know that other branches of humanity have their distinctive ways, and hear rumours of yet stranger ones. But so vast is the galaxy—these two or three spiral arms, a part of which our race has to date thinly occupied—

so vast, that we cannot even keep track of our culture, let alone anyone else's.)

Pelogard, however, was founded on an island off the Branzan mainland, above Serieve's arctic circle: which comes down to almost 56°. Furthermore, it was an industrial centre. Hence most of its buildings were tall and crowded. Laure, standing by the outer wall of Ozer Vandange's office and looking forth across the little city, asked why this location had been chosen.

"You don't know?" responded the physicist. His inflection was a touch too elaborately incredulous.

"I'm afraid not," Laure confessed. "Think how many systems my service has to cover, and how many individual places within each system. If we tried to remember each, we'd never be anywhere but under neuroinductors."

Vandange, seated small and bald and prim behind a large desk, pursed his lips. "Yes, yes," he said. "Nevertheless, I should not think an *experienced* Ranger would dash off to a planet without temporarily mastering a few basic facts about it."

Laure flushed. An experienced Ranger would have put this conceited old dustbrain in his place. But he himself was too aware of youth and awkwardness. He managed to say quietly, "Sir, my ship has complete information. She needed only scan it and tell me no precautions were required here. You have a beautiful globe and I can understand why you're proud of it. But please understand that to me it has to be a way station. My job is with those people from Kirkasant, and I'm anxious to meet them."

"You shall, you shall," said Vandange, somewhat mollified. "I merely thought a conference with you would be advisable first. As for your question, we need a city here primarily because upwelling ocean currents make the arctic waters mineral-rich. Extractor plants pay off better than they would farther south."

Despite himself, Laure was interested. "You're getting your minerals from the sea already? At so early a stage of settlement?"

"This sun and its planets are poor in heavy metals. Most local systems are. Not surprising. We aren't far, here, from the northern verge of the spiral arm. Beyond is the halo—thin gas, little dust; ancient globular clusters very widely scattered. The interstellar medium from which stars form has not been greatly enriched by earlier generations."

Laure suppressed his resentment at being lectured like a child. Maybe it was just Vandange's habit. He cast another glance through the wall. The office was high in one of the buildings. He looked across soaring blocks of metal, concrete, glass, and plastic interlinked, with trafficways and freight cables, down to the waterfront. There bulked the extractor plants, warehouses, and skydocks. Cargo craft moved ponderously in and out. Not many passenger vessels flitted between. Pelogard must be largely automated.

The season stood at late spring. The sun cast brightness across a grey ocean that a wind rumpled. Immense flocks of seabirds dipped and wheeled. Or were they birds? They had wings, anyhow, steely blue against a wan sky. Perhaps they cried or sang, into the wind skirl and wave rush; but Laure couldn't hear it in this enclosed place.

"That's one reason I can't accept their yarn," Vandange declared.

"Eh?" Laure came out of his reverie with a start.

Vandange pressed a button to opaque the wall. "Sit down. Let's get to business."

Laure eased himself into a lounger opposite the desk. "Why am I conferring with you?" he counterattacked. "Whoever was principally working with the Kirkasanters had to be a semanticist. In short, Paeri Ferand. He consulted specialists on your university faculty, in anthropology, history, and so forth. But I should think your own role as a physicist was marginal. Yet you're the one taking up my time. Why?"

"Oh, you can see Ferand and the others as much as you choose," Vandange said. "You won't get more from them than repetitions of what the Kirkasanters have already told. How could you? What else have they got to go on? If nothing else, an underpopulated world like ours can't maintain staffs of experts to ferret out the meaning of every datum, every inconsistency, every outright lie. I had hoped, when our government notified your sector headquarters, the Rangers would have sent a real team, instead of—" He curbed himself. "Of course, they have many other claims on their attention. They would not see at once how important this is."

"Well," Laure said in his annoyance, "if you're suspicious, if you think the strangers need further investigation, why bother with my office? It's just an overworked little outpost. Send them on to a heart world, like Sarnac, where the facilities and people really can be had."

"It was urged," Vandange said. "I, and a few others who felt as I do, fought the proposal bitterly. In the end, as a compromise, the government decided to dump the whole problem in the lap of the Rangers. Who turn out to be, in effect, you. Now I must persuade you to be properly cautious. Don't you see, if those . . . beings . . . have some hostile intent, the very worst move would be to send them on—let them spy out our civilization—let them, perhaps, commit nuclear sabotage on a vital centre, and then vanish back into space." His voice grew shrill. "That's why we've kept them here so long, on one excuse after the next, here on our home planet. We feel responsible to the rest of mankind!"

"But what—" Laure shook his head. He felt a sense of unreality. "Sir, the League, the troubles, the Empire, its fall, the Long Night . . . every such thing—behind us. In space and time alike. The people of the Commonalty don't get into wars."

"Are you quite certain?"

"What makes *you* so certain of any menace in—one antiquated ship. Crewed by a score of men and women. Who came here openly and peacefully. Who, by every report, have been struggling to get past the language and culture barriers and communicate with you in detail—what in cosmos' name makes you worry about them?"

"The fact that they are liars."

Vandange sat awhile, gnawing his thumb, before he opened a box, took out a cigar and puffed it into lighting. He didn't offer Laure one. That might be for fear of poisoning his visitor with whatever local weed he was smoking. Scattered around for many generations on widely differing planets, populations did develop some odd distributions of allergy and immunity. But Laure suspected plain rudeness.

"I thought my letter made it clear," Vandange said. "They insist they are from another continuum. One with impossible properties, including visibility from ours. Conveniently on the far side of the Dragon's Head, so that we don't see it here. Oh, yes," he added quickly, "I've heard the arguments. That the whole thing is a misunderstanding due to our not having an

adequate command of their language. That they're really trying to say they came from—well, the commonest rationalization
is a dense star cluster. But it won't work, you know. It won't
work at all."

"Why not?" Laure asked.

"Come, now. Come, now. You must have learned some astronomy as part of your training. You must know that some things
simply do not occur in the galaxy."

"Uh—"

"They showed us what they alleged were lens-and-film photo-
graphs taken from, ah, inside their home universe." Vandange
bore down heavily on the sarcasm. "You saw copies, didn't you?
Well, now, where in the real universe do you find that kind of
nebulosity—so thick and extensive that a ship can actually lose
its bearings, wander around lost, using up its film among other
supplies, until it chances to emerge in clear space? For that
matter, assuming there were such a region, how could anyone
capable of building a hyperdrive be so stupid as to go beyond
sight of his beacon stars?"

"Uh . . . I thought of a cluster, heavily hazed, somewhat
like the young clusters of the Pleiades type."

"So did many Serievans," Vandange snorted. "Please use
your head. Not even Pleiadic clusters contain that much gas
and dust. Besides, the verbal description of the Kirkasanters
sounds like a globular cluster, insofar as it sounds like anything. But not much. The ancient red suns are there, crowded
together, true. But they speak of far too many younger ones.

"And of far too much heavy metal at home. Which their
ship demonstrates. Their use of alloying elements like aluminium
and beryllium is incredibly parsimonious. On the other hand,
electrical conductors are gold and silver, the power plant is
shielded not with lead but with inertcoated osmium, and it
burns plutonium which the Kirkasanters assert was mined!

"They were astonished that Serieve is such a light-metal
planet. Or claimed they were astonished. I don't know about
that. I do know that this whole region is dominated by light
elements. That its interstellar spaces are relatively free of dust
and gas, the Dragon's Head being the only exception and it
merely in transit through our skies. That all this is even more
true of the globular clusters, which formed in an ultratenuous
medium, mostly before the galaxy had condensed to its present

shape—which, in fact, practically don't *occur* in the main body of the galaxy, but are off in the surrounding halo!"

Vandange stopped for breath and triumph.

"Well." Laure shifted uneasily in his seat and wished *Jaccavrie* weren't ten thousand kilometres away at the only spaceport. "You have a point. There are contradictions, aren't there? I'll bear what you said in mind when I, uh, interview the strangers themselves."

"And you will, I trust, be wary of them," Vandange said.

"Oh, yes. Something queer does seem to be going on." ·

In outward appearance, the Kirkasanters were not startling. They didn't resemble any of the human breeds that had developed locally, but they varied less from the norm than some. The fifteen men and five women were tall, robust, broad in chest and shoulders, slim in waist. Their skins were dark coppery reddish, their hair blue-black and wavy; males had some beard and moustache which they wore neatly trimmed. Skulls were dolichocephalic, faces disharmonically wide, noses straight and thin, lips full. The total effect was handsome. Their eyes were their most arresting feature, large, long-lashed, luminous in shades of grey, or green, or yellow.

Since they had refused—with an adamant politeness they well knew how to assume—to let cell samples be taken for chromosome analysis, Vandange had muttered to Laure about nonhumans in surgical disguise. But that the Ranger classed as the fantasy of a provincial who'd doubtless never met a live xeno. You couldn't fake so many details, not and keep a viable organism. Unless, to be sure, happenstance had duplicated most of those details for you in the course of evolution . . .

Ridiculous, Laure thought. *Coincidence isn't that energetic.*

He walked from Pelogard with Demring Lodden, captain of the *Makt*, and Demring's daughter, navigator Graydal. The town was soon behind them. They found a trail that wound up into steeply rising hills, among low, gnarly trees which had begun to put forth leaves that were fronded and coloured like old silver. The sun was sinking, the air noisy and full of salt odours. Neither Kirkasanter appeared to mind the chill.

"You know your way here well," Laure said clumsily.

"We should," Demring answered, "for we have been held

on this sole island, with naught to do but ramble it when the *reyad* takes us."

"*Reyad?*" Laure asked.

"The need to . . . search," Graydal said. "To track beasts, or find what is new, or be alone in wild places. Our folk were hunters until not so long ago. We bear their blood."

Demring wasn't to be diverted from his grudge. "Why are we thus confined?" he growled. "Each time we sought an answer, we got an evasion. Fear of disease, need for us to learn what to expect— Ha, by now I'm half minded to draw my gun, force my way to our ship, and depart for aye!"

He was erect, grizzled, deeply graven of countenance and bleak of gaze. Like his men, he wore soft boots, a knee-length gown of some fine-scaled leather, a cowled cloak, a dagger and an energy pistol at his belt. On his forehead sparkled a diamond that betokened authority.

"Well, but, Master," Graydal said, "here today we deal with no village witchfinders. Daven Laure is a king's man, with power to act, knowledge and courage to act rightly. Has he not gone off alone with us because you said you felt stifled and spied on in the town? Let us talk as freefolk with him."

Her smile, her words in the husky voice that Laure remembered from his recordings, were gentle. He felt pretty sure, though, that as much steel underlay her as her father, and possibly whetted sharper. She almost matched his height, her gait was tigerish, she was herself weaponed and diademed. Unlike Laure's close cut or Demring's short bob, her hair passed through a platinum ring and blew free at full length. Her clothes were little more than footgear, fringed shorts, and thin blouse. However attractive, the sight did not suggest seductive femininity to the Ranger—when she wasn't feeling the cold that struck through his garments. Besides, he had already learned that the sexes were mixed aboard the *Makt* for no other reason than that women were better at certain jobs than men. Every female was accompanied by an older male relative. The Kirkasanters were not an uncheerful folk, on the whole, but some of their ideals looked austere.

Nonetheless, Graydal had lovely strong features, and her eyes, under the level brows, shone amber.

"Maybe the local government was overcautious," Laure said, "but don't forget, this is a frontier settlement. Not many light-years hence, in that part of the sky you came from, begins the unknown. It's true the stars are comparatively thin in these parts—average distance between them about four parsecs—but still, their number is too great for us to do more than feel our way slowly forward. Especially when, in the nature of the case, planets like Serieve must devote most of their effort to developing themselves. So, when one is ignorant, one does best to be careful."

He flattered himself that was a well-composed conciliatory speech. It wasn't as oratorical as one of theirs, but they had lung capacity for a thinner atmosphere than this. He was disappointed when Demring said scornfully, "*Our* ancestors were not so timid."

"Or else their pursuers were not," Graydal laughed.

The captain looked offended. Laure hastily asked: "Have you no knowledge of what happened?"

"No," said the girl, turned pensive. "Not in truth. Legends, found in many forms across all Kirkasant, tell of battle, and a shipful of people who fled far until at last they found haven. A few fragmentary records—but those are vague, save the Baorn Codex; and it is little more than a compendium of technical information which the Wisemen of Skribent preserved. Even in that case"—she smiled again—"the meaning of most passages was generally obscure until after our modern scientists had invented the thing described for themselves."

"Do you know what records remain in Homeland?" Demring asked hopefully.

Laure sighed and shook his head. "No. Perhaps none, by now. Doubtless, in time, an expedition will go from us to Earth. But after five thousand trouble-filled years— And your ancestors may not have started from there. They may have belonged to one of the first colonies."

In a dim way, he could reconstruct the story. There had been a fight. The reasons—personal, familial, national, ideological, economic, whatever they were—had dropped into the bottom of the millennia between then and now. (A commentary on the importance of any such reasons.) But someone had so badly wanted the destruction of someone else that one ship, or one fleet, hounded another almost a quarter way around the galaxy.

Or maybe not, in a literal sense. It would have been hard

to do. Crude as they were, those early vessels could have made the trip, if frequent stops were allowed for repair and resupply and refilling of the nuclear converters. But to this day, a craft under hyperdrive could only be detected within approximately a light-year's radius by the instantaneous "wake" of space-pulses. If she lay doggo for a while, she was usually unfindable in the sheer stupendousness of any somewhat larger volume. That the hunter should never, in the course of many months, either have overhauled his quarry or lost the scent altogether, seemed conceivable but implausible.

Maybe pursuit had not been for the whole distance. Maybe the refugees had indeed escaped after a while, but—in blind panic, or rage against the foe, or desire to practice undisturbed a brand of utopianism, or whatever the motive was—they had continued as far as they possibly could, and hidden themselves as thoroughly as nature allowed.

In any case, they had ended in a strange part of creation: so strange that numerous men on Serieve did not admit it existed. By then, their ship must have been badly in need of a complete overhaul, amounting virtually to a rebuilding. They settled down to construct the necessary industrial base. (Think, for example, how much plant you must have before you make your first transistor.) They did not have the accumulated experience of later generations to prove how impossible this was.

Of course they failed. A few score—a few hundred at absolute maximum, if the ship had been rigged with suspended-animation lockers—could not preserve a full-fledged civilization while coping with a planet for which man was never meant. And they had to content themselves with that planet. Once into the Cloud Universe, even if their vessel could still wheeze along for a while, they were no longer able to move freely about, picking and choosing.

Kirkasant was probably the best of a bad lot. And Laure thought it was rather a miracle that man had survived there. So small a genetic pool, so hostile an environment . . . but the latter might well have saved him from the effects of the former. Natural selection must have been harsh. And, seemingly, the radiation background was high, which led to a corresponding mutation rate. Women bore from puberty to menopause, and buried most of their babies. Men struggled to keep them alive. Often death harvested adults, too, entire families. But those who were fit tended to survive. And the planet did have an unfilled ecological niche: the one reserved for intelligence. Evolution galloped. Population exploded. In one or two millennia, man was at home on Kirkasant. In five, he crowded it and went looking for new planets.

Because culture had never totally died. The first generation might be unable to build machine tools, but could mine and forge metals. The next generation might be too busy to keep public schools, but had enough hard practical respect for learning that it supported a literate class. Succeeding generations, wandering into new lands, founding new nations and societies, might war with each other, but all drew from a common tradition and looked to one goal: reunion with the stars.

Once the scientific method had been created afresh, Laure thought, progress must have been more rapid than on Earth. For the natural philosophers knew certain things were possible, even if they didn't know how, and this was half the battle. They must have got some hints, however oracular, from the remnants of ancient texts. They actually had the corroded hulk of the ancestral ship for their studying. Given this much, it was not too surprising that they leaped in a single lifetime from the first moon rockets to the first hyperdrive craft—and did so on a basis of wildly distorted physical theory, and embarked with such naïveté that they couldn't find their way home again!

All very logical. Unheard of, outrageously improbable, but in this big a galaxy the strangest things are bound to happen now and again. The Kirkasanters could be absolutely honest in their story.

If they were.

"Let the past tend the past," Graydal said impatiently. "We've tomorrow to hunt in."

"Yes," Laure said, "but I do need to know a few things. It's not clear to me how you found us. I mean, you crossed a thousand light-years or more of wilderness. How did you come on a speck like Serieve?"

"We were asked that before," Demring said, "but then we could not well explain, few words being held in common. Now you show a good command of the Hobrokan tongue, and for our part, albeit none of these villagers will take the responsibility of putting one of us under your educator machine . . . in talking with technical folk we've gained various technical words of yours."

He was silent awhile, collecting phrases. The three people continued up the trail. It was wide enough for them to walk abreast, somewhat muddy with rain and melted snow. The sun was so far down that the woods walled it off; twilight smoked from the ground and from either side, though the sky was still pale. The wind was dying but the chill deepening. Somewhere behind those dun trunks and ashy-metallic leaves, a voice went "K-kr-r-r-*ruk*!" and, above and ahead, the sound of a river became audible.

Demring said with care: "See you, when we could not find our way back to Kirkasant's sun, and at last had come out in an altogether different cosmos, we thought our ancestors might have originated there. Certain traditional songs hinted as much, speaking of space as dark, for instance; and surely darkness encompassed us now, and immense loneliness between the stars. Well, but in which direction might Homeland lie? Casting about with telescopes, we spied afar a black cloud, and thought, if the ancestors had been in flight from enemies, they might well have gone through such, hoping to break their trail."

"The Dragon's Head Nebula," Laure nodded.

Graydal's wide shoulders lifted and fell. "At least it gave us something to steer by," she said.

Laure stole a moment's admiration of her profile. "You had courage," he said. "Quite aside from everything else, how did you know this civilization had not stayed hostile to you?"

"How did we know it ever was in the first place?" she chuckled. "Myself, insofar as I believe the myths have any truth, I suspect our ancestors were thieves or bandits or—".

"Daughter!" Demring hurried on, in a scandalized voice: "When we had fared thus far, we found the darkness was dust and gas such as pervade the universe at home. There was simply an absence of stars to make it shine. Emerging on the far side, we tuned our neutrino detectors. Our reasoning was that a highly developed civilization would use a great many nuclear power plants. Their neutrino flux should be detectable above the natural noise level—in this comparatively empty cosmos—across several score light-years or better, and we could home on it."

First they sound like barbarian bards, Laure thought, *and then like radionicians. No wonder a dogmatist like Vandange can't put credence in them.*

Can I?

"We soon began to despair," Graydal said. "We were nigh to the limit—"

"No matter," Demring interrupted.

She looked steadily first at one man, then the other, and said, "I dare trust Daven Laure." To the Ranger, "Belike no secret anyhow, since men on Serieve must have examined our ship with knowledgeable eyes. We were nigh to our limit of travel without refuelling and refurbishing. We were about to seek for a planet not too unlike Kirkasant where— But then, as if by Valfar's Wings, came the traces we sought, and we followed them here.

"And here were humans!

"Only of late has our gladness faded as we begin to see how they temporize and keep us half prisoner. Wholly prisoner, maybe, should we try to depart. Why will they not rely on us?"

"I tried to explain that when we talked yesterday," Laure said. "Some important men don't see how you could be telling the truth."

She caught his hand in a brief, impulsive grasp. Her own was warm, slender, and hard. "But you are different?"

"Yes." He felt helpless and alone. "They've, well, they've called for me. Put the entire problem in the hands of my organization. And my fellows have so much else to do that, well, I'm given broad discretion."

Demring regarded him shrewdly. "You are a young man," he said. "Do not let your powers paralyse you."

"No. I will do what I can for you. It may be little."

The trail rounded a thicket and they saw a rustic bridge across the river, which ran seaward in foam and clangour. Halfway over, the party stopped, leaned on the rail and looked down. The water was thickly shadowed between its banks, and the woods were becoming a solid black mass athwart a dusking sky. The air smelled wet.

"You realize," Laure said, "it won't be easy to retrace your route. You improvised your navigational co-ordinates. They can be transformed into ours on this side of the Dragon's Head, I suppose. But once beyond the nebula, I'll be off my own charts, except for what few listed objects are visible from either side. No one from this civilization has been there, you see, what with

millions of suns closer to our settlements. And the star sights you
took can't have been too accurate."

"You are not going to take us to Homeland, then," Demring
said tonelessly.

"Don't you understand? Homeland, Earth, it's so far away
that I myself don't know what it's like anymore!"

"But you must have a nearby capital, a more developed
world than this. Why do you not guide us thither, that we may
talk with folk wiser than these wretched Serievans?"

"Well . . . uh . . . Oh, many reasons. I'll be honest, caution
is one of them. Also, the Commonalty does not have anything
like a capital, or— But yes, I could guide you to the heart of
civilization. Any of numerous civilizations in this galactic arm."
Laure took a breath and slogged on. "My decision, though,
under the circumstances, is that first I'd better see your world
Kirkasant. After all . . . .well, certainly, if everything is all right,
we'll establish regular contacts, and invite your people to visit
ours, and— Don't you like the plan? Don't you want to go
home?"

"How shall we, ever?" Graydal asked low.

Laure cast her a surprised glance. She stared ahead of her
and down, into the river. A fish—some kind of swimming
creature—leaped. Its scales caught what kind of light remained
in a gleam that was faint but startling against those murky
waters. She didn't seem to notice, though she cocked her head
instinctively towards the splash that followed.

"Have you not listened?" she said. "Did you not hear us?
How long we searched in the fog, through that forest of suns,
until at last we left our whole small bright universe and came
into this great one that has so much blackness in it—and thrice
we plunged back into our own space, and groped about, and
came forth without having found trace of any star we knew—"
Her voice lifted the least bit. "We are lost, I tell you, eternally
lost. Take us to your home, Daven Laure, that we may try to
make ours there."

He wanted to stroke her hands, which had clenched into fists
on the bridge rail. But he made himself say only: "Our science
and resources are more than yours. Maybe we can find a way
where you cannot. At any rate, I'm duty bound to learn as
much as I can, before I make report and recommendation to
my superiors."

"I do not think you are kind, forcing my crew to return and look again on what has gone from them," Demring said stiffly. "But I have scant choice save to agree." He straightened. "Come, best we start back towards Pelogard. Night will soon be upon us."

"Oh, no rush," Laure said, anxious to change the subject. "An arctic zone, at this time of year— We'll have no trouble."

"Maybe you will not," Graydal said. "But Kirkasant after sunset is not like here."

They were on their way down when dusk became night, a light night where only a few stars gleamed and Laure walked easily through a clear gloaming. Graydal and Demring must needs use their energy guns at minimum intensity for flash-casters. And even so, they often stumbled.

Makt was three times the size of *Jaccavrie*, a gleaming torpedo shape whose curve was broken by boat housings and weapon turrets. The Ranger vessel look like a gig attending her. In actuality, *Jaccavrie* could have outrun, outmanoeuvred, or out-fought the Kirkasanter with ludicrous ease. Laure didn't emphasize that fact. His charges were touchy enough already. He had suggested hiring a modern carrier for them, and met a glacial negative. This craft was the property and bore the honour of the confederated clans that had built her. She was not to be abandoned.

Modernizing her would have taken more time than increased speed would save. Besides, while Laure was personally con-vinced of the good intentions of Demring's people, he had no right to present them with up-to-date technology until he had proof they wouldn't misuse it.

One could not accurately say that he resigned himself to accompanying them in this ship at the plodding pace of theirs. The weeks of travel gave him a chance to get acquainted with them and their culture. And that was not only his duty but his pleasure. Especially, he found, when Graydal was involved.

Some time passed before he could invite her to dinner *à deux*. He arranged it with what he felt sure was adroitness. Two persons, undisturbed, talking socially, could exchange informa-tion of the subtle kind that didn't come across in committee. Thus he proposed to series of private meetings with the officers of *Makt*. He began with the captain, naturally; but after a while came the navigator's turn.

Jaccavrie phased in with the other vessel, laid alongside and made air-lock connections in a motion too smooth to feel. Graydal came aboard and the ships parted company again. Laure greeted her according to the way of Kirkasant, with a handshake. The clasp lasted a moment. "Welcome," he said.

"Peace between us." Her smile offset her formalism. She was in uniform—another obsolete aspect of her society—but it shimmered gold and moulded itself to her.

"Won't you come to the saloon for a drink before we eat?"

"I shouldn't. Not in space."

"No hazard," said the computer in an amused tone. "I operate everything anyway."

Graydal had tensed and clapped hand to gun at the voice. She relaxed, and tried to laugh. "I'm sorry. I am not used to . . . you." She almost bounded on her way down the corridor with Laure. He had set the interior weight at one standard G. The Kirkasanters maintained theirs fourteen per cent higher, to match the pull of their home world.

Though she had inspected this ship several times already, Graydal looked wide-eyed around her. The saloon was small but sybaritic. "You do yourself proud," she said amidst the draperies, music, perfumes, and animations.

He guided her to a couch. "You don't sound quite approving," he said.

"Well—"

"There's no virtue in suffering hardships."

"But there is in the ability to endure them." She sat too straight for the form-fitter cells to make her comfortable.

"Think I can't?"

Embarrassed, she turned her gaze from him, towards the viewscreen, on which flowed a colour composition. Her lips tightened. "Why have you turned off the exterior scene?"

"You don't seem to like it, I've noticed." He sat down beside her. "What will you have? We're fairly well stocked."

"Turn it on."

"What?"

"The outside view." Her nostrils dilated. "It shall not best me."

He spread his hands. The ship saw his rueful gesture and obliged. Space leaped into the screen, star-strewn except where the storm-cloud mass of the dark nebula reared ahead. He heard Graydal suck in a breath and said quickly, "Uh, since you aren't familiar with our beverages, I suggest daiquiris. They're tart, a little sweet—"

Her nod was jerky. Her eyes seemed locked to the screen. He leaned close, catching the slight warm odour of her, not quite identical with the odour of other women he had known, though the difference was too subtle for him to name. "Why does that sight bother you?" he asked.

"The strangeness. The aloneness. It is so absolutely alien to home. I feel forsaken and—" She filled her lungs, forced detachment on herself, and said in an analytical manner: "Possibly we are disturbed by a black sky because we have virtually none of what you call night vision." A touch of trouble returned. "What else have we lost?"

"Night vision isn't needed on Kirkasant, you tell me," Laure consoled her. "And evolution there worked fast. But you must have gained as well as atrophied. I know you have more physical strength, for instance, than your ancestors could've had." A tray with two glasses extended from the side. "Ah, here are the drinks."

She sniffed at hers. "It smells pleasant," she said. "But are you sure there isn't something I might be allergic to?"

"I doubt that. You didn't react to anything you tried on Serieve, did you?"

"No, except for finding it overly bland."

"Don't worry," he grinned. "Before we left, your father took care to present me with one of your saltshakers. It'll be on the dinner table."

Jaccavrie had analysed the contents. Besides sodium and potassium chloride—noticeably less abundant on Kirkasant than on the average planet, but not scarce enough to cause real trouble —the mixture included a number of other salts. The proportion of rare earths and especially arsenic was surprising. An ordinary human who ingested the latter element at that rate would lose quite a few years of life expectancy. Doubtless the first refugee generations had, too, when something else didn't get them first. But by now their descendants were so well adapted that food didn't taste right without a bit of arsenic trioxide.

"We wouldn't have to be cautious—we'd know in advance what

you can and cannot take—if you'd permit a chromosome analysis," Laure hinted. "The laboratory aboard this ship can do it."

Her cheeks turned more than ever coppery. She scowled. "We refused before," she said.

"May I ask why?"

"It . . . violates integrity. Humans are not to be probed into."

He had encountered that attitude before, in several guises. To the Kirkasanter—at least, to the Hobrokan clansman; the planet had other cultures—the body was a citadel for the ego, which by right should be inviolable. The feeling, so basic that few were aware of having it, had led to the formation of reserved, often rather cold personalities. It had handicapped if not stopped the progress of medicine. On the plus side, it had made for dignity and self-reliance; and it had caused this civilization to be spared professional gossips, confessional literature, and psychoanalysis.

"I don't agree," Laure said. "Nothing more is involved than scientific information. What's personal about a DNA map?"

"Well . . . maybe. I shall think on the matter." Graydal made an obvious effort to get away from the topic. She sipped her drink, smiled, and said, "Mm-m-m, this *is* a noble flavour."

"Hoped you'd like it. I do. We have a custom in the Commonalty—" He touched glasses with her.

"Charming. Now we, when good friends are together, drink half what's in our cups and then exchange them."

"May I?"

She blushed again, but with pleasure. "Certainly. You honour me."

"No, the honour is mine." Laure went on, quite sincere: "What your people have done is tremendous. What an addition to the race you'll be!"

Her mouth drooped. "If ever my folk may be found."

"Surely—"

"Do you think we did not try?" She tossed off another gulp of her cocktail. Evidently it went fast to her unaccustomed head. "We did not fare forth blindly. Understand that *Makt* is not the first ship to leave Kirkasant's sun. But the prior ones went to nearby stars, stars that can be seen from home. They are many. We had not realized how many more are in the Cloud Universe, hidden from eyes and instruments, a few light-years farther on. We, our ship, we intended to take the next step. Only the next step. Barely beyond that shell of suns we could see from Kirkasant's system. We could find our way home again without trouble. Of course we could! We need but steer by those suns that were already charted on the edge of instrumental perception. Once we were in their neighbourhood, our familiar part of space would be visible."

She faced him, gripping his arm painfully hard, speaking in a desperate voice. "What we had not known, what no one had known, was the imprecision of that charting. The absolute magnitudes, therefore the distances and relative positions of those verge-visible stars . . . had not been determined as well as the astronomers believed. Too much haze, too much shine, too much variability. Do you understand? And so, suddenly, our tables were worthless. We thought we could identify some suns. But we were wrong. Flitting towards them, we must have bypassed the volume of space we sought . . . and gone on and on, more hopelessly lost each day, each endless day—"

"What makes you think you can find our home?"

Laure, who had heard the details before, had spent the time admiring her and weighing his reply. He sipped his own drink, letting the sourness glide over his palate and the alcohol slightly, soothingly burn him, before he said: "I can try. I do have instruments your people have not yet invented. Inertial devices, for example, that work under hyperdrive as well as at true velocity. Don't give up hope." He paused. "I grant you, we might fail. Then what will you do?"

The blunt question, which would have driven many women of his world to tears, made her rally. She lifted her head and said—haughtiness rang through the words: "Why, we will make the best of things, and I do not think we will do badly."

Well, he thought, *she's descended from nothing but survivor types. Her nature is to face trouble and whip it.*

"I'm sure you will succeed magnificently," he said. "You'll need time to grow used to our ways, and you may never feel quite easy in them, but—"

"What are your marriages like?" she asked.

"Uh?" Laure fitted his jaw back into place.

She was not drunk, he decided. A bit of drink, together with these surroundings, the lilting music, odours and pheromones in the air, had simply lowered her inhibitions. The huntress in her was set free, and at once attacked whatever had been most deeply perturbing her. The basic reticence remained. She looked straight at him, but she was fiery-faced, as she said:

"We ought to have had an equal number of men and women along on *Makt*. Had we known what was to happen, we would have done so. But now ten men shall have to find wives among foreigners. Do you think they will have much difficulty?"

"Uh, why no. I shouldn't think they will," he floundered. "They're obviously superior types, and then, being exotic— glamourous . . ."

"I speak not of amatory pleasure. But . . . what I overheard on Serieve, a time or two . . . did I miscomprehend? Are there truly women among you who do not bear children?"

"On the older planets, yes, that's not uncommon. Population control—"

"We shall have to stay on Serieve, then, or worlds like it." She sighed. "I had hoped we might go to the pivot of your civilization, where your real work is done and our children might become great."

Laure considered her. After a moment, he understood. Adapting to the uncountably many aliennesses of Kirkasant had been a long and cruel process. No blood line survived which did not do more than make up its own heavy losses. The will to reproduce was a requirement of existence. It, too, became an instinct.

He remembered that, while Kirkasant was not a very fertile planet, and today its population strained its resources, no one had considered reducing the birthrate. When someone on Serieve had asked why, Demring's folk had reacted strongly. The idea struck them as obscene. They didn't care for the notion of genetic modification or exogenetic growth either. And yet they were quite reasonable and noncompulsive about most other aspects of their culture.

Culture, Laure thought. *Yes. That's mutable. But you don't change your instincts; they're built into your chromosomes. Her people* must *have children.*

"Well," he said, "you can find women who want large families on the central planets, too. If anything, they'll be eager to marry your friends. They have a problem finding men who feel as they do, you see."

Graydal dazzled him with a smile and held out her glass. "Exchange?" she proposed.

"Hoy, you're way ahead of me." He evened the liquid levels. "Now."

They looked at each other throughout the little ceremony. He nerved himself to ask, "As for you women, do you necessarily have to marry within your ship?"

"No," she said. "It would depend on . . . whether any of your folk . . . might come to care for one of us."

"That I can guarantee!"

"I would like a man who travels," she murmured, "if I and the children could come along."

"Quite easy to arrange," Laure said.

She said in haste: "But we are buying grief, are we not? You told me perhaps you can find our planet for us."

"Yes. I hope, though, if we succeed, that won't be the last I see of you."

"Truly it won't."

They finished their drinks and went to dinner. *Jaccavrie* was also an excellent cook. And the choice of wines was considerable. What was said and laughed at over the table had no relevance to anyone but Laure and Graydal.

Except that, at the end, with immense and tender seriousness, she said: "If you want a cell sample from me . . . for analysis . . . you may have it."

He reached across the table and took her hand. "I wouldn't want you to do anything you might regret later," he said.

She shook her head. The tawny eyes never left him. Her voice was slow, faintly slurred, but bespoke complete awareness of what she was saying. "I have come to know you. For you to do this thing will be no violation."

Laure explained eagerly: "The process is simple and painless, as far as you're concerned. We can go right down to the lab. The computer operates everything. It'll give you an anaesthetic spray and remove a small sample of flesh, so small that tomorrow you won't be sure where the spot was. Of course, the analysis will take a long while. We don't have all possible equipment aboard. And the computer does have to devote most of her—most of its attention to piloting and interior work. But at the end, we'll be able to tell you—"

"Hush." Her smile was sleepy. "No matter. If you wish this,

that's enough. I ask only one thing."

"What?"

"Do not let a machine use the knife, or the needle, or whatever it is. I want you to do that yourself."

". . . Yes. Yonder is our home sky." The physicist Hirn Oran's son spoke slow and hushed. Cosmic interference seethed across his radio voice, nigh drowning it in Laure's and Graydal's earplugs.

"No," the Ranger said. "Not off there. We're already in it."

"What?" Silvery against rock, the two space-armoured figures turned to stare at him. He could not see their expressions behind the faceplates, but he could imagine how astonishment flickered above awe.

He paused, arranging words in his mind. The star noise in his receivers was like surf and fire. The landscape overwhelmed him.

Here was no simple airless planet. No planet is ever really simple, and this one had a stranger history than most. Eons ago it was apparently a subjovian, with a cloudy hydrohelium and methane atmosphere and an immense shell of ice and frozen gases around the core; for it orbited its sun at a distance of almost a billion and a half kilometres, and though that primary was bright, at this remove it could be little more than a spark.

Until stellar evolution—hastened, Laure believed, by an abnormal infall of cosmic material—took the star off the main sequence. It swelled, surface cooling to red but total output growing so monstrous that the inner planets were consumed. On the farther ones, like this, atmosphere fled into space. Ice melted; the world-ocean boiled; each time the pulsations of the sun reached a maximum, more vapour escaped. Now nothing remained except a ball of metal and rock, hardly larger than a terrestrial-type globe. As the pressure of the top layers was removed, frightful tectonic forces must have been liberated. Mountains—the younger ones with crags like sharp teeth, the older ones worn by meteorite and thermal erosion—rose from a cratered plain of gloomy stone. Currently at a minimum, but nonetheless immense, a full seven degrees across, blue core surrounded and dimmed by the tenuous ruddy atmosphere, the sun smouldered aloft.

Its furnace light was not the sole illumination. Another star was passing sufficiently near at the time that it showed a perceptible disc . . . in a stopped-down viewscreen, because no human eye could directly confront that electric cerulean intensity. The outsider was a B_8, newborn out of dust and gas, blazing with an intrinsic radiance of a hundred Sols.

Neither one helped in the shadows cast by the pinnacled upthrust which Laure's party was investigating. Flashcasters were necessary.

But more was to see overhead, astride the dark. Stars in thousands powdered the sky, brilliant with proximity. And they were the mere fringes of the cluster. It was rising as the planet turned, partly backgrounding and partly following the sun. Laure had never met a sight to compare. For the most part, the individuals he could pick out in that enormous spheroidal cloud of light were themselves red: long-lived dwarfs, dying giants like the one that brooded over him. But many glistened exuberant golden, emerald, sapphire. Some could not be older than the blue which wandered past and added its own harsh hue to this land. All those stars were studded through a soft glow that pervaded the entire cluster, a nacreous luminosity into which they faded and vanished, the fog wherein his companions had lost their home but which was a shining beauty to behold.

"You live in a wonder," Laure said.

Graydal moved towards him. She had had no logical reason to come down out of *Makt*'s orbit with him and Hirn. The idea was simply to break out certain large groundbased instruments that *Jaccavrie* carried, for study of their goal before travelling on. Any third party could assist. But she had laid her claim first, and none of her shipmates argued. They knew how often she and Laure were in each other's company.

"Wait until you reach our world," she said low. "Space is eldritch and dangerous. But once on Kirkasant— We will watch the sun go down in the Rainbow Desert; suddenly, in that thin air, night has come, our shimmering star-crowded night, and the auroras dance and whisper above the stark hills. We will see great flying flocks rise from dawn mists over the salt marshes, hear their wings thunder and their voices flute. We will stand on the battlements of Ey, under the banners of those very knights who long ago rid the land of the firearms, and watch the folk dance welcome to a new year—"

"If the navigator pleases," said Hirn, his voice sharpened

by an unadmitted dauntedness, "we will save our dreams for later and attend now to the means of realizing them. At present, we are supposed to choose a good level site for the observing apparatus. But, ah, Ranger Laure, may I ask you what you meant by saying we are already back in the Cloud Universe?"

Laure was not as annoyed to have Graydal interrupted as he might normally have been. She'd spoken of Kirkasant so often that he felt he had almost been there himself. Doubtless it had its glories, but by his standards it was a grim, dry, storm-scoured planet where he would not care to stay for long at a time. Of course, to her it was beloved home; and he wouldn't mind making occasional visits if— No, chaos take it, there was work on hand!

Part of his job was to make explanations. He said: "In your sense of the term, Physicist Hirn, the Cloud Universe does not exist."

The reply was curt through the static. "I disputed that point on Serieve already, with Vandange and others. And I resented their implication that we of *Makt* were either liars or incompetent observers."

"You're neither," Laure said quickly. "But communication had a double barrier on Serieve. First, an imperfect command of your language. Only on the way here, spending most of my time in contact with your crew, have I myself begun to feel a real mastery of Hobrokan. The second barrier, though, was in some ways more serious: Vandange's stubborn preconceptions, and your own."

"I was willing to be convinced."

"But you never got a convincing argument. Vandange was so dogmatically certain that what you reported having seen was impossible, that he didn't take a serious look at your report to see if it might have an orthodox explanation after all. You naturally got angry at this and cut the discussions off short. For your part, you had what you had always been taught was a perfectly good theory, which your experiences had confirmed. You weren't going to change your whole concept of physics just because the unlovable Ozer Vandange scoffed at it."

"But we were mistaken," Graydal said. "You've intimated as much, Daven, but never made your meaning clear."

"I wanted to see the actual phenomenon for myself, first,"

Laure said. "We have a proverb—so old that it's reputed to have originated on Earth—'It is a capital mistake to theorize in advance of the data.' But I couldn't help speculating, and what I see shows my speculations were along the right lines."

"Well?" Hirn challenged.

"Let's start with looking at the situation from your viewpoint," Laure suggested. "Your people spent millennia on Kirkasant. You lost every hint, except a few ambiguous traditions, that things might be different elsewhere. To you, it was natural that the night sky should be like a gently shining mist, and stars should crowd thickly around. When you developed the scientific method again, not many generations back, perforce you studied the universe you knew. Ordinary physics and chemistry, even atomistics and quantum theory, gave you no special problems. But you measured the distance of the visible stars as light-months—at most, a few light-years—after which they vanished in the foggy background. You measured the concentration of that fog, that dust and fluorescing gas. And you had no reason to suppose the interstellar medium was not equally dense everywhere. Nor had you any hint of receding galaxies.

"So your version of relativity made space sharply curved by the mass packed together throughout it. The entire universe was two or three hundred light-years across. Stars condensed and evolved—you could witness every stage of that—but in a chaotic fashion, with no particular overall structure. It's a wonder to me that you went on to gravities and hyperdrive. I wish I were scientist enough to appreciate how different some of the laws and constants must be in your physics. But you did plough ahead. I guess the fact you knew these things were possible was important to your success. Your scientists would keep fudging and finagling, in defiance of theoretical niceties, until they made something work."

"Um-m-m . . . as a matter of fact, yes," Hirn said in a slightly abashed tone. Graydal snickered.

"Well, then *Makt* lost her way, and emerged into the outer universe, which was totally strange," Laure said. "You had to account somehow for what you saw. Like any scientists, you stayed with accepted ideas as long as feasible—a perfectly correct principle which my people call the razor of Occam. I imagine that the notion of contiguous space-times with varying properties looks quite logical if you're used to thinking of a

universe with an extremely small radius. You may have been
puzzled as to how you managed to get out of one 'bubble' and
into the next, but I daresay you cobbled together a tentative
explanation."

"I did," Hirn said. "If we postulate a multidimensional—"

"Never mind," Laure said. "That's no longer needful. We
can account for the facts much more simply."

"How? I have been pondering it. I think I can grasp the idea
of a universe billions of light-years across, in which the stars
form galaxies. But our home space—"

"Is a dense star cluster. And as such, it has no definite
boundaries. That's what I meant by saying we are already in it.
In the thin verge, at least." Laure pointed to the diffuse,
jewelled magnificence that was rising higher above these wastes,
in the wake of the red and blue suns. "Yonder's the main body,
and Kirkasant is somewhere there. But this system here is asso-
ciated. I've checked proper motions and I know."

"I could have accepted some such picture while on Serieve,"
Hirn said. "But Vandange was so insistent that a star cluster
like this cannot be." Laure visualized the sneer behind his faceplate. "I thought that he, belonging to the master civilization,
would know whereof he spoke."

"He does. He's merely rather unimaginative," Laure said.
"You see, what we have here is a globular cluster. That's a
group made up of stars close together in a roughly spherical
volume of space. I'd guess you have a quarter million, packed
into a couple of hundred light-years' diameter.

"But globular clusters haven't been known like this one. The
ones we know lie mostly well off the galactic plane. The space
within them is much clearer than in the spiral arms, almost a
perfect vacuum. The individual members are red. Any normal
stars of greater than minimal mass have gone off the main
sequence long ago. The survivors are metal-poor. That's another
sign of extreme age. Heavy elements are formed in stellar
cores, you know, and spewed back into space. So it's the younger
suns, coalescing out of the enriched interstellar medium, that
contain a lot of metal. All in all, everything points to the
globular clusters being relics of an embryo stage in the galaxy's
life.

"Yours, however—! Dust and gas so thick that not even a
giant can see be seen across many parsecs. Plenty of main-

sequence stars, including blues which cannot be more than a few million years old, they burn out so fast. Spectra, not to mention planets your explorers visited, showing atomic abundances far skewed towards the high end of the periodic table. A background radiation too powerful for a man like me to dare take up permanent residence in your country.

"Such a cluster shouldn't be!"

"But it is," Graydal said.

Laure made bold to squeeze her hand, though little of that could pass through the gauntlets. "I'm glad," he answered.

"How do you explain the phenomenon?" Hirn asked.

"Oh, that's obvious . . now that I've seen the things and gathered some information on its path," Laure said. "An improbable situation, maybe unique, but not impossible. This cluster happens to have an extremely eccentric orbit around the galactic centre of mass. Once or twice a gigayear, it passes through the vast thick clouds that surround that region. By gravitation, it sweeps up immense quantities of stuff. Meanwhile, I suppose, perturbation causes some of its senior members to drift off. You might say it's periodically rejuvenated.

"At present, it's on its way out again. Hasn't quite left our spiral arm. It passed near the galactic midpoint just a short while back, cosmically speaking; I'd estimate less than fifty million years. The infall is still turbulent, still condensing out into new stars like that blue giant shining on us. Your home sun and its planets must be a product of an earlier sweep. But there've been twenty or thirty such since the galaxy formed, and each one of them was responsible for several generations of giant stars. So Kirkasant has a lot more heavy elements than the normal planet, even though it's not much younger than Earth. Do you follow me?"

"Hm-m-m . . . perhaps. I shall have to think." Hirn walked off, across the great tilted block on which the party stood, to its edge, where he stopped and looked down into the shadows below. They were deep and knife sharp. The mingled light of red and blue suns, stars, starfog played eerie across the stone land. Laure grew aware of what strangeness and what silence—under the hiss in his ears—pressed in on him.

Graydal must have felt the same, for she edged close until their armours clinked together. He would have liked to see her face. She said: "Do you truly believe we can enter that realm and conquer it?"

"I don't know," he said, slow and blunt. "The sheer number of stars may beat us."

"A large enough fleet could search them, one by one."

"If it could navigate. We have yet to find out whether that's possible."

"Suppose. Did you guess a quarter million suns in the cluster? Not all are like ours. Not even a majority. On the other coin side, with visibility as low as it is, space must be searched back and forth, light-year by light-year. We of *Makt* could die of eld before a single vessel chanced on Kirkasant."

"I'm afraid that's true."

"Yet an adequate number of ships, dividing the task, could find our home in a year or two."

"That would be unattainably expensive, Graydal."

He thought he sensed her stiffening. "I've come on this before," she said coldly, withdrawing from his touch. "In your Commonalty they count the cost and the profit first. Honour, adventure, simple charity must run a poor second."

"Be reasonable," he said. "Cost represents labour, skill, and resources. The gigantic fleet that would go looking for Kirkasant must be diverted from other jobs. Other people would suffer need as a result. Some might suffer sharply."

"Do you mean a civilization as big, as productive as yours could not spare that much effort for a while without risking disaster?"

She's quick on the uptake, Laure thought. *Knowing what machine technology can do on her single impoverished world, she can well guess what it's capable of with millions of planets to draw on. But how can I make her realize that matters aren't that simple?*

"Please, Graydal," he said. "Won't you believe I'm working for you? I've come this far, and I'll go as much farther as need be, if something doesn't kill us."

He heard her gulp. "Yes. I offer apology. *You* are different."

"Not really. I'm a typical Commonalty member. Later, maybe, I can show you how our civilization works, and what an odd problem in political economy we've got if Kirkasant is to be rediscovered. But first we have to establish that locating it is physically possible. We have to make long-term observations from here, and then enter those mists, and— One trouble at a time, I beg you!"

She laughed gently. "Indeed, my friend. And you will find a way." The mirth faded. It had never been strong. "Won't you?" The reflection of clouded stars glistened on her faceplate like tears.

Blindness was not dark. It shone.

Standing on the bridge, amidst the view of space, Laure saw nimbus and thunderheads. They piled in cliffs, they eddied and streamed, their colour was a sheen of all colours overlying white—mother-of-pearl—but here and there they darkened with shadows and grottoes; here and there they glowed dull red as they reflected a nearby sun. For the stars were scattered about in their myriads, dominantly ruby and ember, some yellow or candent, green or blue. The nearest were clear to the eye, a few showing tiny discs, but the majority were fuzzy glows rather than lightpoints. Such shimmers grew dim with distance until the mist engulfed them entirely and nothing remained but mist.

A crackling noise beat out of that rolling formlessness, like flames. Energies pulsed through his marrow. He remembered the old, old myth of the Yawning Gap, where fire and ice arose and out of them the Nine Worlds, which were doomed in the end to return to fire and ice; and he shivered.

"Illusion," said *Jaccavrie*'s voice out of immensity.

"What?" Laure started. It was as if a mother goddess had spoken.

She chuckled. Whether deity or machine, she had the great strength of ordinariness in her. "You're rather transparent to an observer who knows you well," she said. "I could practically read your mind."

Laure swallowed. "The sight, well, a big, marvellous, dangerous thing, maybe unique in the galaxy. Yes, I admit I'm impressed."

"We have much to learn here."

"Have you been doing so?"

"At a near-capacity rate, since we entered the denser part of the cluster." *Jaccavrie* shifted to primness. "If you'd been less immersed in discussions with the Kirkasanter navigation officer, you might have got running reports from me."

"Destruction!" Laure swore. "I was studying her notes from their trip outbound, trying to get some idea of what configuration to look for, once we've learned how to make allowances for what this material does to starlight— Never mind. We'll have our conference right now, just as you requested. What'd you mean by 'an illusion'?"

"The view outside," answered the computer. "The concentration of mass is not really as many atoms per cubic centimetre as would be found in a vaporous planetary atmosphere. It is only that, across light-years, their absorption and reflection effects are cumulative. The gas and dust do, indeed, swirl, but not with anything like the velocity we think we perceive. That is due to our being under hyperdrive. Even at the very low pseudospeed at which we are feeling our way, we pass swiftly through varying densities. Space itself is not actually shining; excited atoms are fluorescing. Nor does space roar at you. What you hear is the sound of radiation counters and other instruments which I've activated. There are no real tangible currents working on our hull, making it quiver. But when we make quantum microjumps across strong interstellar magnetic fields, and those fields vary according to an extraordinarily complex pattern, we're bound to interact noticeably with them.

"Admittedly the stars are far thicker than appears. My instruments can detect none beyond a few parsecs. But what data I've gathered of late leads me to suspect the estimate of a quarter million total is conservative. To be sure, most are dwarfs—"

"Come off that!" Laure barked. "I don't need you to explain what I knew the minute I saw this place."

"You need to be drawn out of your fantasizing," *Jaccavrie* said. "Though you recognize your daydreams for what they are, you can't afford them. Not now."

Laure tensed. He wanted to order the view turned off, but checked himself, wondered if the robot followed that chain of his impulses too, and said in a harshened voice: "When you go academic on me like that, it means you're postponing news you don't want to give me. We have troubles."

"We can soon have them, at any rate," *Jaccavrie* said. "My advice is to turn back at once."

"We can't navigate," Laure deduced. Though it was not unexpected, he nonetheless felt smitten.

"No. That is, I'm having difficulties already, and conditions ahead of us are demonstrably worse."

"What's the matter?"

"Optical methods are quite unsuitable. We knew that from the experience of the Kirkasanters. But nothing else works, either. You recall, you and I discussed the possibility of identifying supergiant stars through the clouds and using them for beacons. Though their light be diffused and absorbed, they should produce other effects—they should be powerful neutrino sources, for instance—that we could use."

"Don't they?"

"Oh, yes. But the effects are soon smothered. Too much else is going on. Too many neutrinos from too many different sources, to name one thing. Too many magnetic effects. The stars are so close together, you see; and so many of them are double, triple, quadruple, hence revolving rapidly and twisting the force lines; and irradiation keeps a goodly fraction of the interstellar medium in the plasma state. Thus we get electromagnetic action of every sort, plus synchrotron and betatron radiation, plus nuclear collisions, plus—"

"Spare me the complete list," Laure broke in. "Just say the noise level is too high for your instruments."

"And for any instruments that I can extrapolate as buildable," *Jaccavrie* replied. "The precision their filters would require seems greater than the laws of atomistics would allow."

"What about your inertial system? Bollixed up, too?"

"It's beginning to be. That's why I asked you to come take a good look at what's around us and what we're headed into, while you listen to my report." The robot was not built to know fear, but Laure wondered if she didn't spring back to pedantry as a refuge: "Inertial navigation would work here at kinetic velocities. But we can't traverse parsecs except hyperdrive. Inertial and gravitational mass being identical, too rapid a change of gravitational potential will tend to cause uncontrollable precession and nutation. We can compensate for that in normal parts of space. But not here. With so many stars so closely packed, moving among each other on paths too complex for me to calculate, the variation rate is becoming too much."

"In short," Laure said slowly, "if we go deeper into this stuff, we'll be flying blind."

"Yes. Just as *Makt* did."

"We can get out into clear space any time, can't we? You can follow a more or less straight line till we emerge."

"True. I don't like the hazards. The cosmic ray background is increasing considerably."

"You have screen fields."

"But I'm considering the implications. Those particles have to originate somewhere. Magnetic acceleration will only account for a fraction of their intensity. Hence the rate of nova production in this cluster, and of supernovae in the recent past, must be enormous. This in turn indicates vast numbers of lesser bodies—neutron stars, rogue planets, large meteoroids, thick dust banks—things that might be undetectable before we blunder into them."

Laure smiled at her unseen scanner. "If anything goes wrong, you'll react fast," he said. "You always do."

"I can't guarantee we won't run into trouble I can't deal with."

"Can you estimate the odds on that for me?"

Jaccavrie was silent. The air sputtered and sibilated. Laure found his vision drowning in the starfog. He needed a minute to realize he had not been answered. "Well?" he said.

"The parameters are too uncertain." Overtones had departed from her voice. "I can merely say that the probability of disaster is high in comparison to the value for travel through normal regions of the galaxy."

"Oh, for chaos' sake!" Laure's laugh was uneasy. "That figure is almost too small to measure. We knew before we entered this nebula that we'd be taking a risk. Now what about coherent radiation from natural sources?"

"My judgment is that the risk is out of proportion to the gain," *Jaccavrie* said. "At best, this is a place for scientific study. You've other work to do. Your basic—and dangerous—fantasy is that you can satisfy the emotional cravings of a few semi-barbarians."

Anger sprang up in Laure. He gave it cold shape: "My order was that you report on coherent radiation."

Never before had he pulled the rank of his humanness on her.

She said like dead metal: "I have detected some in the visible and short infra-red, where certain types of star excite pseudo-quasar processes in the surrounding gas. It is dissipated as fast as any other light."

"The radio bands are clear?"

"Yes, of that type of wave, although—"

"Enough. We'll proceed as before, towards the centre of the cluster: Cut this view and connect me with *Makt*."

The hazy suns vanished. Laure was alone in a metal compartment. He took a seat and glowered at the outercom screen before him. What had got into *Jaccavrie*, anyway? She'd been making her disapproval of this quest more and more obvious over the last few days. She wanted him to turn around, report to HQ, and leave the Kirkasanters there for whatever they might be able to make of themselves in a lifetime's exile. Well . . . her judgments were always conditioned by the fact that she was a Ranger vessel, built for Ranger work. But couldn't she see that his duty, as well as his desire, was to help Graydal's people?

The screen flickered. The two ships were so differently designed that it was hard for them to stay in phase for any considerable time, and thus hard to receive the modulation imposed on space-pulses. After a while the image steadied to show a face. "I'll switch you to Captain Demring," the communications officer said at once. In his folk, such lack of ceremony was as revealing of strain as haggardness and dark-rimmed eyes.

The image wavered again and became the Old Man's. He was in his cabin, which had direct audiovisual connections, and the background struck Laure anew with outlandishness. What history had brought forth the artistic conventions of that bright-coloured, angular-figured tapestry? What song was being sung on the player, in what language, and on what scale? What was the symbolism behind the silver mask on the door?

Worn but indomitable, Demring looked forth and said, "Peace between us. What occasions this call?"

"You should know what I've learned," Laure said. "Uh, can we make this a three-way with your navigator?"

"Why?" The question was machine steady.

"Well, that is, her duties—"

"She is to help carry out decisions," Demring said. "She does not make them. At maximum, she can offer advice in discussion." He waited before adding, with a thrust: "And you have been having a great deal of discussion already with my daughter, Ranger Laure."

"No . . . I mean, yes, but—" The younger man rallied. He
did have psych training to call upon, although its use had
not yet become reflexive in him. "Captain," he said, "Graydal
has been helping me understand your ethos. Our two cultures
have to see what each other's basics are if they're to cooperate,
and that process begins right here, among these ships. Graydal
can makes things clearer to me, and I believe grasps my intent
better, than anyone else of your crew."

"Why is that?" Demring demanded.

Laure suppressed pique at his arrogance—he was her father
—and attempted a smile. "Well, sir, we've got acquainted to
a degree, she and I. We can drop formality and just be friends."

"That is not necessarily desirable," Demring said.

Laure recollected that, throughout the human species, sexual
customs are among the most variable. And the most emotionally
charged. He put himself inside Demring's prejudices and said
with what he hoped was the right slight note of indignation:
"I assure you nothing improper has occurred."

"No, no." The Kirkasanter made a brusque, chopping gesture.
"I trust her. And you, I am sure. Yet I must warn that close
ties between members of radically different societies can prove
disastrous to everyone involved."

Laure might have sympathized as he thought, *He's afraid
to let down his mask—is that why their art uses the motif so
much?—but underneath, he is a father worrying about his little
girl.* He felt too harassed. First his computer, now this! He said
coolly, "I don't believe our cultures are that alien. They're both
rational-technological, which is a tremendous similarity to begin
with. But haven't we got off the subject? I wanted you to hear
the findings this ship has made."

Demring relaxed. The unhuman universe he could cope with.
"Proceed at will, Ranger."

When he had heard Laure out, though, he scowled, tugged
his beard, and said without trying to hide distress: "Thus we
have no chance of finding Kirkasant by ourselves."

"Evidently not," Laure said. "I'd hoped that one of my
modern locator systems would work in this cluster. If so, we
could have zigzagged rapidly between the stars, mapping them,
and had a fair likelihood of finding the group you know within

months. But as matters stand, we can't establish an accurate enough grid, and we have nothing to tie any such grid to. Once a given star disappears in the fog, we can't find it again. Not even by straight-line backtracking, because we don't have the navigational feedback to keep on a truly straight line."

"Lost." Demring stared down at his hands, clenched on the desk before him. When he looked up again, the bronze face was rigid with pain. "I was afraid of this," he said. "It is why I was reluctant to come back at all. I feared the effect of disappointment on my crew. By now you must know one major respect in which we differ from you. To us, home, kinfolk, ancestral graves are not mere pleasures. They are an important part of our identities. We are prepared to explore and colonize, but not to be totally cut off." He straightened in his seat and turned the confession into a strategic datum by finishing dry-voiced: "Therefore, the sooner we leave this degree of familiarity behind us and accept with physical renunciation the truth of what has happened to us—the sooner we get out of this cluster —the better for us."

"No," Laure said. "I've given a lot of thought to your situation. There *are* ways to navigate here."

Demring did not show surprise. He, too, must have dwelt on contingencies and possibilities. Laure sketched them nevertheless:

"Starting from outside the cluster, we can establish a grid of artificial beacons. I'd guess fifty thousand, in orbit around selected stars, would do. If each has its distinctive identifying signal, a spaceship can locate herself and lay a course. I can imagine several ways to make them. You want them to emit something that isn't swamped by natural noise. Hyperdrive drones, shuttling automatically back and forth, would be detectable in a light-year's radius. Coherent radio broadcasters on the right bands should be detectable at the same distance or better. Since the stars hereabouts are only light-weeks or light-months apart, an electromagnetic network wouldn't take long to complete its linkups. No doubt a real engineer, turned loose on the problem, would find better answers than these."

"I know," Demring said. "We on *Makt* have discussed the matter and reached similar conclusions. The basic obstacle is the work involved, first in producing that number of beacons, then—more significantly—in planting them. Many man-years, much shipping, must go to that task, if it is to be accomplished in a reasonable time."

"Yes."

"I like to think," said Demring, "that the clans of Hobrok would not haggle over who was to pay the cost. But I have talked with men on Serieve. I have taken heed of what Graydal does and does not relay of her conversations with you. Yours is a mercantile civilization."

"Not exactly," Laure said. "I've tried to explain—"

"Don't bother. We shall have the rest of our lives to learn about your Commonalty. Shall we turn about, now, and end this expedition?"

Laure winced at the scorn but shook his head. "No, best we continue. We can make extraordinary findings here. Things that'll attract scientists. And with a lot of ships buzzing around—"

Demring's smile had no humour. "Spare me, Ranger. There will never be that many scientists come avisiting. And they will never plant beacons through the cluster. Why should they? The chance of one of their vessels stumbling on Kirkasant is negligible. They will be after unusual stars and planets, information on magnetic fields and plasmas and whatever else is readily studied. Not even the anthropologists will have any strong impetus to search out our world. They have many others to work on, equally strange to them, far more accessible."

"I have my own obligations," Laure said. "It was a long trip here. Having made it, I should recoup some of the cost to my organization by gathering as much data as I can before turning home."

"No matter the cost to my people?" Demring said slowly. "That they see their own sky around them, but nonetheless are exiles—for weeks longer?"

Laure lost his patience. "Withdraw if you like, Captain," he snapped. "I've no authority to stop you. But I'm going on. To the middle of the cluster, in fact."

Demring retorted in a cold flare: "Do you hope to find something that will make you personally rich, or only personally famous?" He reined himself in at once. "This is no place for impulsive acts. Your vessel is undoubtedly superior to mine. I am not certain, either, that *Makt*'s navigational equipment is equal to finding that advanced base where we must refuel her. If you continue, I am bound in simple prudence to accompany you, unless the risks you take become gross. But I urge that we confer again."

"Any time, Captain." Laure cut his circuit.

He sat then, for a while, fuming. The culture barrier couldn't be that high. Could it? Surely the Kirkasanters were neither so stupid nor so perverse as not to see what he was trying to do for them. Or were they? Or was it his fault? He'd concentrated more on learning about them than on teaching them about him. Still, Graydal, at least, should know him by now.

The ship sensed an incoming call and turned Laure's screen back on. And there she was. Gladness lifted in him until he saw her expression.

She said without greeting, winter in the golden gaze: "We officers have just been given a playback of your conversation with my father. What is your" (outphasing occurred, making the image into turbulence, filling the voice with staticlike ugliness, but he thought he recognized) "intention?" The screen blanked.

"Maintain contact," Laure told *Jaccavrie*.

"Not easy in these gravitic fields," the ship said.

Laure jumped to his feet, cracked fist in palm, and shouted, "Is everything trying to brew trouble for me? Bring her back or so help me, I'll scrap you!"

He got a picture again, though it was blurred and wavery and the voice was streaked with buzzes and whines, as if he called to Graydal across light-years of swallowing starfog. She said—was it a little more kindly?—"We're puzzled. I was deputed to inquire further, since I am most . . . familiar . . . with you. If our two craft can't find Kirkasant by themselves, why are we going on?"

Laure understood her so well, after the watches when they talked, dined, drank, played music, laughed together, that he saw the misery behind her armour. For her people—for herself—this journey among mists was crueller than it would have been for him had he originated here. He belonged to a civilization of travellers; to him, no one planet could be the land of lost content. But in them would always stand a certain ridge purple against sunset, marsh at dawn, ice cloud walking over windgnawed desert crags, ancient castle, wingbeat in heaven . . . and always, always, the dear bright nights that no other place in man's universe knew.

They were a warrior folk. They would not settle down to be pitied; they would forge something powerful for themselves in their exile. But he was not helping them forget their uprootedness.

Thus he almost gave her his true reason. He halted in time and, instead, explained in more detail what he had told Captain Demring. His ship represented a considerable investment, to be amortized over her service life. Likewise, with his training, did he. The time he had spent coming hither was, therefore, equivalent to a large sum of money. And to date, he had nothing to show for that expense except confirmation of a fairly obvious guess about the nature of Kirkasant's surroundings.

He had broad discretion—while he was in service. But he could be discharged. He would be, if his career, taken as a whole, didn't seem to be returning a profit. In this particular case, the profit would consist of detailed information about a unique environment. You could prorate that in such terms as: scientific knowledge, with its potentialities for technological progress; spacefaring experience; public relations—

Graydal regarded him in a kind of horror. "You cannot mean . . . we go on . . . merely to further your private ends," she whispered. Interference gibed at them both.

"No!" Laure protested. "Look, only look, I want to help you. But you, too, have to justify yourselves economically. You're the reason I came so far in the first place. If you're to work with the Commonalty, and it's to help you make a fresh start, you have to show that that's worth the Commonalty's while. Here's where we start proving it. By going on. Eventually, by bringing them a bookful of knowledge they didn't have before."

Her gaze upon him calmed but remained aloof. "Do you think that is right?"

"It's the way things are, anyhow," he said. "Sometimes I wonder if my attempts to explain my people to you haven't glided right off your brain."

"You have made it clear that they think of nothing but their own good," she said thinly.

"If so, I've failed to make anything clear." Laure slumped in his chair web. Some days hit a man with one club after the next. He forced himself to sit erect again and say:

"We have a different ideal from you. Or no, that's not correct. We have the same set of ideals. The emphases are different. You believe the individual ought to be free and ought to help his fellowman. We do, too. But you make the service basic, you give it priority. We have the opposite way. You give a man, or a woman, duties to the clan and the country from birth. But you protect his individuality by frowning on slavishness and on anyone who doesn't keep a strictly private side to his life. We give a person freedom, within a loose framework of common-sense prohibitions. And then we protect his social aspect by frowning on greed, selfishness, callousness."

"I know," she said. "You have—"

"But maybe you haven't thought how we *must* do it that way," he pleaded. "Civilization's got too big out there for anything but freedom to work. The Commonalty isn't a government. How would you govern ten million planets? It's a private, voluntary, mutual-benefit society, open to anyone anywhere who meets the modest standards. It maintains certain services for its members, like my own space rescue work. The services are widespread and efficient enough that local planetary governments also like to hire them. But I don't speak for my civilization. Nobody does. You've made a friend of me. But how do you make friends with ten million times a billion individuals?"

"You've told me before," she said.

And it didn't register. Not really. Too new an idea for you, I suppose, Laure thought. He ignored her remark and went on:

"In the same way, we can't have a planned interstellar economy. Planning breaks down under the sheer mass of detail when it's attempted for a single continent. History is full of cases. So we rely on the market, which operates as automatically as gravitation. Also as efficiently, as impersonally, and sometimes as ruthlessly—but we didn't make this universe. We only live in it."

He reached out his hands, as if to touch her through the distance and the distortion. "Can't you see? I'm not able to help your plight. Nobody is. No individual quadrillionaire, no foundation, no government, no consortium could pay the cost of finding your home for you. It's not a matter of lacking charity It's a matter of lacking resources for that magnitude of effort. The resources are divided among too many people, each of whom has his own obligations to meet first.

"Certainly, if each would contribute a pittance, you could buy your fleet. But the tax mechanism for collecting that pittance doesn't exist and can't be made to exist. As for free-will donations—how do we get your message across to an entire civilization, that big, that diverse, that busy with its own affairs?—which include cases of need far more urgent than yours.

"Graydal, we're not greedy where I come from. We're helpless."

She studied him at length. He wondered, but could not see through the ripplings, what emotions passed across her face. Finally she spoke, not altogether ungently, though helmeted again in the reserve of her kindred, and he could not hear anything of it through the buzzings except: ". . . proceed, since we must. For a while, anyhow. Good watch, Ranger."

The screen blanked. This time he couldn't make the ship repair the connection for him.

At the heart of the great cluster, where the nebula was so thick as to be a nearly featureless glow, pearl-hued and shot with rainbows, the stars were themselves so close that thousands could be seen. The spaceships crept forward like frigates on unknown seas of ancient Earth. For here was more than fog; here were shoals, reefs, and riptides. Energies travailed in the plasma. Drifts of dust, loose planets, burnt-out suns lay in menace behind the denser clouds. Twice *Makt* would have met catastrophe had not *Jaccavrie* sensed the danger with keener instruments and cried a warning to sheer off.

After Demring's subsequent urgings had failed, Graydal came aboard in person to beg Laure that he turn homeward. That she should surrender her pride to such an extent bespoke how worn down she and her folk were. "What are we gaining worth the risk?" she asked shakenly.

"We're proving that this is a treasure house of absolutely unique phenomena," he answered. He was also hollowed, partly from the long travel and the now constant tension, partly from the half estrangement between him and her. He tried to put enthusiasm in his voice. "Once we've reported, expeditions are certain to be organized. I'll bet the foundations of two or three whole new sciences will get laid here."

"I know. Everything astronomical, in abundance, close together and interacting." Her shoulders drooped. "But our task isn't research. We can go back now, we could have gone back already, and carried enough details with us. Why do we not?"

14

"I want to investigate several planets yet, on the ground, in different systems," he told her. "Then we'll call a halt."

"What do they matter to you?"

"Well, local stellar spectra are freakish. I want to know if the element abundances in solid bodies correspond."

She stared at him. "I do not understand you," she said. "I thought I did, but I was wrong. You have no compassion. You led us, you lured us so far in that we can't escape without your ship for a guide. You don't care how tired and tormented we are. You can't, or won't, understand why we are anxious to live."

"I am myself," he tried to grin. "I enjoy the process."

The dark head shook. "I said you won't understand. We do not fear death for ourselves. But most of us have not yet had children. We do fear death for our bloodlines. We *need* to find a home, forgetting Kirkasant, and begin our families. You, though, you keep us on this barren search—why? For your own glory?"

He should have explained then. But the strain and weariness in him snapped: "You accepted my leadership. That makes me responsible for you, and I can't be responsible if I don't have command. You can endure another couple of weeks. That's all it'll take."

And she should have answered that she knew his motives were good and wished simply to hear his reasons. But being the descendant of hunters and soldiers, she clicked heels together and flung back at him: "Very well, Ranger. I shall convey your word to my captain."

She left, and did not again board *Jaccavrie*.

Later, after a sleepless "night", Laure said, "Put me through to *Makt*'s navigator."

"I wouldn't advise that," said the woman-voice of his ship.

"Why not?"

"I presume you want to make amends. Do you know how she —or her father, or her young male shipmates that must be attracted to her—how they will react? They are alien to you, and under intense strain."

"They're human!"

Engines pulsed. Ventilators whispered. "Well?" said Laure.

"I'm not designed to compute about emotions, except on an elementary level," *Jaccavrie* said. "But please recollect the diver-

sity of mankind. On Reith, for example, ordinary peaceful men
can fall into literally murderous rages. It happens so often
that violence under those circumstances is not a crime in their
law. A Talatto will be patient and cheerful in adversity, up to
a certain point: after which he quits striving, contemplates
his God, and waits to die. You can think of other cultures. And
they are within the ambience of the Commonalty. How foreign
might not the Kirkasanters be?"

"Um-m-m—"

"I suggest you obtrude your presence on them as little as
possible. That makes for the smallest probability of provoking
some unforeseeable outburst. Once our task is completed, once
we are bound home, the stress will be removed and you can
safely behave towards them as you like."

"Well . . . you may be right." Laure stared dull-eyed at a bulkhead. "I don't know. I just don't know."

Before long, he was too busy to fret much. *Jaccavrie* went at
his direction, finding planetary systems that belonged to various
stellar types. In each, he landed on an airless body, took analytical readings and mineral samples, and gave the larger worlds
a cursory inspection from a distance.

He did not find life. Not anywhere. He had expected that. In
fact, he was confirming his whole guess about the inmost part
of the cluster.

Here gravitation had concentrated dust and gas till the rate
of star production became unbelievable. Each time the cluster
passed through the clouds around galactic centre and took on a
new load of material, there must have been a spate of supernovae, several per century for a million years or more. He could
not visualize what fury had raged: he scarcely dared put his
estimate in numbers. Probably radiation had sterilized every
abode of life for fifty light-years around. (Kirkasant must, therefore, lie farther out—which fitted in with what he had been
told, that the interstellar medium was much denser in this
core region than in the neighbourhood of the vanished world.)

Nuclei had been cooked in stellar interiors, not the two, three,
four star-generations which have preceded the majority of the
normal galaxy—here, a typical atom might well have gone
through a dozen successive supernova explosions. Transformation built on transformation. Hydrogen and helium remained

the commonest elements, but only because of overwhelming initial abundance. Otherwise the lighter substances had mostly become rare. Planets were like nothing ever known before. Giant ones did not have thick shells of frozen water, nor did smaller ones have extensive silicate crusts. Carbon, oxygen, nitrogen, sodium, aluminium, calcium were all but lost among ... iron, gold, mercury, tungsten, bismuth, uranium and transuranics— On some little spheres Laure dared not land. They radiated too fiercely. A heavily armoured robot might some day set foot on them, but never a living organism.

The crew of *Makt* didn't offer to help him. Irrational in his hurt, he didn't ask them. *Jaccavrie* could carry on any essential communication with their captain and navigator. He toiled until he dropped, woke, fuelled his body, and went back to work. Between stars, he made detailed analyses of his samples. That was tricky enough to keep his mind off Graydal. Minerals like these could have formed nowhere but in this witchy realm.

Finally the ships took orbit around a planet that had atmosphere. "Do you indeed wish to make entry there?" the computer asked. "I would not recommend it."

"You never recommend anything I want to do," Laure grunted. "I know air adds an extra factor to reckon with. But I want to get some idea of element distribution at the surface of objects like that." He rubbed bloodshot eyes. "It'll be the last. Then we go home."

"As you wish." Did the artificial voice actually sigh? "But after this long a time in space, you'll have to batten things down for an aerodynamic landing."

"No, I won't. I'm taking the sled as usual. You'll stay put."

"You are being reckless. This isn't an airless globe where I can orbit right above the mountaintops and see everything that might happen to you. Why, if I haven't misgauged, the ionosphere is so charged that the sled radio can't reach me."

"Nothing's likely to go wrong," Laure said. "But should it, you can't be spared. The Kirkasanters need you to conduct them safely out."

"I—"

"You heard your orders." Laure proceeded to discuss certain basic precautions. Not that he felt they were necessary. His objective looked peaceful—dry, sterile, a stone spinning around a star.

Nevertheless, when he departed the main hatch and gunned his gravity sled to kill velocity, the view caught at his breath.

Around him reached the shining fog. Stars and stars were caught in it, illuminating caverns and tendrils, aureoled with many-coloured fluorescences. Even as he looked, one such point, steely blue, multiplied its brilliance until the intensity hurt his eyes. Another nova. Every stage of stellar evolution was so richly represented that it was as if time itself had been compressed—cosmos, what an astrophysical laboratory!

(For unmanned instruments, as a general rule. Human flesh couldn't stand many months in a stretch of the cosmic radiation that sleeted through these spaces, the synchrotron and betatron and Cerenkov quanta that boiled from particles hurled in the gas across the intertwining magnetism of atoms and suns. Laure kept glancing at the cumulative exposure meter on his left wrist.)

The solar disc was large and lurid orange. Despite thermostating in the sled, Laure felt its heat strike at him through the bubble and his own armour. A stepdown viewer revealed immense prominences licking flame-tongues across the sky, and a heartstoppingly beautiful corona. A Type K shouldn't be that spectacular, but there were no normal stars in sight—not with this element distribution and infall.

Once the planet he was approaching had been farther out. But friction with the nebula, over gigayears, was causing it to spiral inward. Surface temperature wasn't yet excessive, about 50° C., because the atmosphere was thin, mainly noble gases. The entire world hadn't sufficient water to fill a decent lake. It rolled before him as a gloom little relieved by the reddish blots of gigantic dust storms. Refracted light made its air a fiery ring.

His sled struck that atmosphere, and for a while he was busy amidst thunder and shudder, helping the autopilot bring the small craft down. In the end, he hovered above a jumbled plain. Mountains bulked bare on the near horizon. The rock was black and brown and darkly gleaming. The sun stood high in a deep purple heaven. He checked with an induction probe, confirmed that the ground was solid—in fact, incredibly hard—and landed.

When he stepped out, weight caught at him. The planet had less diameter than the least of those on which men live, but was so dense that gravity stood at 1.22 standard G. An unexpec-

tedly strong wind shoved at him. Though thin, the air was
moving fast. He heard it wail through his helmet. From afar
came a rumble, and a quiver entered his boots and bones. Landslide? Earthquake? Unseen volcano? He didn't know what was
or was not possible here. Nor, he suspected, did the most expert
planetologist. Worlds like this had not hitherto been trodden.

Radiation from the ground was higher than he liked. Better
do his job quickly. He lugged forth apparatus. A power drill
for samples—he set it up and let it work while he assembled a
pyroanalyser and fed it a rock picked off the chaotic terrain.
Crumbled between alloy jaws, flash heated to vapour, the mineral
gave up its fundamental composition to the optical and mass
spectrographs. Laure studied the printout and nodded in satisfaction. The presence of atmosphere hadn't changed matters.
This place was loaded with heavy metals and radioactives. He'd
need a picture of molecular and crystalline structures before
being certain that they were as easily extractable as he'd found
them to be on the other planets; but he had no reason to doubt
it.

Well, he thought, aware of hunger and aching feet, *let's relax
awhile in the cab, catch a meal and a nap, then go check a few
other spots, just to make sure they're equally promising; and
then—*

The sky exploded.

He was on his belly, faceplate buried in arms against that flash,
before his conscious mind knew what had happened. Rangers
learn about nuclear weapons. When, after a minute, no shock
wave had hit him, no sound other than a rising wind, he dared
sit up and look.

The sky had turned white. The sun was no longer like an
orange lantern but molten brass. He couldn't squint anywhere
near it. Radiance crowded upon him, heat mounted even as
he climbed erect. *Nova,* he thought in his rocking reality, and
caught Graydal to him for the moment he was to become a wisp
of gas.

But he remained alive, alone, on a plain that now shimmered
with light and mirage. The wind screamed louder still. He felt
how it pushed him, and how the mass of the planet pulled, and
how his mouth was dry and his muscles tautened for a leap.
The brilliance pained his eyes, but was not unendurable behind

a self-adapting faceplate and did not seem to be growing greater. The infra-red brought forth sweat on his skin, but he was not being baked.

Steadiness came. Something almighty strange was happening. It hadn't killed him yet, though. As a check, with no hope of making contact, he tuned his radio. Static brawled in his ear-plugs.

His heart thudded. He couldn't tell whether he was afraid or exhilarated. He was, after all, quite a young man. But the coolness of his training came upon him. He didn't stop feeling. Wildness churned beneath self-control. But he did methodically begin to collect his equipment and to reason while he acted.

Not a nova burst. Main sequence stars don't go nova. They don't vary in seconds, either . . . but then, every star around here is abnormal. Perhaps, if I'd checked the spectrum of this one, I'd have seen indications that it was about to move into another phase of a jagged output cycle. Or perhaps I wouldn't have known what the indications meant. Who's studied astrophysics in circumstances like these?

What had occurred might be akin to the Wolf-Rayet phenomenon, he thought. The stars around him did not evolve along ordinary lines. They had strange compositions to start with. And then matter kept falling into them, changing that composition, increasing their masses. That must produce instability. Each spectrum he had taken in this heart of the cluster showed enormous turbulence in the surface layers. So did the spots, flares, prominences, coronas he had seen. Well, the turbulence evidently went deeper than the photospheres. Actual stellar cores and their nuclear furnaces might be affected. Probably every local sun was a violent variable.

Even in the less dense regions, stars must have peculiar careers. The sun of Kirkasant had apparently been stable for five thousand years—or several million, more likely, since the planet had well-developed native life. But who could swear it would stay thus? Destruction! The place had to be found, had to, so that the people could be evacuated if need arose. You can't let little children fry—

Laure checked his radiation meter. The needle climbed ominously fast up the dial. Yonder sun was spitting X-rays, in appreciable quantity, and the planet had no ozone layer to block them. He'd be dead if he didn't get to shelter—for choice, his ship and her forcescreens—before the ions arrived. Despite its density, the globe had no magnetic field to speak of, either, to ward them off. Probably the core was made of stuff like osmium and uranium. Such a weird blend might well be solid rather than molten. *I don't know about that. I do know I'd better get my tail out of here.*

The wind yelled. It began driving ferrous dust against him, borne from somewhere else. He saw the particles scud in darkling whirls and heard them click on his helmet. Doggedly, he finished loading his gear. When at last he entered the sled cab and shut the air lock, his vehicle was trembling under the blast and the sun was reddened and dimmed by haze.

He started the motor and lifted. No sense in resisting the wind. He was quite happy to be blown towards the night side. Meanwhile he'd gain altitude, then get above the storm, collect orbital velocity and—

He never knew what happened. The sled was supposedly able to ride out more vicious blows than any this world could produce. But who could foretell what this world was capable of? The atmosphere, being thin, developed high velocities. Perhaps the sudden increased irradiation had triggered paroxysm in a cyclone cell. Perhaps the dust, which was conductive, transferred energy into such a vortex at a greater rate than one might believe. Laure wasn't concerned about meteorological theory.

He was concerned with staying alive, when an instant blindness clamped down upon him with a shriek that nigh tore the top off his skull, and he was whirled like a leaf and cast against a mountainside.

The event was too fast for awareness, for anything but reaction. His autopilot and he must somehow have got some control. The crash ruined the sled, ripped open its belly, scattered its cargo, but did not crumple the cab section. Shock harness kept the man from serious injury. He was momentarily unconscious, but came back with no worse than an aching body and blood in his mouth.

Wind hooted. Dust went hissing and scouring. The sun was a dim red disc, though from time to time a beam of pure fire struck through the storm and blazed off metalic cliffsides.

Laure fumbled with his harness and stumbled out. Half seen, the slope on which he stood caught at his feet with cragginess. He had to take cover. The beta particles would arrive at any moment, the protons within hours, and they bore his death.

He was dismayed to learn the stowed equipment was gone. He dared not search for it. Instead, he made his clumsy way into the murk.

He found no cave—not in this waterless land—but by peering and calculating (odd how calm you can grow when your life depends on your brain) he discovered in what direction his chances were best, and was rewarded. A one-time landslide had piled great slabs of rock on each other. Among them was a passage into which he could crawl.

Then nothing to do but lie in that narrow space and wait.

Light seeped around a bend, with the noise of the storm. He could judge thereby how matters went outside. Periodically he crept to the entrance of his dolmen and monitored the radiation level. Before long it had reached such a count that—space armour, expert therapy, and all—an hour's exposure would kill him.

He must wait.

Jaccavrie knew the approximate area where he intended to set down. She'd come looking as soon as possible. Flitting low, using her detectors, she'd find the wrecked sled. More than that she could not do unaided. But he could emerge and call her. Whether or not they actually saw each other in this mountainscape, he could emit a radio signal for her to home on. She'd hover, snatch him with a forcebeam, and reel him in.

But . . . this depended on calm weather. *Jaccavrie* could overmaster any wind. But the dust would blind both her and him. And deafen and mute them; it was conductive, radio could not get through. Laure proved that to his own satisfaction by experimenting with the miniradar built into his armour.

So everything seemed to depend on which came first, the end of the gale or the end of Laure's powerpack. His air renewer drew on it. About thirty hours' worth of charge remained before he choked on his own breath. If only he'd been able to grab a spare accumulator or two, or better still, a hand-cranked recharger! They might have rolled no more than ten metres off. But he had decided not to search the area. And by now, he couldn't go back. Not through the radiation.

He sighed, drank a bit from his water nipple, ate a bit through his chow lock, wished for a glass of beer and a comfortable bed, and went to sleep.

*   *   *

When he awoke, the wind had dropped from a full to a half gale; but the dust drift was so heavy as to conceal the glorious starfog night that had fallen. It screened off some of the radiation, too, though not enough to do him any good. He puzzled over why the body of the planet wasn't helping more. Finally he decided that ions, hitting the upper air along the terminator, produced secondaries and cascades which descended everywhere.

The day-side bombardment must really have got fierce!

Twenty hours left. He opened the life-support box he had taken off his shoulder rack, pulled out the sanitary unit, and attached it. Men don't die romantically, like characters on a stage. Their bodies are too stubborn.

So are their minds. He should have been putting his thoughts in order, but he kept being disturbed by recollections of his parents, of Graydal, of a funny little tavern he'd once visited, of a gaucherie he'd rather forget, of some money owing to him, of Graydal—He ate again, and drowsed again, and the wind filled the air outside with dust, and time closed in like a hand.

Ten hours left. No more?

Five. Already?

What a stupid way to end. Fear fluttered at the edge of his perception. He beat it off. The wind yammered. How long can a dust storm continue, anyhow? Where'd it come from? Daylight again, outside his refuge, coloured like blood and brass. The charged particles and X-rays were so thick that some diffused in to him. He shifted cramped muscles, and drank the stench of his unwashed skin, and regretted everything he had wanted and failed to do.

A shadow cast on the cornering rock. A rustle and slither conducted to his ears. A form, bulky and awkward as his own, crawling around the tunnel bend. Numb, shattered, he switched on his radio. The air was fairly clear in here and he heard her voice through the static: "... you are, you are alive! Oh, Valfar's Wings upbear us, you live!"

He held her while she sobbed, and he wept, too. "You shouldn't have," he stammered. "I never meant for *you* to risk yourself—"

"We dared not wait," she said when they were calmer. "We saw, from space, that the storm was enormous. It would go on in this area for days. And we didn't know how long you had to live. We only knew you were in trouble, or you'd have been back with us. We came down. I almost had to fight my father, but I won and came. The hazard wasn't so great for me. Really, no, believe me. She protected me till we found your sled. Then I did have to go out afoot with a metal detector to find you. Because you were obviously sheltered somewhere, and so you could only be detected at closer range than she can come. But the danger wasn't that great, Daven. I can stand much more radiation than you. I'm still well inside my tolerance, won't even need any drugs. Now I'll shoot off this flare, and she'll see, and come so close that we can make a dash—You are all right, aren't you? You swear it?"

"Oh, yes," he said slowly. "I'm fine. Better off than ever in my life." Absurdly, he had to have the answer, however footling all questions were against the fact that she had come after him and was here and they were both alive. "We? Who's your companion?"

She laughed and clinked her faceplate against his. "*Jaccavrie;* of course. Who else? You didn't think your womenfolk were about to leave you alone, did you?"

The ships began their trek homeward. They moved without haste. Best to be cautious until they had emerged from the nebula, seen where they were, and aimed themselves at the Dragon's Head.

"My people and I are pleased at your safety," said Demring's image in the outercom screen. He spoke under the obligation to be courteous, and could not refrain from adding: "We also approve your decision not to investigate that planet further."

"For the first, thanks," Laure answered. "As for the second—" He shrugged. "No real need. I was curious about the effects of an atmosphere, but my computer has just run off a probability analysis of the data I already have, which proves that no more are necessary for my purposes."

"May one inquire what your purposes are?"

"I'd like to discuss that first with your navigator. In private."

The green gaze studied Laure before Demring said, unsmiling: "You have the right of command. And by our customs, she having been instrumental in saving your life, a special relationship exists. But again I counsel forethought."

Laure paid no attention to that last sentence. His pulse was beating too gladly. He switched off as soon as possible and ordered the best dinner his ship could provide.

"Are you certain you want to make your announcement through her?" the voice asked him. "And to her in this manner?"

"I am. I think I've earned the pleasure. Now I'm off to make myself presentable for the occasion. Carry on." Laure went whistling down the corridor.

But when Graydal boarded, he took both her hands and they looked long in silence at each other. She had strewn jewels in her tresses, turning them to a starred midnight. Her clothes were civilian, a deep blue that offset coppery skin, amber eyes, and suppleness. And did he catch the least woodsy fragrance of perfume?

"Welcome," was all he could say at last.

"I am so happy," she answered.

They went to the saloon and sat down on the couch together. Daiquiris were ready for them. They touched glasses. "Good voyage," he made the old toast, "and merry landing."

"For me, yes." Her smile faded. "And I hope for the rest. How I hope."

"Don't you think they can get along in the outside worlds?"

"Yes, undoubtedly." The incredible lashes fluttered. "But they will never be as fortunate as . . . as I think I may be."

"You have good prospects yourself?" The blood roared in his temples.

"I am not quite sure," she replied shyly.

He had intended to spin out his surprise at length, but suddenly he couldn't let her stay troubled, not to any degree. He cleared his throat and said, "I have news."

She tilted her head and waited with that relaxed alertness he liked to see. He wondered how foolish the grin was on his face. Attempting to recover dignity, he embarked on a roundabout introduction.

"You wondered why I insisted on exploring the cluster centre, and in such detail. Probably I ought to have explained myself from the beginning. But I was afraid of raising false hopes. I'd no guarantee that things would turn out to be the way I'd guessed. Failure, I thought, would be too horrible for you, if you knew what success could mean. But I was working on your behalf, nothing else.

"You see, because my civilization is founded on individualism, it makes property rights quite basic. In particular, if there aren't any inhabitants or something like that, discoverers can claim ownership within extremely broad limits.

"Well, we . . . you . . . our expedition has met the requirements of discovery as far as those planets are concerned. We've been there, we've proven what they're like, we've located them as well as might be without beacons—"

He saw how she struggled not to be too sanguine. "That isn't a true location," she said. "I can't imagine how we will ever lead anybody back to precisely those stars."

"Nor can I," he said. "And it doesn't matter. Because, well, we took an adequate sample. We can be sure now that practically every star in the cluster heart has planets that are made of heavy elements. So it isn't necessary, for their exploitation, to go to any particular system. In addition, we've learned about hazards and so forth, got information that'll be essential to other people. And therefore"—he chuckled—"I guess we can't file a claim on your entire Cloud Universe. But any court will award you . . . us . . . a fair share. Not specific planets, since they can't be found right away. Instead, a share of everything. Your crew will draw royalties on the richest mines in the galaxy. On millions of them."

She responded with thoughtfulness rather than enthusiasm. "Indeed? We did wonder, on *Makt*, if you might not be hoping to find abundant metals. But we decided that couldn't be. For why would anyone come here for them? Can they not be had more easily, closer to home?"

Slightly dashed, he said, "No. Especially when most worlds in this frontier are comparatively metal-poor. They do have some veins of ore, yes. And the colonists can extract anything from the oceans, as on Serieve. But there's a natural limit to such a process. In time, carried out on the scale that'd be required when population has grown . . . it'd be releasing so much heat that planetary temperature would be affected."

"That sounds farfetched."

"No. A simple calculation will prove it. According to historical records, Earth herself ran into the problem, and not terribly long after the industrial era began. However, quite aside from remote prospects, people will want to mine these cluster worlds immediately. True, it's a long haul, and operations will have to be totally automated. But the heavy elements that are rare elsewhere are so abundant here as to more than make up for those extra costs." He smiled. "I'm afraid you can't escape your fate. You're going to be . . . not wealthy. To call you 'wealthy' would be like calling a supernova 'luminous'. You'll command more resources than many whole civilizations have done."

Her look upon him remained grave. "You did this for us? You should not have. What use would riches be to us if we lost you?"

He remembered that he couldn't have expected her to carol about this. In her culture, money was not unwelcome, but neither was it an important goal. So what she had just said meant less than if a girl of the Commonalty had spoken. Nevertheless, joy kindled in him. She sensed that, laid her hand across his, and murmured, "But your thought was noble."

He couldn't restrain himself any longer. He laughed aloud. "Noble?" he cried. "I'd call it clever. Fiendishly clever. Don't you see? I've given you Kirkasant back!"

She gasped.

He jumped up and paced exuberant before her. "You could wait a few years till your cash reserves grow astronomical and buy as big a fleet as you want to search the cluster. But it isn't needful. When word gets out, the miners will come swarming. They'll plant beacons, they'll have to. The grid will be functioning within one year, I'll bet. As soon as you can navigate, identify where you are and where you've been, you can't help finding your home—in weeks!"

She joined him, then, casting herself into his arms, laughing and weeping. He had known of emotional depth in her, beneath the schooled reserve. But never before now had he found as much warmth as was hers.

Long, long afterwards, air locks linked and she bade him good night. "Until tomorrow," she said.

"Many tomorrows, I hope."

"And I hope. I promise."

He watched the way she had gone until the locks closed again and the ships parted company. A little drunkenly, not with alcohol, he returned to the saloon for a nightcap.

"Turn off that colour thing," he said. "Give me an outside view."

The ship obeyed. In the screen appeared stars, and the cloud from which stars were being born. "Her sky," Laure said. He flopped on to the couch and admired.

·"I might as well start getting used to it," he said. "I expect I'll spend a lot of vacation time, at least, on Kirkasant."

"Daven," said *Jaccavrie*.

She was not in the habit of addressing him thus, and so gently. He started. "Yes?"

"I have been—" Silence hummed for a second. "I have been wondering how to tell you. Any phrasing, any inflection, could strike you as something I computed to produce an effect. I am only a machine."

Though unease prickled him, he leaned forward to touch a bulkhead. It trembled a little with her engine energy. "And I, old girl," he said. "Or else you also are an organism. We're both people."

"Thank you," said the ship, almost too low to be heard.

Laure braced himself. "What did you have to tell me?"

She forgot about keeping her voice humanized. The words clipped forth: "I finished the chromosome analysis some time ago. Thereafter I tried to discourage certain tendencies I noticed in you. But now I have no way to avoid giving you the plain truth. They are not human on that planet."

"What?" he yelled. The glass slipped from his hand and splashed red wine across the deck. "You're crazy! Records, traditions, artifacts, appearance, behaviour—"

The ship's voice came striding across his. "Yes, they are human descended. But their ancestors had to make an enormous adaptation. The loss of night vision is merely indicative. The fact that they can, for example, ingest heavy metals like arsenic unharmed might be interpreted as simple immunity. But you will recall that they find unarsenated food tasteless. Did that never suggest to you that they have developed a metabolic requirement for the element? And you should have drawn a conclusion from their high tolerance for ionizing radiation. It cannot be due to their having stronger proteins, can it? No, it must be because they have evolved a capacity for extremely rapid and error-free repair of chemical damage from that source. This in turn is another measure of how different their enzyme system is from yours.

"Now the enzymes, of course, are governed by the DNA of the cells, which is the molecule of heredity—"

"Stop," Laure said. His speech was as flat as hers. "I see what you're at. You are about to report that your chromosome study proved the matter. My kind of people and hers can't reproduce with each other."

"Correct," *Jaccavrie* said.

Laure shook himself, as if he were cold. He continued to look at the glowing fog. "You can't call them nonhuman on that account."

"A question of semantics. Hardly an important one. Except for the fact that Kirkasanters apparently are under an instinctual compulsion to have children."

"I know," Laure said.

And after a time: "Good thing, really. They're a high-class breed. We could use a lot of them."

"Your own genes are above average," *Jaccavrie* said.

"Maybe. What of it?"

Her voice turned alive again. "I'd like to have grandchildren," she said wistfully.

Laure laughed. "All right," he said. "No doubt one day you will." The laughter was somewhat of a victory.